CAME
MONSTERS

ALSO BY PETE ALDIN

Black Marks

(audiobook, eBook, paperback)

Nine Tales

(eBook only)

Illegal

(eBook only, with Kevin Ikenberry)

The Doomsday's Child series

Doomsday's Child

(eBook, paperback)

Rescue Mission

(eBook only)

Came Monsters

(eBook, paperback)

CAME MONSTERS

PETE ALDIN

Cover design by Melody Simmons

Cover layout by coversbychristian.com

Paperback layout by Ebook Launch

To JR Jackson

Author's Note

In this novel, Elliot uses a mix of imperial measurements and metric measurements. This mixed usage is due to various influences on Elliot: growing up in the USA (imperial); a career in the military (metric); more than three years of living in Australia among Aussies (metric again).

Most spelling is American since we view the story from Elliot's point of view. Other spelling (such as "Centre") is Australian for local accuracy and authenticity.

Also, in Australian cars, the driver sits on the right.

- Pete Aldin, September 2018

God lay dead in heaven;
Angels sang the hymn of the end;
Purple winds went moaning,
Their wings drip-dripping with blood
That fell upon the earth.
It, groaning thing,
Turned black and sank.
Then from the far caverns of dead sins
Came monsters,
Livid with desire.
They fought,
Wrangled over the world,
A morsel...

- Stephen Crane, Poet, 1895 CE
(Christian/Common Era)

Monday's child is fair of face,
Tuesday's child is full of grace,
Wednesday's child is full of woe,
Thursday's child has far to go,
Friday's child is loving and giving,
Saturday's child works hard for a living,
But the child who is born to survive Doomsday
Is blessed and cursed in every way.

- Children's Rhyme circa 66 PC
(Post-Collapse)

PROLOGUE

Al-Kasrah, Syria
Nine years ago ...

E lliot had complete trust in the man beside him driving the Humvee, Eames. He had complete trust in the man seated directly behind the shotgun seat, Radler. He even trusted that wiseass, McGovern, manning the tri-barreled GAU-19 mounted on the roof. Between the four of them, they made a solid fire team. Which is no doubt why the Major had sent *them* to babysit the final man in the party, the man in the passenger seat behind Eames, the man McGovern kept calling The Guy.

Elliot had zero trust in The Guy. He wasn't one of them. And he wasn't giving any clues as to what the hell this trip was about.

No briefing, he complained to himself. *No prep time. Not even a goddamn name for our passenger. Just orders.*

Simple orders, too: *Get your team in the Humvee out there. Escort the passenger to this town. Watch his ass and yours while he's there.* When Elliot had asked

PETE ALDIN

for more, the Major had repeated the same orders, but with a dozen cusswords strategically added. Elliot's response the second time had been a simple "Yes, sir."

Elliot was jolted from the memory as the Humvee hit another basketball-sized pothole in the godforsaken excuse for a highway. He jounced from his seat and came down swearing while Radler barked laughter behind him.

"Sparkles," Radler said, using the nickname the team had given Elliot, "you got to concentrate!"

Half-seated, half-squatting, with his ass in the eight-inch-wide gunner's sling seat, McGovern called down in a fair imitation of Elliot's voice, "Concentrate! It's important to concentrate!"

It was one of the two words that Elliot had drummed into his team, whether they needed that drumming or not. The other was *circumspection*: see everything. Elliot fidgeted, trying for a more comfortable position. "Yeah, well, maybe Eames could concentrate on the goddamn road and avoid getting us airborne."

Eames's eyes flashed his way, brief, apologetic. Elliot couldn't tell if the sweat gleaming on the Corporal's dark skin was due to the heat, the efforts of keeping the vehicle steady, or the quiet terror they all shared of IEDs. Eames raised his voice above the road noise: "More holes than highway out here."

"Damn straight." Elliot put his face to his window, scanning the Syrian badlands, checking on the second team's Humvee bobbing around in his side mirror.

"Are we there yet?" McGovern called down.

"Four klicks," Eames replied.

"Shit. Four? That's like three more minutes up here! Why am I the one always has to man the gun on long trips, Sparkles?"

"Assholes always man the gun on long trips," Elliot replied.

"Roger that," Radler said.

"Massage my feet, Rads?"

"Fuck off, Mac," Radler replied.

McGovern farted, loudly.

"Goddamnit!" Eames complained. He twisted so he could elbow Mac in the knee.

Simultaneously Radler said, "Again with this? What do you eat that we don't?"

"Keep a store of beans to eat before road trips like this, where my ass gets to be at your mouth level."

"Beans?" Eames said. "Man, I think you been eating dogshit."

"That too. How's the air in first class now, boys?"

Breathing through his mouth now, Elliot had to admit the air wasn't good.

"Will you please ask your men to shut *up*?" It was the first time The Guy had spoken. The first time he'd interacted with anything other than his seatbelt and phone.

Elliot turned to study him. Because The Guy wore wraparound goggles over one half of his face and a checkered bandana over the other, Elliot couldn't read any expression there. Whatever the expression was, Elliot wanted to punch it from The Guy's heavily-disguised head.

"You're a guest here," he told him.

"Then treat me like one."

3

Up until he'd spoken, Elliot had thought The Guy might be local. The skin on his hands, neck and forehead was tanned like the Syrians. The one time he'd put his cell to his ear, the voice on the other end had spoken exclusively in Arabic. At the time, Radler had pointed to him and mouthed *Terp?*, but Elliot considered it more likely he was CIA than an interpreter. Maybe private contractor. His ballistic vest was US military issue. And his accent was now identifiable as educated American.

CIA, then. It wasn't the first time they'd played taxi service to one of them.

Certainly not a journalist, he thought and flipped The Guy the bird. That gesture provoked a mild headshake before the man turned his head away.

Elliot cuffed Eames to get his attention, then he mouthed the word *Spook*. Eames curled a hand into the shape of a pistol and mimed popping the man through the back of his seat.

A burst of chatter babbled from the commo gear in the transmission tunnel between Elliot and Eames. A weather report for the region, broadcast to all units. Same as yesterday and same as today: hot and dry.

"Three klicks to destination," Eames called to McGovern.

For a moment, Elliot thought he saw movement outside, but it was only a dust devil, wind whipping up dirt. He pressed against the window, looking up and around for the drone he knew was overhead. It wasn't visible; that put it behind them somewhere. This was supposedly clear territory, so the threat of ambush or IED was as low as it could be in this part of the world.

Three kilometers. They'd made it this far. What was it about, though? What was it for?

He turned in his chair so he could see their passenger clearly. Loud enough for all the men to hear, he said, "Hey, boys, you know those things called briefings? They take the team sergeant into a tent where a senior officer talks through the mission with them?"

"Heard of them," Eames said. He kept his eyes on the country ahead, being circumspect. But he was smiling, playing along.

"Well, that's good," Elliot continued. "I was starting to think I'd dreamed about those."

"Wait a darn minute, Sergeant." Radler's surprised tone was wonderfully theatrical. "Are you telling me that we have embarked upon a trip into god-knows-where *without* a briefing?"

"Without a briefing. Without intel."

Radler released an exaggerated groan. "Gosh darn it! That is reprehensible. You are the team leader, for gosh darn sakes."

"Insulting, right?"

Eames pretended to shoot the spook through the seatback again. "Just plain rude, you ask me, Sergeant."

"Shut the hell up, ass clowns." The Guy's accent was definitely New England. It was an educated voice, a nasal voice, but it carried … and it carried authority. "It's not a difficult mission. No secrets. You take me to Al-Kasrah to pick up a friendly. We put him in the other Humvee. We go back. Your Major said you could handle that." He adjusted position, sitting forward to get air to his back beneath his vest. "I'd appreciate it if we could drop the play-acting."

5

"I'd like to know what's *in* Al-Kasrah before we get there." Radler was all seriousness now. "In fact, our sergeant shoulda known that before we even got in this vehicle."

"Nothing to worry about," The Guy said, settling back. He stuck a finger in one ear, digging at wax or an itch.

"Nothing to—?" Something banged Radler's window, no doubt his elbow. Elliot couldn't see it, but he smiled when The Guy jumped a little.

Elliot said, "Maybe you're new, mister? Plenty to worry about round here, I'd say."

The spook withdrew the finger, checked it over. "Dial it down. This is very friendly territory, I vouch for that. Discussion over." He pointed the ear-mining finger at the windscreen. Elliot turned forward to see a row of sand-colored buildings come into view over a rise.

"If this territory is so friendly," he asked The Guy, "then why are you wearing a vest?"

McGovern laughed above them. "Burn!"

"That's why we call him Sparkles," Radler replied. "Coz the man has a sparkling wit and the sparkling personality to match it."

The smells of cooking wafted from the middle of the busy market square they'd pulled into—burning fat, spices, onions, meat. Elliot's fire team stood in a rectangle, watching the angles, their slice of pie. Each had their own corner of the vehicle, Mac the corner where The Guy had sat. Thirty meters back by the gates to the market, the second team stood in identical arrangement around their own vehicle. The spook leaned against the Humvee's hood, speaking hushed Arabic into his cell. Apart from the cooking smells, the area stank from their own vehicle exhaust and the piles of dung baking in the stifling heat.

Eames pointed to some of the animal droppings. "Hey, McGovern. Lunch."

"Hey, Eames. Bite me."

"You fellas frosty?" Elliot said. A bright flash drew his attention across the marketplace to the top floor of a building, but it was only a woman opening a window to hang washing from the sill.

"We're snowmen, Sparkles," McGovern replied.

When he'd exited the Humvee, Mac's 1970s mustache had been turned up in a sneer of distrust for their surroundings. Elliot couldn't see Mac now through the vehicle between them, so he didn't know if the man still wore that expression. Knowing Mac, he probably did.

Elliot felt the same distrust. Locals milled, keeping their distance, conducting their business with their own suspicious eye on these intruders. Were any of these people insurgents? Extremists? Informants for the enemy? Lookouts?

McGovern added loudly, "Is it cliché to say I don't like this?"

"It absolutely is," said Radler. "Mainly because you never like anything."

"You don't even like my coffee," Eames said. "Best in any unit and you won't drink it."

"That's coz tastes like battery-acid. It burns my eyes just thinking about it."

"Says the man with the dogshit-farts," Eames replied.

"I'm with Mac on this one," Radler added. "It's so thick, we keep wondering if you filter it through your dirty shorts."

"Fuckin' barbarians, the both of you. It's Turkish coffee. It's a goddamn luxury."

"It's a goddamn travesty," McGovern said.

"Hey, what's my buzzwords, fellas?" Elliot said.

"Trust me, we're heeding them buzzwords, Sparkles," said McGovern.

Radler added, "We are concentrating circumspectly."

The only people in the whole square who didn't seem at least a little on edge were the children. There were a dozen or more of them in among the stalls, kicking a soccer ball, helping their parents, watching adults work. There were always kids. Living and working and playing in the midst of danger. Their faces were carefree, happy, though they must have felt the anxiety of their elders; anxiety was elemental here; everyone in this goddamn country swam in it.

The Guy cleared his throat, turning Elliot's head. Sun bounced off the man's desert goggles. The bandana still covered his lower face. "All right. What comes next is so simple, even a child could do it. So perhaps it's good I have you." His right hand was on the butt of his sidearm, belying the calm in his tone. He pointed with his left hand across the market to an alley opening. "We walk that way to meet my friend. We escort him back here."

"Because it's such friendly territory," Elliot replied.

Eames asked, "How far?"

"Fifty meters down that laneway."

"Babysitting." Radler spat in the dirt as he came around the Hummer.

The goggles turned his way. "You think you can handle that?"

Radler bristled, but Elliot stepped in. "Let's just get this over with, CIA-man. You're in the middle of our diamond. Eames, you have point."

"Why me?" Eames mock-complained, but the spook started off and Eames had to jog a little to get ahead of him.

"McGovern, you're left. Radler, you're right. I'm at the rear."

"So you can stare at our asses," McGovern said and set off in a fast walk, swinging left and closest to the market stalls. To their right was open ground all the way to a wall of apartments. Windows. Flat roofs. A hundred places for a sniper.

"Much prettier than your faces," Elliot called after him and got a chuckle from Radler headed right.

Elliot turned and signaled the second team leader to watch his Humvee. The sergeant gave a thumbs-up and told his driver to wander over. Civilians were always surprised to hear that military Humvees required no key to start them and had no door locks. The instructions for starting the damn thing were right there on the dash for anyone who read English, along with the switch labeled *Start, Run, Stop*. Elliot gave the vehicle a last pat on the hood. He said, "See you soon" and started off.

There were several other vehicles in the market-place besides the Hummers: battered, sand-scoured cars that wouldn't have been out of place in a wrecking yard. Ahead of Eames and close to where the team's path would take them, a rust-riddled Mercedes had its trunk up while three men leaned over it and all talked at once. Elliot tensed, fingers tightening on his rifle. Eames and McGovern were watching it too.

"God, I hate cars in the Middle East," Elliot muttered.

One of the men brought out an old boom box stereo, nodding and smiling over it. His companion paid the third man from a roll of notes.

"Shit," he breathed. "Don't these people have eBay?"

At least four other vehicles were parked amongst the stalls with trunks open like the Mercedes. Any of them could contain an IED. The spook had said this area was friendly. The map the Major had pointed to agreed.

"But the twin towers were in friendly territory too," Elliot said to himself.

He tensed at movement near Mac: a kid detaching from a market stall, chattering Arabic, offering something from a basket. Mac flashed the kid a grin and called, "Very hungry!" in bad Arabic.

Elliot barked, "On task!"

A brief scowl of disappointment from Mac over his shoulder, but he waved the kid away as instructed.

Rather than return to his stall, the kid came toward Elliot. He was close enough now for Elliot to see he was a boy, maybe four, maybe six, maybe somewhere in between. The basket contained dried fruit, dates. Elliot hated dates. And he hated distractions. But …

Another careful three-sixty. A scan of the roofs, the windows, the cars. The kid chattered faster as he neared. Elliot could give this boy a lucky break. The mood in the market had relaxed a few notches since the Americans' first appearance. Locals had turned their focus fully to their trading, their banter. He took a hand from his weapon to pull two US dollars from the pocket where he kept them folded. For moments like this.

"Here." He stopped walking, aimed, and flipped the money into the basket, judging wind direction so that it landed dead center. The boy cooed, lifting the basket to his face as if to smell the notes.

A shout. Elliot stiffened. All his men were looking past the Mercedes. The man who'd sold the boom box was marching after his buyers, a hand in the air and waving the notes they'd given him. The two buyers sent him *screw you* gestures and started running. The seller sped off in pursuit.

"Assholes," Elliot said.

"*A soles*," the boy said in mimicry.

Elliot relaxed a notch, told the kid to spend his money wisely, started forward again as he realized he'd drifted back from the team. There was a girl nearby, a little older than the boy, crouched beside one of the car-trunk stalls and staring at him with hard eyes. A spotter's eyes. But she wasn't anyone's spotter. She was just a kid, like the boy, watching an alien creature in full battle rig walking through her world and—

Impact!

Blackness.

Bright light, nausea.

Ringing.

Salt and copper on his tongue.

Something tugged at his shoulder.

He opened gummy eyes to stare into a bleached-out sky and wonder why he was on his back beneath it. Why he was hot and cold at the same time, with dust in his nostrils, blood in his mouth, ringing in his ears. Clods of dirt and brick pattered the hard earth around him. The pull on his shoulder was a child, a girl, a … a … Syrian girl. Pulling at his rifle strap, looting his dead body, only—

"I'm not dead," he said, or he thought he said. His tongue felt rough and thick as pumice. His legs were on the ground, but his head was at a funny angle above it, prevented from touching it by the bulk of his gear. He bent his limbs to turn over onto his hands and knees, tried to see what had happened to him. The girl was fleeing, picking her way across a wide black scorch mark, a *crater*, between blackened cars and pieces of market stalls and merchandise … and pieces of people.

He had somehow gotten to his feet, swaying there. Through the ringing in his ears came screaming. Wailing. Some people were alive. Some had made it. His team? What the hell were their names again?

To his left, the date-seller boy lay with lacerations across his face and his left arm sliced off at the elbow. The stump spurted blood while the other arm reached for something only he could see. Elliot had to help him.

Had to stop that bleeding. Had to check the rooftops for hostiles. Had to ... Had to check his men.

Radler.

Eames.

McGovern.

That was it. Their names.

But they were not there.

Although that, that over there, that was a piece of kit. That was a boot. A US Army boot. And that, that there, that might be a sleeve with an arm inside.

Somebody grabbed him by the vest, turned him, shouting in his face. The other sergeant. Elliot couldn't remember his name. And his words were just noise. Was it even English, or Arabic? Elliot pulled free of him and stumbled, falling on hands and knees again. The Guy? The spook? Was that him there, that battered ballistic vest with raw mincemeat leaking out of it?

He blinked and he was upright, the sergeant and another soldier at each arm, forcing him back to the Hummers. They were fine, the vehicles were fine. A shadow passed over him, so he squinted up: the drone, low and headed to the other side of the market. He blinked again and found himself slumped in his Humvee's shotgun seat. The other team's driver was beside him, shouting into the comms, calling for support. "That's what I should do," Elliot told him but the man just frowned as if it were Elliot's turn to speak Arabic.

He grabbed the door frame and levered himself out. The driver tried to restrain him, but Elliot easily jerked his sleeve from the man's grip.

The market had filled with new people, local people, dragging bodies to the edges. None of those bodies were his team. His team, his men, they were dead men and there wasn't much left to see of them.

Radler.

Eames.

McGovern.

Dead.

Gone.

Friendly territory, The Guy's voice asserted inside Elliot's head.

He shook his head. Cleared the voice. Started up a headache.

It felt like all his bones were rattling. His skull vibrated with fragmented thoughts and that goddamned ringing.

This can't be real, a voice told all the other thoughts. Perhaps the voice was pleading with the universe. *It's not. No way is this real. It's not!*

But it was real.

It was very goddamned real.

And it always would be.

PART ONE

SETTLERS DOWNS

1

The dog froze, growling, her hackles raised, her head angled left.

Elliot tightened his grip on her leash. "Wassup, Bess?"

She stopped growling, but didn't move, her ears up. And he waited her out. Maybe it would be another rabbit. Maybe another dog. If they were lucky it wouldn't be a claymore—or *drybones* as the rest of the camp called them.

The long grass around him hissed in the wind, waving and dancing to a melody only it could hear. Stalks brushed his jacket sleeves, the side pocket of his cargo pants. This was always risky, walking through land that hadn't been marked off their maps as safe. But risk was part of scouting. Three years and no one had wanted to come in here, because it was empty space, a green patch on the map between two sets of wooded hills, just grass overgrown and ready for wild fire someday. Also, some said, because it was so close to the Esk Highway, and therefore close to land frequented by the pot-head group who called themselves Vikes. This was at the western limits of the territory that had fallen to The Downs, the original name for the converted sheep ranch the others now called *Settlers* Downs—but it *was* their territory.

The dog was sniffing, listening. He gave her more time, plucked a grain head and rolled it around his palm. It might be barley, he thought. They might have planted this for cattle fodder, it might be useful. Up ahead, a silo rose above the sea of green. He'd been using the old farm's rutted driveways to hike along— until he'd seen the tall cylinder out in the middle of the field, a half klick behind the homestead. A silo was worth investigating. A silo might have useful stuff: seed stocks; a forgotten weapons cache. Someone had to be first, and he did have Bess. Problem was, long grass occasionally hid *claymores*, unseen like a landmine until a person stepped on them and got a bite. It had happened. It had happened a lot last summer and autumn, though only one bite had reached skin and that was because poor dead Alan had gone scouting wearing shorts. That was asking for a bite—from deaders or snakes.

One more poor dead idiot to add to the rest of them. Survival of the smartest.

Elliot thanked Christ and all the saints that any undead still haunting the earth these days had lost the bite strength to puncture most fabrics. And he hadn't seen one walking in well over a year.

The dog glanced back at him with a short whine. He dropped the grain and rested his hand on his holstered SIG, eyes and ears straining toward whatever was in the grass there. If it was a wallaby or a hare, it might break and reveal its position, handing him a chance at bagging it. But, it also might be feral cats, a litter. Or a tiger snake. Or—however remote the chance these days—it might be a mobile deader.

Bess growled again and Elliot decided a detour was in order. That silo was right there, a hundred and fifty yards away. But it wasn't worth this. He could always come back with a tractor and someone riding shotgun. They could muscle across the field that way.

Probably nothing in it but mulch anyway.

"Move," he said, jerking the lead right. With relief it seemed, she complied, allowing him to turn her away from whatever hazard she'd sensed and toward the bitumen road on the hill a kilometre ahead. "Good girl," he soothed and her ears flicked down at the praise.

His pack was heavy with rabbit carcasses and a coil of aluminum wire for the farm's mig welders. His long bow's string rubbed across his jacket zipper, the quiver at his left hip catching in the grass from time to time. The SIG sat on the opposite hip in front of his machete.

Six rabbits, some welding materials. Actually not bad for a days' work and about as much as he wanted to carry on foot. He'd left the car in the woods off road and up the hill beyond the roadway ahead, and tried to cover some territory they hadn't yet cleared on their maps. There was very little of that left these days, at least within the bounds set by the Council. If it was old-world supplies they wanted, they'd have to start traveling further afoot like he'd been advocating. They could try making peace with the Nine Mile River folks north again, try trading with them. Or else venture south toward Hobart and hope the coastal scavengers they'd skirmished with were long gone or had calmed down a little. With the biker gangs gone, things should have been more civilized these days among the living. Should have been.

Bess growled again and surged against the lead. He gave it a little slack, let the Alsatian-cross drag him forward until a whitened lump amidst the grass resolved as a head. A weathered and unmoving head with hair like cobwebs. He jerked the lead hard and ordered, "*sit!*" She complied. She was one of the better dogs he'd bred: loyal, obedient, predictable. And she didn't demand idle chitchat.

He slipped off the bow, dropped it, then lowered his shoulders with his arms held back. The pack's straps slid down until it fell the final couple of feet to the ground. Bess glanced at the rabbits, but never truly considered taking one. He scratched her neck and told her, "*stay*". She was by far his favorite—she listened to him the way people should. She'd stay there until he said otherwise, come what may. He grabbed the bow and passed the dog, getting his machete out.

His inner Unconventional Warfare Instructor said, *Go back to the tractor path. Forget the shortcut. Long way is usually the right way.*

But he was tired and the highway was right up there and taking the direct route would shave fifteen minutes off the walk. And it was only one deader. He pushed the hay aside to reveal the claymore in all its lack-of-glory, lying perpendicular to him with its peeling-paint skull near his right boot. It shuddered, wanting him but unable to act upon it. The ex-human was a husk really, all ribs and hips and a snapping jaw without much muscle strength or fiber left. The damn thing couldn't even turn its head to look at him, much less use its arms and legs. Not for the first time, Elliot wondered how they survived so long once they lost the ability to move. And feed. Did field mice come a-nibblin' and get more than they bargained for once they got near the face? Did deaders eat *grass*?

He braced, about to stomp its head, when the dog barked. Then yipped. Then howled in pain and terror. He pivoted, machete high. Bess was on her side, legs kicking and muzzle snapping at the two naked deaders who'd fallen onto her.

What in-?

They'd sprung from the thick vegetation to the dog's left while she was focused on Elliot. He hadn't heard them with the wind hissing in the grass and the dog's quiet growling. Neither, apparently, had she. One had dropped across her, pinning her. She tore at the other one's ribs while it clawed and snapped at her.

He started forward, but instinct made him jerk left, almost toppling him. Another deader had reached for him from the grass. It was standing, moving, jaw clacking, coming for him. He slashed at it, taking off a hand, then split the skull with the back of the blade. He turned back to her and froze. Bess was in bad shape, blood in her fur. They hadn't gotten her fully open yet, maybe didn't have the strength, but could still damn-well scratch—and bite too from the looks. If he got her away now, she might survive this. One of the farmers might treat her. Reaching her, he took one drybones down with a blow to the base of the skull. Bess pulled free then, fast-crawling away and into the grass, vanishing.

"Come!" he called in desperation, and raised the machete to take out the other deader so he could follow her. But the grass parted to his right in multiple places and heads appeared at ankle-height, knee-height, and then one at shoulder-height. He recoiled, cried out. Croaking, stumbling undead came at him—three, then five, then eight, then *more*—and Elliot himself was stumbling, crashing through stalks and clumps of long grass, his bow and his pack and his dog abandoned. He was running for the far side of the field, running for the black ribbon of asphalt visible up on the hill. He glanced back, saw nothing, slowed, then stopped. The noise was all back by the pack where there was enough meat in the six rabbits to keep the pusbags happy. Bess yelped, then wailed. Bile burned his throat as he put one hand on his thigh, bent over, gasping.

Should he go back? Should he run?

The decision was made for him when the grass-lands came alive around him, alive with the snarls and gurgles of the long-dead. Rustling. Scraping. They were everywhere. Dozens of them. Maybe hundreds.

Elliot stumbled backwards as the familiar tinnitus and white-vision of a flashback came at him hard. He twisted round and ran as the dry brown of the grass merged with the terracotta walls of Al-Kasrah. Bess's cries became the wailing of mothers and the boy with no arm.

He cried out in agony and shock and wasn't sure if he was yelling now or back then or both. Surging forward on legs he couldn't feel, he saw the ruined faces of deaders through the Syrian dust as he shoulder-charged them and vaulted them and hacked at them, registered the impacts against them only distantly, and just as distantly hoped none of the impacts were bites.

And then he was on the road, having somehow gotten over the wire fence. He was sinking to his knees on rough bitumen, a headache slamming at his temples, his machete gone, cursing the moment he'd ever decided to head into terrain where he couldn't see more than a couple of yards in any direction.

He'd lost the rabbits, the bow and the pack.

He'd lost the dog.

He'd lost another friend.

2

He drove home with dulled emotions, a churning stomach and a head full of self-recrimination. No bites. Some bruises. A tear along the bottom of his shirt where it had caught on the fence. It wasn't fair he'd escaped this unscathed—not when Bess had died. Not when he'd gotten her killed. It wasn't goddamned fair that he got off so lightly every time.

It was near sunset when he arrived. Slowing twenty metres out from the Settlers Downs main gate, he flashed the headlights five times—two long, one short, two long—the code for *scout returning*. Today was Wednesday because Sturgis was on sniper duty up on the Windmill. The former Navy man's red hair stood out against the scaffolding as much as his dirty-white pullover—neither was best practice in camouflage.

Who are you to talk about best practice? he asked himself. *Went wandering through a sea of claymores. Lost your dog...*

There was no excuse for the lapse of judgment, the lapse of caution, the risk he'd taken. Same as there wasn't for Sturgis up there. The Council should give the man holy hell about it.

Holding onto the gate as he crept past, one of the Cambodian moms gave him a broad smile and called "Suas dae!"—*hey there* in the Khmer language. A shotgun swung from the strap on her shoulder. He and Lewis had met Chariya and her extended family on a bridge more than three years ago. Lewis had instantly adopted them as his own family. Elliot had taken a lot longer to warm to them than they had to him.

Elliot acknowledged her with a brief raise of his fingers from the wheel and kept the Land Rover moving—past the tarp-covered piles of steel and aluminum scrap on his left, ready for future smelting; past the four-metre-long smokehouse on his right, the building that housed pottery kilns and meat smokers leaking its rich and pleasant-smelling stream of grey into the still air; past the long line of burners and trestles set up beneath canopies and along the outside of the smokehouse, their pans and sifters and pots set for evaporating seawater for salt, for separating potash from wood ash to mix with fats for soap, for separating soda ash from seawater to be used in laundry and in controlling pests and mildew; past the jumble of equipment piled under yet another tarp after being stripped months ago from the nearby Iron Devil Brewery.

Above, the clouds sagged, pregnant with rain. He nosed the Rover inside the garage. Two younger men had their heads buried under the hood of an Audi SUV. The one holding the work lamp straightened and snatched the keys from the air when Elliot tossed them.

"There's stuff in the back," Elliot told him. But there wasn't much. No, the really good stuff, the rabbits and the aluminum were with his pack in the middle of that field. Them and—

"Where's Bess?" the man with the lamp asked. His friend raised his head and Elliot saw that he was talking to both of the two "Daves". With typical Aussie humor, the community had nicknamed them Dave One and Dave Two. Dave One held the work lamp.

Ignoring the question, Elliot said, "Where is everyone?"

The Yard was deserted. At this time on a Wednesday, Lewis and his girlfriend Krystal should be sitting with a ring of children in the homestead's front garden, finishing off a math lesson. No doubt that was because the weather was threatening rain. Maybe they were in the small classroom inside the homestead. Slinging his bow, he thought briefly about stopping by to say hello. Briefly. It was a dumbass idea. The days he could have a conversation with Lewis were long gone.

"Most are at dinner," said Dave One and pointed the lamp at nearby empty bowls and then the car engine. "We ate here so we could finish this."

Dave Two wiped his hands on a rag and added, "Nance and Woodsy are walking the fence."

That put Woodsy as far away as possible. That was very good.

"How about Faye?" he asked.

The friends exchanged a glance. Dave One said, "Infirmary."

The transportable classroom-turned-sickbay had been dumped in the paddock directly behind the sheep sheds in the main Yard. Elliot took two steps in that direction and Dave One stepped out to intercept him, his expression apologetic.

"You can't go there."

"Off limits," said Dave Two.

Jesus. "It's got *that* bad?"

The two men nodded back at him.

"How many?"

Dave Two held up nine greasy fingers, wincing. "Not good."

"Well, I'd say that's a goddamn understatement." Three people had come down with flu symptoms the day he'd left. Only three. "Claire there, too?"

"Nope, she's at dinner."

Elliot turned an about-face and left the garage.

"Good stew tonight!" Dave Two called after him. "They caught ten trevally this morning!"

"They were all bream, you tool," Dave One corrected him.

Their argument over fish species faded as Elliot marched across the Yard's turning circle then hooked around the barn toward "Main Street".

The double row of small studio cabins had been lined up between the Yard's barn and the apple, plum, and cherry orchard, accommodating the burgeoning population. Two and a half years earlier, Sturgis, his wife Tina, her sister Ilsa and Ilsa's boyfriend Mike had left Barnabas Island to come knocking on the farm's metaphorical door. This event came at the start of an influx of non-threatening wanderers, most found by The Downs's scouts in their travels. Sturgis—with navy experience including relief aid—had been a godsend in design and construction, as had Mike, a carpenter who'd been renovating a house on the island at the time of the Collapse. Isla was a professional chef, and Tina's berry farming and home brewing background had come in handy, too. Main Street had been the fledgling community's first real infrastructure project, something to be proud of.

Elliot's boots crunched on the pressed-gravel path between the cabins. He remembered that month of Aussie-style scones and jam and American-style lemonade which they called cordial, of backslapping and high fives. Twenty single-roomed huts, all occupied now. Meager furniture, a single or double bed, sometimes a baby's cradle, a small table and a chair or two, a set of drawers or closet pilfered from other farming properties. Two rows of ten homes with twelve-foot gaps between them and their neighbors and a ten-foot wide path down the middle, clusters of water tanks at either end for washing and drinking water.

The deathly quiet in the Street was a relief to Elliot who really wasn't in a mood for people; normally at this time of day, there were coughs and murmurs, lamplight spilling through an open door, the tang of someone having a quiet cigarette, the good-natured banter around a game of cards. But most were at dinner, the Daves had said. A few worked.

And the others were sick.

Nine, now? How bad is this shit gonna get?

As he cleared the end of Main Street, a sudden scuffling made him whirl with hand on SIG. Then he blew out a breath and reached out to the two dogs running his way. They were sister and brother, two years old. He ruffled their fur, then told them to go patrol. If they'd been humans, they'd have been asking after the other dog, the one he'd left with. Dogs were so much better that way than people. He sighed and continued on—past the experimental Zeer pots used for unpowered refrigeration; past the rows of tomato vines; past the series of concrete-floored and ground-hugging cages for rabbits, for chickens, guarded by a dog run to keep away foxes. He paused to acknowledge the pooch inside the dog run, Wilma, then straightened to stare at the Community Centre and work up the motivation to continue toward it.

The Centre had been erected as a multipurpose hall in the exact middle of the farm where it couldn't be seen from any perimeters, where the creek and dam made it defensible against grass fires. His own digs were over the small creek and hill to his right, a five-minute wander, tantalizingly close. He'd really like to lie down, use up enough of his medicinal stash of bourbon to close his eyes and forget the world…and to shut off the slideshow of faces and bodies he'd been seeing again, ever since the field full of claymores.

Bess.

Radler.

Eames.

McGovern.

The little girl from the resort, just after he'd left Hobart. The burly guy from the same resort.

Lewis and Alyssa's parents.

Tommy Harrison.

Birdy.

"For Christ's sake, stop it," he muttered with one hand in his hair and the other on the Community

Centre's doorknob. There was noise from inside but not much of it. Some voices. Dishes and chairs scraped. He smelled fried onions and fish as he took a couple of deep breaths and let them out slow. He twisted the knob and leaned inside, chest constricting.

As the Daves had said, most of the community was here. Conversation was subdued, but still the sound pressed on his head as if the words and noise were pressurizing the room. The air was decidedly warmer and thick with the smells of food and unwashed people. Scanning the tables for Claire, he expected a couple of kids to rush him, fleecing him for any candy he may have found out there. But there were no kids at all. No one under—

He looked around and caught Jimmy's eye before the young man dropped his head, allowing his long hair to cover his face—

No one under eighteen.

A couple people noticed him, smiling tentatively. He nodded, too. Angie had her back to him, deep in conversation with her former-boyfriend Dylan and with a fifty-something mining company accountant named Neil.

Finally, he located Claire in the very back corner, her broad shoulders hunched over a book. A big book. A textbook, maybe. Of course she'd be right back there, like in the old days when convenience stores and supermarkets put the thing you most wanted in the furthest place from the door so you'd have to pass all the other crap and end up buying some of it on impulse. Only here, it was people he'd have to pass, interact with. Twenty people he didn't want to talk to who'd want to talk to him. They'd ask about his mission. They'd ask if he came across any Vikes or scav-rats. They'd ask what he found.

They'd ask how Bess had performed.

She performed admirably. I just didn't listen to her. I focused on one thing when they attacked, one deader, instead of the many things that make up a situation.

He locked eyes with Kim sitting closest to the door. The Cambodian man smiled and opened his mouth, ready to start up the questions, but Elliot interrupted and asked him to tell Claire to meet him outside. A concerned narrowing of the eyes, but Kim rose to do as asked. And Elliot returned outside to the blessed relief of crisp air and no crowds.

Claire greeted him with a smile, but eyed him carefully, offering him a glass of lemon cordial. She was wearing latex gloves. "The prodigal scout returns. You're back just now?"

"Yep." He took the glass, swallowed some. It was a perfect combo of sweet and sour. "The other two?"

"Back a few hours ago."

"Injuries?"

Claire grimaced. "Both sick."

"Jesus. Same symptoms? But they were gone three days, like me."

"Long incubation period, Faye says. They would have had it when they left."

"And there's nine now?"

"Nine," she confirmed. "One of them's little Abby."

"Jesus," he repeated, picturing the three-year-old's chubby face.

"Yeah. Her mum, too. So. How about you?"

He shook his head, understanding the reason now for her close scrutiny. And the gloves. It wasn't his soul she was worried about for once, just his body. "I'm fine. Who's with them?"

"Only Faye. But we're quarantining."

"It's that bad?"

Claire did a check over her shoulder, then closed the door and stepped away from it. "Two of them could die. Little Abby ..." She reached around to massage a crick from one shoulder. Dark circles marred the skin beneath her eyes. "I wish this wasn't happening."

"Well ... Faye's a nurse. Isn't she training you, too? Just goddamn ... do something."

Elliot recoiled from the uncharacteristic anger in her eyes. "What d'you think we're doing, Elliot?"

"Okay, I'm—"

"It's not like we're working in an emergency department."

"Okay."

"We don't even have a doctor. We're doing all we can."

"I know. I shouldn't have said that."

"Damn right you shouldn't."

"Damn right," he agreed.

She growled, plunging her gloved fists into her cardigan pockets, but her fury was spent.

"New sweater?" he asked and tried a smile.

She laughed once. "See, I told you you're good at small talk. Alyssa made this."

"Thought she might have," he said, gaze running across all the circles in the pattern. Lewis's sister did love her circles. "One more question."

"What?" she sighed.

"You checked the other scouts for bites?"

"Elliot."

"I'm just saying. The symptoms are similar. Remember Alan? What if one of them got bit out there?"

"Elliot, they weren't bitten."

"It can still happen."

"And it didn't. And if the *first* ones sick had the zombie virus, they'd have turned by now. It's been four friggin' days. They're plain old-fashioned sick and it's probably a version of the virus that tore up the group that Neil and Dave Two came from. The idiots probably brought it with them." It was very unlike her to cuss anyone for anything; Claire was normally a study in patience and compassion. She growled again and pulled out a hand to slap him in the chest. "Like you reminded me, Faye and I, we know what we're doing."

"Yeah," he said. "You do. You're two thirds of a Council that's doing a damn good job. Although, someone should tell Sturgis to wear better camouflage when he's up on the windmill."

"I'm happy for you to tell him."

"More your job than mine."

"What, you can't tell people what to do? Not the Elliot I know."

"Actually, I wanted to talk to you about that."

She raised her eyebrows, waiting him out.

"Mind if we walk?" he asked and started off anyway, aimed toward the thin creek bisecting the property. He was self-aware enough to know he hated standing still, but not enough to know whether the habit stemmed from Army training or from avoiding Uncle John as a kid. Or perhaps from being male.

When she fell in step with him, he said, "I've been thinking it might be time for me to move on."

"Move on?"

"Leave. I was only ever going to stay a few weeks. That was three years ago."

She didn't reply.

"Three years is a long time, Claire."

"I been here as long, remember? Heng, too. You were already here when Faye arrived. Far as us three Council-bigwigs are concerned, you're part of the furniture."

"See, that's where I disagree. I'm not so much furniture as satellite."

She cocked an eyebrow.

"In orbit," he explained. "Never really settled in."

"Wonderful metaphor. But it's bullshit. You have Angie."

He frowned. "That's ... casual. Angie doesn't care about me, one way or the other." Few women had over the course of his life. And with good reason.

"Really? I'm not so sure about that."

Elliot was. Wasn't he? And what did he feel for her? She had certainly not turned out to be the sociopath he'd feared she was early on. No, sir, she had turned out to be complex, witty, sassy, resourceful.

And goddamn if she didn't turn his head each time she passed.

But I'm a card-carrying loner, he told himself. And behind the thought, Uncle John's #1 maxim reminded him *in the end, you're all you have*. Which made him a little too like John for his own comfort.

"Also," Claire was saying, "you have your five-star tent over there."

"Yeah. You might have noticed that's in the back paddock and a fair distance from the other billets. And you might have noticed I spend as much time outside the fences as in."

"Some people find that makes you mysterious and enigmatic."

"I avoid them the most."

"So you're an introvert. Doesn't mean this isn't your home. We need you here."

"You don't. You have weapons. A secure base. Competent people. You need to tighten things up a little, but you Councilors know what you're doing, you said so yourself."

Waving it off, she added, "You're our family and we are yours."

"See, that's not a good thing. I don't really do family."

"Bullshit," she said again.

"Claire, you don't know me. Not really. My original family didn't do a great job, and I don't think that sets me up to get how families work."

"Elliot. I'm not asking you to be the patriarch."

"The what now?"

"To be our big daddy."

"I'm trying to talk sensibly here."

"Elliot, you had this same conversation last year with Heng when he was Council Head: I'm no good here; I need my space; I never intended to stay."

Elliot ignored that, though he cursed the old coot for sharing the info. "Bottom line. You three are smart and experienced and battle-hardened. So are other people. Like Sturgis. And Angie."

"Sure, but—"

"The Downs hasn't—"

"Settlers Downs," she corrected.

"*Settlers* Downs hasn't been attacked since we took it. The closest people groups want to leave us alone. Nine Mile River think we're scav-rats, and they keep their distance. And me..."

"You what."

"Never mind."

"You *what*, Elliot?"

"I'm making mistakes, all right? I'm goddamn sloppy. They started when I met Lewis and they haven't stopped. And lately they're getting worse."

"I'm not aware of any mistakes. What mistakes?"

"You know the biggest one: lying to Lewis about his sister."

"Sure and he might be angry, but I'm not so sure it was a mistake. Can you imagine *him* walking into that Druid compound and trading fire? Imagine if there'd been more of them than there was. You got Alyssa back for him. He's a smart young man. He owes you his life and hers. One day he'll see it."

"I got the dog killed today." He rubbed at his throat, surprised at the constriction there, the break in his voice.

She flinched at that, missing her step on the creek bank. "Bess? Oh-Kay. How'd that happen?"

He told her about the field as they wandered the creek, while the encroaching dusk snuffed out what was left of the daylight. It was almost dark by the time he'd finished and they'd turned back toward the Centre.

She said, "Bess was a fine animal. But she was an animal. One of the reasons you're breeding and training them is to protect us. I'd say that made today a success."

"You don't get it." He didn't know why he opened up to Claire. It had become a habit, a bad one. She had a way of getting around his goddamn defenses. Maybe she was a little bit like Tommy Harrison's mother. Maybe it was some kind of life change that went with being in his forties now—and *that* was a really shitty idea.

"No, I don't get it," she agreed. "So elucidate."

"I need time out there. To sharpen up. No safety net. No dogs. No Downs to come running back to."

"Sharpening up your skill set, check. What else?"

"If I'm on my own, if I get myself hurt or killed, then fine. But if I get someone else hurt or killed, not fine. Not at all fine. And it'll happen. Sometime. I'll screw up when—"

"Elliot, this is about Woodsy, isn't it?"

"What?"

"You didn't want to let him in, but everyone else voted against you."

"It's not about him. What am I, some limp-ass who cares about being outvoted? You people want to let a guy like him in, that's your business."

"It's your business, too. That's the problem. You don't want him here, but he's here. To stay."

"Folks are entitled to their opinion. Even if it's stupid."

"Sure. That's democracy."

"In its very essence."

"And the fact that even Angie didn't listen to you?"

"Why should that matter?"

"You do care about her."

"Do I, now?"

"She cares about you. I see the way she looks at you when you're getting ready to go out that gate."

He laughed outright at that. Angie and warm fuzzy feelings: not a correlation he'd ever observed.

"You've been an item how long?" she pressed gently.

"Item! Don't confuse the occasional roll in the hay with romance, Councilor Claire. And don't confuse me with a brain-dead kid who needs your mothering."

Her expression and her posture hardened, the shift obvious even in the failing light. "And don't confuse me with some village biddy who wants you to settle down and raise rosy-cheeked children. For good or bad, I was one of the people elected to run this place this year. If our best warrior, our best scout, our best tactician decides to run away into the bush, then we've got a much harder job. Our job's hard e-bloody-nuff as it is."

"And maybe I've done enough for other people. Maybe it's time to think about me. I need my goddamn space."

"You wanna roam around out there among the bikers and scav-rats?"

"The scav-rats are too crazy to be much threat. The bikers killed each other off ages ago."

"We don't know that."

"Dave One and Janice said they did. The aftermath looked pretty obvious to me when I saw it. Pretty sure you were there, too. That's right—you had a front row seat. And then there's the one time I got a decent conversation with a Vike and he confirmed it, too."

"Vikes could *be* bikers."

The Centre was back in sight now, the door open and clusters of people dribbling from within. The lights were running, powered by the solar panels on the roof. Elliot had no intention of going in there, so he stopped. He was thinking of the next thing to say when Claire jumped in.

"Elliot. You have one reason for leaving. I have several for you to stay. We're facing a possible epidemic. We lose people and it could make us vulnerable to the Nine Mile River group if they come calling. Or the Vikes and scavs, if they're not as harmless as you think they are. And if you really believe Woodsy is bad people, and you really don't want us to get hurt, why would you leave with him still here?"

Elliot ground his heel into the soil and his teeth together. Goddamnit, she had him there. Woodsy was out there now, walking the fence and no doubt carrying a weapon Elliot had liberated from the Death Druids.

"Exactly why do you think he's so bad anyway?"

"I talked this through with Faye—"

"Talk it through with me."

He took a deep breath and blew it out slow. "All right. A guy shows up on a police bike, carrying police-issue handguns and everyone believes he's a cop. *Believing* he's a cop somehow makes him trustworthy."

"Not answering my question, Elliot."

"He says he was part of a bigger group and they're all dead. How do we know he's not the killer?"

"Woodsy's a serial killer?"

"How do we know he didn't kill three cops and take a bike? How do we know he wasn't a *crooked* cop?"

There was always the small possibility of incursion from an unknown group to their south. There'd been two old women left alive at the end of the Battle for The Downs—enemies. Favoring mercy, they had released the women to wander south and never return. They might have died. Or they may have joined a coastal faction, provided intel on their former home, prompted someone in their group like Woodsy to eventually infiltrate.

"How do we know anything about anyone?" Claire asked. "How do we know Neil was really an accountant or Dave Two a mechanic?"

"Well, now, that's pretty simple. Neil teaches the teenagers complex math. Dave Two fixes cars."

"All right, smartarse. According to your logic, because Woodsy isn't handing out speeding tickets, he can't be highway patrol. So what we *don't know* and *can't prove* about him definitely makes him a potential serial killer."

"Yeah. That. Or a spy from another faction."

"Oh, now Faye did tell me your concerns about that. And I'll tell you what *she* told you. How do we know anyone isn't a spy for another faction, apart from you original guys? Faye could be from Nine Mile River. Perhaps Krystal's gathering intel for a scav-rat group. Maybe—oo, maybe I'm really a biker chick!"

"Sarcasm doesn't suit you, Claire. Don't take me seriously then. But the guy is a complete dick at the very least. Tell me you can stand in his presence and *not* smell bullshit?"

She shrugged. "I do smell something. But I honestly think it's the bullshit of a damaged man who has lost everything, just like the rest of us. He puts on bravado and bluster to get people to like him and to block out the bad thoughts. I don't think there's a person here who is completely honest with everyone. Not even you."

"Your tarots told you that?"

She raised her chin. "Maybe they did. And maybe people who deride other people's beliefs should be considered 'dicks', too."

Elliot scratched at his stubble and made a face. "Think I'll go take a shower."

"You do that, mate. Woodsy's bullshit isn't the only thing I'm smelling."

He handed her his empty glass and started off.

"Sure, I'll do your dishes, too."

He turned and held out a hand.

She waved his offer a way. "It's okay, Elliot. I'm going back there anyway. Look, I didn't want an argument with you."

"Me neither," he said. "Sorry about the tarots thing."

"Go freshen up and I'll send someone to get you some clean clothes from the laundry. Do you want dinner?"

"Not if it's fish," he said and she smiled. "A little tired of it."

"I think we have some rabbit and plain rice. Actually, Elliot, the Council's meeting at 7.00. Faye said if you were back to invite you, so I'll have the rice waiting in the Office."

"Thank you, Claire," he said.

"You're very welcome, my friend," she said and patted his shoulder as she passed.

My friend.

Much as he didn't want to admit it, she was. And she was probably a better friend than Bess and the other dogs who he spent most of his time with. Angie would be too, if he'd let her. And Kim, Rit, Heng.

Shit.

Heading toward the shower block, Elliot thought that he was damn lucky in a time and a place like this to have friends. But if Bess's experience—and Birdy's and his fire team's—was anything to go by, he just wasn't sure having him around made *them* lucky.

3

He left his filthy clothes in the shower block laundry bin, dressed in the clean ones left for him, then slid his fleece jacket back on over the tee. Whoever had left the clothes also left him a bowl of rice and rabbit strips with a handful of old raisins on top. He scraped the raisins to the side. Since his dive watch told him there was twenty minutes until 7.00, he sat on the bench seat and ate slowly and thought about Woodsy and the community at The Downs.

They were nice people. He'd gotten lucky, as had they. They were not chained up in some Death Druid compound. They were not a bunch of good-for-nothings. Nor were they heartless bastards. They worked hard. They cooperated, combining skills and energy. And they trusted each other. And that's where letting Woodsy in irked him. They were *too* trusting. What was stopping those aggressive assholes up past Nine Mile River sending in a spy or two? Or some not-so-messed-up scav group? Nine Mile and the Vikes were at their borders but they were factions Settlers Downs knew virtually nothing about. On the other hand, what was stopping a charming solo psychopath coming in and winning everyone's confidence? After all, if an animal like Jock could fool Elliot …

He shoveled more rice into his face and changed the subject in his head. Jock was not something he ever wanted to think about—not Jock, and not the things he had seen in that basement. Instead he thought of the challenges facing Settlers Downs. If this illness didn't set them back three years, or wipe them out completely, what really was the future here? Were they going to rebuild a civilization from this? There wasn't nearly enough genetic diversity here to reboot the human race. He'd watched enough Discovery Channel as a teenager to know that. If there'd been multiple nuclear reactor meltdowns across the world—and there probably had been—if the surviving populations out there had been further decimated by fallout, by starvation, by disease, then what future was there for the race, especially if white bread Tasmania was all that was left? Perhaps if they hooked up with the Nine Milers and the scav-rats and the Vikes—and whatever other small groups were out there—perhaps there might be enough diversity to relaunch the species and enough for a larger society to specialize in tech areas and to improve on the agriculture they were attempting here.

"The problem's not enough people," he told his dish as he scraped the final grains of rice together, still avoiding the raisins. The Settlers, as they'd come to call themselves, were so preoccupied with growing food and scavenging their region that education and manufacture were falling by the wayside. They were jerry-rigging technology instead of crafting it. It took a much larger community to break out of subsistence and start manufacturing and research and science and medicine … "If all the factions team up and play nice. Yeah. That'll happen."

He rinsed the dish and spoon under a shower and left it on the laundry basket for someone else to collect.

Kind people here. So kind they'd do his dishes for him. So kind that one day they'd let their own murderers walk through the front gates.

They'd trucked in the materials for The Office twelve days earlier. And "Mike the Builder" had overseen its construction. The glass, plastic and wooden box sat between homestead and shearing shed, lit inside by lanterns since it wasn't yet hooked up to solar. Heng and Claire sat at the map table in the center, nursing steaming mugs of tea. So did Woodsy.

As much as Claire had complained about Elliot's post-mission stink, Woodsy's b.o. was competing. A couple hours wandering around a fence even in cool conditions seemed to have made him work up a sweat. Perhaps it was the combination of skinny legs and middle age paunch. Woodsy had been a traffic cop, or so he claimed, so he probably wasn't used to walking. He'd certainly looked comfortable on the motorcycle he had ridden up to the gates a month back. And his straight looks and heavy frame fit a cop stereotype, as did his bluster. He ran a chubby hand through his long thinning hair and mumbled a hello.

Elliot didn't reply. The rice and meat grumbled in his gut as he closed the door and took the only free seat between Woodsy and Heng.

"Welcome back," Heng said. He pointed at the pot amidst the maps, then at the pile of mugs on a shelf. "Tea?"

When was the old coot going to learn that Elliot hated tea?

"You trying to piss me off?" Elliot asked him.

Heng shrugged as if to say, *Your loss.*

"Faye running late?" Elliot asked.

"Not coming," said Heng.

"What? Why?"

Claire cleared her throat. "She's placed herself in quarantine." Lines had appeared at the corners of her eyes, lines Elliot had never noticed before. Worry lines?

"She's …?"

"She doesn't want to spread it if she's already got it. We're to leave food and water at a distance and she'll come out and get it every morning."

"God Almighty."

Heng said, "This get worse every day."

"Before we talk about that situation, let's get your report, Elliot. You found a bad area today."

"You got my map there?"

Claire pushed the topmost one toward him. Elliot leaned over and traced with his finger. "Here. By this access road. Old dairy farm, judging by the milking sheds. But no animals. Tall grass, and some of it may be barley. But there's plenty of claymores."

"You mean drybones," Woodsy corrected him. "We should all use the same term."

Elliot ignored him.

"A little close to Vike territory," Claire observed.

Elliot grunted. "Nothing left in the middle of our territory to explore. If we want fresh resources…"

"So drybones killed your dog?" Woodsy pressed, eyes on the spot where Elliot's finger rested.

Elliot felt like raising a different finger, but refrained for Claire's sake.

"How many of them?" she asked.

"Didn't stop to count. But a lot. Enough to be leftovers from the Dead Line."

Woodsy looked from one to the other for an explanation. "Deadline?"

"How you not know about that?" Heng said. "You never talk to anybody here? Dead Line. Two word. Big crowd of zombie. Maybe ten or twenty or thirty thousand."

"Oh, that. Headed south, weren't they?"

"Does it matter where they were headed at first?" Elliot said. "I doubt they all had a particular destination in mind. They probably wandered round and round till they got stuck behind the fences or turned dormant and started rotting."

"What condition were they in?" asked Claire.

"A couple I saw were too far gone to move much. But dozens of others came at me. Enough were in good enough condition to get the dog."

"Shit," said Woodsy. "Dogs are valuable."

Grinding his teeth, Elliot pressed on. "Anyway, mark it. Avoid it."

"Wouldn't catch me dead in a place like that," Woodsy muttered.

Elliot continued, "Maybe wild fire will come through and clean them up for us. Meantime, the fences looked like they'd hold them. And the mobile ones have no reason to head all the way here."

"We could set that fire," Woodsy suggested. "Burn 'em out."

"Yeah, and risk it blowing this way."

"Just a thought. Bush fire's gunna happen sometime anyway. This is Australia, mate."

Elliot clenched a fist under the table, wishing the asshole would keep his pie hole firmly closed. He flashed Claire a look, asking if they could get rid of this tool. She gave a little shake of her head as she dragged the paper back and shaded the area indicated with an orange marker.

"Question is," he said, "where do we scavenge now, since there's nowhere left we haven't looked except a few gorges along the boundaries of our territory. I don't wanna climb into them, but if I have to... Or do we simply stop?"

She exchanged a glance with the other two. "We have bigger fish at the moment, Elliot."

"The illness?"

"Indeed."

"It's like a flu, right? Exactly how bad is this?"

"Bad," Heng said.

Woodsy added, "The kids are camping on the far side of the farm with Lewis and a couple of others watching them. They seem okay so far. I've been leaving food, water and supplies at a distance so they don't catch it from me."

"You have the bug?"

Woodsy frowned. "No. I mean in *case* I do."

Damn shame, Elliot thought.

"And how are you?" he asked Claire pointedly.

She brushed hair from her eyes. It had more grey in it than a week ago, he was sure. Just like those worry lines weren't there back then, either.

"I'm fine."

She was flushed, but that could have been stress.

"And we're sure this isn't, you know, *the* Sickness."

Woodsy scoffed. "Not every bug is the zombie virus, mate. We did have other illnesses before the breakdown, you know."

"What the hell are you doing in here, anyway? When did you get voted onto the Council?"

Woodsy sniffed. "When did you? You're in here, too."

"I was invited to update intel."

Woodsy sipped tea and offered no more than a grunt.

Claire cleared her throat. "Everyone's welcome in here, Elliot."

"Especially when they can help like I can," Woodsy said into his cup.

He sipped again while Claire poured herself more tea.

"Elliot," she said, "there was another reason Faye wanted you here. We've been discussing the medical situation. The antibiotic and antiviral situation."

"We don't have any," he said.

"Exactly."

There were more exchanged looks.

"Christ," he gasped. "You want to go find some." He combed a hand through his short and shower-damp hair. "I get that we need it. But where from? I'm telling you, we've looked everywhere. There could still be some useful crap out there within our limits, but none of it's pharmaceuticals. And any medication we'd find would be pretty useless by now. Wouldn't it?"

"Antibiotics and antivirals might still be okay. If they were dry and cool. Or especially if they were engineered to last this long."

A pause.

Again, he asked, "What?"

She gestured toward Woodsy.

The big man said, "Was just telling them that the Federal Government kept cool rooms full of high-grade antivirals and antibiotics in every state. Prevention in case something like a terrorist biological attack happened."

"Where?"

"You mean where in *Tassie*? Inland. Halfway between here and Hobart."

"You're not serious."

"As long as the facility's solar power is still working—"

"And if it's not?"

"If it *is*, mate, we can supply ourselves with serious medication."

"We don't know what's happening out there, past our territory."

Claire said, "Elliot, an hour ago you told me the biker gangs were all gone."

"And you said maybe some are left. I'll admit you had a point. Helluva lot we don't know about the world outside our region. How do we know there's not a bunch of leftover bikers watching the roads down there?

50

How do we know some other faction hasn't found and liberated all that good stuff?"

"If you let me explain, I'll talk you through that," said Woodsy.

"How do we know whether there's not still a thousand mobile deaders hanging out near these 'cool rooms'?"

"The dead are dead," the ex-cop sighed.

"Well, I just lost my dog to a field full of 'em."

"We call those drybones for a reason. You were unlucky, but mostly they're innocuous these days. Slow. Rotted. I saw enough of 'em on my way here to know that."

"Yeah, and I'm still not satisfied I know exactly where you came from."

"Christ, I told all of this when—"

Heng slapped the table. "Stop. We must think about this serious. People in quarantine can die. But we find medicine, we can save them. Not argue. We do something."

Elliot growled. "Yeah, well, the dumbasses heading out on this fool's errand could also die."

"Or they could save everyone's arses," Woodsy returned evenly.

"Let's say you bring them back here. Twelve months later, outside their refrigeration they're useless and we're back to square one."

"The fridges are on solar power, Elliot," Claire said.

"And they break down?"

"What, all of them? At once?"

Elliot turned his face to the ceiling, breaking contact, unwilling to concede that point.

"We also have the Zeer pots," she added.

To Elliot, Woodsy said, "You don't have to go. No one's asking you. I'm going. I'll travel light and take one other person with me—"

"Not Lewis."

Woodsy blinked. "No, not Lewis. I was thinking of Jimmy."

Jimmy. The kid that Elliot had found chained up with Claire, the kid repeatedly abused by both male and female Druids in the gang. The kid who for some reason had never bonded with anyone in this community—anyone, that was, except for Woodsy.

"Yeah, that kid'll go with you all right. For some reason, he thinks the sun shines outa your hairy ass. And he will until the day you get him killed doing something stupid like this."

Claire tried: "Gentlemen."

"I got here okay, didn't I?" Woodsy said. "Three and a half years, and I survived."

"Sure. And the rest of your group?"

For the first time, Woodsy grew angry, straightening in his chair. "What's that s'posed to mean?"

"Gentlemen!"

"When you arrived, you mentioned a larger group, all dead now but you."

"Two died on raids. Three died from running into the undead. The other died of a bloody heart attack. You're blaming me for all of that?"

Claire shouted this time. "Gentlemen, enough!"

The room lapsed into silence apart from the wall clock ticking.

Heng grinned.

Elliot eyeballed him. "What are you smiling at!"

"This like having TV again." He chuckled. "Who get kicked out of house next?"

Woodsy slumped, released a chuckle of his own. "Good one."

Claire said, "If we can keep on topic. We were just starting to consider the sorts of obstacles you're thinking of, Elliot. What if someone else has taken all of it? What if the facility is occupied by armed factions? What if it's full of eaters?"

Elliot added, "What if it caught fire, or broke down?"

"We mentioned that, too. So we can sit here and ask our questions. And never know. Or someone can go look. And maybe—maybe—come back with enough medicine to save our people from this bug and from the next five or ten."

"You're deciding on this as a Council?"

"We already have, Elliot. Faye cast her vote this afternoon. Woodsy has volunteered to go since he knows location and codes."

"Don't expect me to go with him."

"Jesus," Woodsy muttered.

She said, "But we would like your thoughts."

Woodsy started, "I'm fine, Claire, I know what—"

Claire stopped him with a raised palm. "Elliot?"

Elliot scratched at his beard and said, "Take a Land Rover—"

"Thought of it," Woodsy said.

"—they're tough and have a big gas tank. Think about moving the vehicle from cover to cover like an infantryman: plan your drive and then drive from what looks like safe place to safe place fast, keep moving. Scope it quickly, reassess, move on. You run before shooting anyone or thing. You get into firefights only as last resort."

"I've thought this through a million—"

"And I'll keep talking about it, because Claire asked me to and because drilling it into you might save someone's life besides yours, dumbass." Why was there always someone who wouldn't listen to him? "Worst thing is to get bogged down, pinned down, or flanked. Keep moving and if you have to abandon the vehicle, you do."

Woodsy sat with his mug in his lap, lips pressed together, like a schoolboy getting a dressing down.

Elliot stood. "And I'm goddamned tired and I'm going to bed. Just tell me tomorrow what you decide to do. But," he added with his hand on the door, "my best piece of advice is this. Don't. Take. Jimmy."

4

It felt like someone had turned up gravity. With bowed head and slumped shoulders, Elliot trudged across the Yard toward Main Street, forcing himself to take that route. He could have diverted through the orchards and across the paddocks, making a beeline for his tent. But he had one more person to visit before he could collapse into welcome unconsciousness.

With the rain holding off, the Street now showed the signs of life he expected from it. Light spilled from behind curtains. Shaz and Tania—the women rescued from Waxer's van following the battle for The Downs—sat shoulder to shoulder on their step, sharing a cigarette. He dug a half empty packet of them from a pocket, considered it for a moment: it had gotten a little crushed in his escape from the field. Well, *he* wasn't going to smoke them. He tossed the pack to Shaz. "Found these in a car."

She looked it over then flashed him the inside of the pack on the step beside her. It had one left. "Good timing. Appreciate it."

"De nada," he responded and stopped at the last hut on the left. A candle flickered inside. He knocked gently and said, "It's Elliot."

The voice from within was soft and all it said was: "Okay."

He opened the door and left it open, leaning on the jamb—no point inviting idiot speculation about booty calls.

Lewis's sister sat cross-legged on her single bed, surrounded by wool. Knitting another pullover from the looks. Her long hair hid the very edges of her face so that her dark and serious eyes had a narrow gap to peer at him. In a voice barely above a whisper, she asked, "Anything?"

He made a sorry face. Then smiled and pulled a charm from his pocket. The tight silver spiral was actually an earring he'd found in the claymore property's homestead. But it would connect to her pandora bracelet fine, and he figured she'd like it. And she did; he was practiced enough in reading her body language. She didn't squeal, like a different nineteen-year-old girl might. She didn't clap her hands. Not even a smile in acknowledgment of his teasing. But there was a sudden and ever so slight widening of her eyes—a sign of pleasure and of innocence, there and gone again like a gust of breeze. Elliot leaned forward and placed the charm on the foot of her bed. She stretched for it, then lay it on top of her bracelet where it sat on her bedside drawers.

"Doing okay?" he asked.

She nodded, hands busy with knitting again.

"Need anything?"

Her hair rippled with the single shake of her head.

"Well, you let Claire know if you do and I'll get it for you."

A nod.

This was their ritual, their dance. It never changed. She'd never given him much sign that she trusted him, but she'd told Claire that she did.

He had one foot reaching for the step behind him when she spoke again.

"Find anything for yourself?"

He balked. She'd never asked anything like that before. She'd barely ever spoken. "Er, no. Oh, a half-bottle of Jim Beam hidden under a car seat. But I promise I'll share that."

She made a face. "Not with me."

"No. I'll find you some soda next time I'm out. Soft drink."

Her needles started up their clacking again. She said, "Coke."

He smiled at that.

The silence lengthened until he was certain nothing else would be forthcoming. "Sure you don't need anything else?"

"I'm good," she murmured.

Yes, you are, sweetheart. These days, you're doing pretty damn good, all things considered.

His eyes caught then on an object on the chair beside the door. A grey and red striped pullover, folded neat. His pullover. He disliked that pullover. Very much. It was one of the ugliest objects he'd ever seen. Jen had made it, the woman who'd taken a shine to him, who looked at him with wedding cake eyes every chance she got. The pullover didn't fit properly and was scratchy, but at Claire and Faye's insistence, he'd been wearing it recently during some fence wiring. And he'd been proud of how credibly he'd snagged it on the fence and torn it up.

Damn shame, he'd told Faye as he'd handed it to her to repurpose.

He tapped the chair beside the sweater. "You repaired this?"

A nod.

Shee-it.

He picked it up and tied the arms round his waist. "Well. Thanks."

I guess.

A murmur. Something that might even have been *de nada.*

He engaged the door lock before closing it, then stood outside on her step. He pulled his flashlight, ready for the trek across the unlit paddocks to his tent. The first few drops of the rain he'd been expecting spattered against his jacket, his face. Shaz and Tania had retreated indoors. Someone laughed in another cabin and complained about cheating: cards, no doubt.

In the room behind him, there came a soft tinkling from the pandora bracelet as Alyssa fitted her new addition.

De nada.

She had never recovered from her ordeal with the Death Druids. But occasionally he caught glimpses of the girl—and woman—who might have been. It made him angry. What that girl had lost made him truly angry. And if Elliot found a million Death Druid bikers—a million Waxers—and if he killed each and everyone one, it was an anger he would never ever purge.

He whistled once as he entered the paddock where this tent and the dog pens lay. Recognizing his tone, the dogs locked in their pens started up barking but he shouted once for them to quiet and they did. A few seconds later the two dogs he'd seen roaming found him again, coming in to nuzzle.

"Hope you two can forgive me," he said, giving both a chest and belly rub. "Bess ain't coming—"

He stood, clearing his throat.

During his absence, Sturgis and his wife had been tasked with caring for the dogs, so Elliot felt comfortable leaving their upkeep until tomorrow. He wanted that belt of bourbon and a decent night's sleep. If his mind would let him.

He said, "Follow" and the two animals fell in behind him. They could be his ears while he rested. Dogs, he'd found, were like soldiers: they did what they were trained to do, they followed orders. Even when it got them killed.

The sight of his tent pitched in the flat between two tea trees never failed to bring him a sense of relief. His own space. A place to rest—rest and forget. It was huge, a deluxe model's deluxe model. Two large "rooms": a kitchen-and-storage area at the front, plus a large sleeping and living area behind it, separated by zips and flaps.

The male dog growled. Something stirred inside, brushing and sliding against the rear wall. Elliot's hand was halfway to his SIG when he realized who it'd be.

"Quiet," he told the dog. He reached for the front flap, already half unzipped. "Shit, Angie. You gotta stop just turning up. One of these days, I'll accidentally—"

Inside, commotion exploded—claws scratching across plastic flooring, tins clattering to the floor from a shelf. The dogs barked. A small form shot through the opening, vaulting off one of Elliot's boots before disappearing into the grass nearby. His flashlight had only just caught it: the grey-brown fuzz of a goddamn possum. Both dogs took off after it across the paddock. Elliot let them go while his pulse hammered in his throat and he hurried inside, groaning, "Christ, no, no, no."

The flashlight beam revealed disaster. His personal stash of jerky strips spread through the kitchen area, the dried plums container opened and fruit spread all over. Jar of bullet casings turned over. Possum shit on his favorite hoody—he bundled that up and tossed it out the entrance. In the sleeping room, more mess, the worst of it possum piss on his bedding. Fortunately, he kept the suitcase he used for a wardrobe closed at all times. But his bed was history.

"Christ on a crutch!"

An animal had made the mess, but it hadn't opened the tent zippers. Who had?

Did some lunatic scav-rat come over the fences? Nothing seemed to be taken.

Was it Lewis? But why would he? Lewis hadn't given Elliot the time of day for three years, and he'd never do anything like this.

Was it Woodsy, being a dick because Elliot had opposed his suggestions in community meetings a couple of times?

Was it young Jimmy, being a freak?

No. It was kids, probably. Kids being kids, being curious. Which means his home had been open to the elements since before the kids were quarantined, a couple days ago. He kicked the plums container out through the door and followed it to pace outside, fuming.

The dogs weren't back yet, and wouldn't be unless he called them. They'd be after that possum for an hour if Elliot let them. And Elliot was going to let them.

Exhausted, he gathered a spare blanket and pillow from his suitcase-cupboard—he couldn't sleep here tonight. Maybe not ever, the way it stank. He'd have to sleep in the homestead living room for a while. Heading back across the paddocks and leaving the dogs to run free for the night, he realized he was back to feeling the way he'd felt for most of his adult life.

Displaced.

5

He came into a crowded Community Centre, air bitey with woodsmoke from the fireplace and thick with low conversation and the scrape of cutlery on crockery. The windows hissed with morning rain; the drainpipes sang. He shook his parka off and hung it on the racks with the others. No kids again, Lewis and Krystal out with them. A quick headcount: the four adults who'd be on watch duty were missing, as was Claire. He figured she'd be leaving supplies for Faye outside the infirmary.

Without small children there to harass it, one of the farm cats had curled up on the floor before the wood-burning heater.

As was often the case at breakfast, small groups with something in common had drawn together around different tables. Those with practical skills: the Daves, Wendy the plumber who'd come in with Dave Two, Mike, and Phil. The quiet people, the ones who got things done and bent their skills to whatever the task was that most needed doing right then: Sturgis, Kim, Tina, Heng, Angie. The farmers like late-sixties Nance, who worked with their hands in the soil and whose fingernails were lined with black. The ones who had once worked with words or numbers or ideas, and now lived in a more practical reality: Di and Neil and Dylan. But the cliques were not really cliques; there was no Them-and-Us here, only We. A group of people who'd got lucky—or made their own luck—by finding each other, creating a community without power plays, hubris, control freaks, divisiveness. Thirty-five damaged but decent adults—not counting messed-up Jimmy, who was nonetheless cared for and tolerated here— thirty-five cooperative people without one asshole among them ... until Woodsy came along.

And there the man was, holding court at the words-and-numbers table in the exact center of the hall, where he'd been for some time from the look of his empty plate and glass. Woodsy seated with those polite middle-classers who'd tolerate his out-of-phase humor and know-it-all attitude.

Elliot wiped recalcitrant night grit from his eyes as he stepped up to the kitchen servery window. The homestead couch had been badly sprung, sagging in the middle. He rubbed at his back, thinking that he'd clean the tent later. Or maybe burn it and pull a smaller tent out of storage.

From the servery, Rit adjusted his Disney baseball cap and said, "Your normal cheerful self, I see." Chariya by the sink laughed at her husband's jibe and nodded hello. Alyssa drying dishes, just stared.

"And you're still a smart ass," Elliot growled, but there was no sting in it. "Gimme some of everything."

"Even the fish?"

"Sure."

"You hate fish."

"Don't hate it, just *tired* of it. But I need the protein."

"Protein, we have," Rit said, spooning a small portion of scrambled eggs on to the plate. As he followed it with a slim white fillet and five slices of apple, he lowered his voice. "We used up the last of the oats while you were gone."

"I expected that."

"And we're nearly out of rice."

At that moment, Woodsy leaned past Elliot to slide his plate and mug onto the counter. With a friendly grin, he said, "Jeez, how will you Asians survive without rice?" and headed back to his table. Only Elliot and Rit heard it. Maybe Alyssa and Chariya, too.

"Racist dickhead." Rit's head shake was sincere, but dismissive. "Running out of grain isn't great for any of us."

Elliot glanced aside, but the next men in line—the Daves, with their mugs in hand for a refill—were busy arguing over old sports stats. He told Rit, "And so far we're not doing that well growing any. Not nearly enough to feed this many people. I did come across a big field of barley out there. I think it's barley anyway, but probably only good for animals."

"Looks like it's gonna be lots more fish, rabbit and potatoes to tide us over for a few years while we sort this out."

Elliot pushed food around his plate with his fork. "Don't forget apples. No shortage of goddamn apples in Tasmania." He was tired of those as well.

Chariya slid a cup beside Elliot's plate. "Cocoa. Weak."

"Cause the cocoa's nearly gone, too." Rit added. "Going to be a low-carb diet for a while."

Elliot picked up the cup and plate. "We've survived worse. Heng's generation in Cambodia survived much worse."

"Sure." Rit leaned on the bench. "I'd still kill for a donut and a packet of corn flakes."

The Daves moved up to take his place and Elliot surveyed the room for a suitable seat. Usually he liked to eat at the small foldout table facing the back wall to discourage conversation. Eating outside was even better. But as the patter on the tin roof testified, the rain would make outside dining unpleasant—steamed fish was bad enough without getting it waterlogged. His usual table was occupied. All of them were, though there were plenty of spare chairs. Two were spare at Woodsy's table.

Screw it. He'd eat outside, rain or no rain. A little water wouldn't hurt him. But when he reached the door, he found it blocked by Claire.

Above the filter-mask she wore, her face was drawn, her eyes black-rimmed and bloodshot. There were fresh gloves on her hands. She asked, "Where you headed?"

"Thought I'd get some fresh air."

She shook her head and took a step forward, forcing him back. "Not yet, please. Community meeting."

"Now?"

"Everyone's here that's gonna be."

"How about I relieve someone on the gate?"

He tried to step around. She reached back and tugged the door shut. "Already spoken to. I need you here."

He grumped a little as he stepped to the side, then put his back against the wall. *Bland food, weak cocoa, and a morning meeting. Just like the goddamn Middle East.* He jammed a chunk of fish fillet in his mouth: getting the worst food down first was an old Army trick, same as learning to eat most anything when choices were slim.

Claire rang the discussion bell that hung by the door. Conversation petered out. Plates clattered in the kitchen. All eyes turned her way, a few darting to Elliot near her. He dropped his head to dissuade attention.

Her tone formal, Claire said loudly, "We belong to Settlers Downs."

"A place where peaceful people settle down," most of the room responded in unison.

"A lighthouse of hope," she continued, in reference to the lighthouse and small beach three hundred metres beyond their front gate.

"In a dark world," the room responded.

"May we increase the light and decrease the darkness."

Murmurs of agreement. One *Amen*.

It might have been a little cheesy, Elliot thought, but Claire's idea for this introduction to meetings served an important cultural purpose. It was clever of her.

The ritual over, her tone lost its formality without losing its gravity. Or weariness. "We have some things to discuss before we get on with the day's busyness."

"The sick people?" farmer Nance asked.

"Them, mainly, yes." As if requested, the rain abated a little outside, so that the main noise Claire had to contend with was the shifting of chairs and occasional coughs and sniffles. "I've been to check on Faye and the Infirmary this morning. And I've been round the sentries to tell them what I'll be telling you. And consult on what I'll be consulting about. We now have ten sick."

"Ten?" Nance again.

"As of last night, Faye is officially down with the same thing."

A chorus of interruptions, cries of alarm and inquiries into Claire's own health status. When it didn't immediately drop off, Elliot adopted a parade ground voice and barked for quiet.

"Thank you," Claire said as the hubbub choked off. "And I'm fine. Yes, I've been in there a bit lately, so I'll stay over this side of the room right now, then isolate myself in my cabin afterwards for a couple of days to see if it develops. Heng is in charge till then, I guess. But, no. No symptoms. We need to keep our distance from the Infirmary, leaving food and water ten metres from the hut. Faye, Jen, and Raj are still mobile enough to fetch and distribute it."

That drew a teary "thank god" from Raj's wife.

"Is anyone actually getting better?" Dave 1 asked. "Tony?" The first person to get sick.

Claire pursed her lips ruefully and a collective sigh passed around the room. "But it's been seven days now since the first case, and everyone is still alive. I hate to be that blunt. But maybe it's not as bad as we feared, on that score. However, no improvement is not a good sign either. Dehydration is probably their biggest danger. Obviously we don't want this spreading further. We've got the kids in quarantine thanks to Lewis and Krystal and Huy."

He'd gotten the fish down; now Elliot sipped cocoa, swishing it around his tongue and teeth to cleanse them before starting on the eggs. He wanted to be out of here as quick as he could. There were three small hamlets within their territory he should comb through again, check inside drywall and under floor boards, in case they'd missed something that could help the sick.

"As is the case with all viruses," Claire was saying, "it's the very young and the elderly that are at most risk."

"The elderly: that'd be me," Nance piped up, drawing a ripple of nervous laughter. Although she was in her late sixties, Elliot considered her one of the fittest people on site, a lifelong workhand, hard as stone.

Rit called out from the servery window, "And Heng. He's older than the rest of us put together."

More laughter, brighter this time. And some cussing from Heng in the corner.

Claire continued, "So we're at the point of needing medicine. To protect Heng and Nance mainly." This time the laughter was decidedly more relaxed. Elliot thought it good leadership. "As you know, we've scoured every inch of the two veterinarian's rooms near here. Every pharmacy and doctor's office. Every farm. We don't have what we need. Antivirals to fight the bug. And if this goes on much longer, we'll be out of acetaminophen and ibuprofen for the fever. And before you all tell me that's impossible to find those things now, Woodsy has an idea that's worth following up. Woodsy?"

The ex-cop stood. Elliot's stomach clenched. Jimmy, two years older than Lewis, but nowhere near as together, straightened in his chair. Nance and Neil watched Woodsy with respect. Others sat back, eyes wide with interest. Woodsy outlined the plan, explaining that as a cop he knew the government facility's door codes, about how they would use chiller bags to transport whatever they found back to Settlers Downs. "But I need help, folks."

Who would help him? Who *could* help him? Elliot had already been inventorying the room. Most people like Rit or Kim or the two Daves would be perfectly fine defending The Downs against incursion. But very few of them made decent scouts, despite Elliot's best efforts at training them, and infiltrating hostile territory was a long way outside their skillset.

A few were so hapless, they were barely able to contribute meaningfully to the community: Alyssa, folded into a corner of the kitchen worrying at the tea towel; Tania, who'd never recovered fully from her ordeal in Waxer's van; Neil, who was likely to hit his thumb more times than the nail, to break the eggs when closing the coop; and Jimmy, who spent a lot of his time alone doing God knew what and the time they did monitor rereading old comic books. Few of those remaining were competent enough for a mission of this magnitude. And the ones who were, were also the ones Elliot would least like to lose. The best choice for

Woodsy, and worst choice for the camp, would be Sturgis with his Australian Navy experience.

"I need two people," Woodsy was saying. Eyes had dropped, opting out of consideration. Elliot was disheartened to see Sturgis chewing his lips as he thought it over while Tina gripped his hand tight, willing him to stay.

Jimmy shot to his feet, arms crossed over a puffed-out chest "I'm in, Woodsy!" The outburst was uncharacteristic in volume, though typical in intensity. He bobbed on his feet, eyes blazing with zealot fire. Perhaps he hoped to come across a few leftover Death Druids he could stab to death.

A few people murmured approval, perhaps relief. Elliot cursed. Well, the kid was as stupid as the man he idolized. Let him go. Elliot had done enough rescuing in his life and rarely been thanked for it.

Woodsy tossed the young man a wink. "Thought you would be, matey. Good on ya. Just need one more, folks. Rules are rules. Only three people outside the fences at once."

Smartass prick. I was the one came up with that rule and he knows it.

"Course, I can go ask the sentries if no one here feels up to it. It's perfectly—"

"I'm in!"

Heads turned. Elliot gaped.

Angie was on her feet.

Christ Almighty.

"Wonderful," Woodsy beamed. "Brave girl."

What was she thinking?

"All right," said Claire as she waved Woodsy toward his seat. "That's three."

She's crazy, she can't do this!

Claire continued, her voice dull in Elliot's ears, "We'll let you get set up to leave by lunch. Kitchen crew can prep traveling food for them."

Holy Christ, that fool will get her killed. Or worse!

"Everyone else can work out duties and cover those people going on mission and in quarantine. But any symptoms, come see me at my cabin immediately."

"I'll go, too," Elliot said.

Claire didn't hear him at first. She kept on talking for another ten seconds while faces turned his way until finally she picked up on it. She fell silent like the rest of the room.

"I said I'll go, too."

Woodsy came to his feet. "You said last night you didn't want to."

"Changed my mind."

"We only need three."

"Four's better."

"The rule's no more than three outside the fences at any one time."

"And you made that rule, Elliot," Nance chimed in.

"Then I'll be the first to break it." Elliot stared down the crowd, avoiding Angie's fierce gaze. "Besides, this is a bigger mission than scouting for Mars bars and tampons."

Some murmurs of objection to his choice of subject matter, but Elliot didn't care.

Woodsy turned his attack on Heng and then Claire. "Can we discuss this privately?"

71

"Why?" one of the Daves asked.

Claire said, "Sure," then pointed at the door. "I'm heading outside anyway."

Elliot followed her out and waited until Woodsy joined them a few metres away from the door so that people wouldn't have to brush past Claire if she was infected.

As people began leaving the Centre, Woodsy stage-whispered, "We don't need a fourth person."

"More the merrier," Elliot said dismissively.

Claire said, "If you want to drop someone, drop Jimmy."

"Amen," Elliot said.

"The lad wants to come."

"Then four it is," she said. "I trust you boys will cooperate."

"Cooperation's my middle name," said Elliot.

Woodsy stormed away without further comment.

Jimmy's head poked from the Centre before he located Woodsy and jogged off after him.

Claire jerked her head to steer Elliot out of earshot from anyone at the door. "I mean it, Elliot. You need each other. And *we* need both of you."

"Message received," he said. Noticing Angie in the doorway, trying to push past Neil and Nance with murder in her eyes, he added quickly, "Gotta go get the Rover prepped. I'll see ya."

He turned and walked.

Fast.

6

___

S plashing through puddles, he'd made it no more than twenty paces before Angie braked his progress with a fistful of his shirt. Her hair had grown out from the buzz cut she'd had the first time they'd met. That had been in the back of a sheep truck, both captured by allies of the Death Druids. Her new blonde locks would have reached past her shoulders if she hadn't gathered them into a samurai-style topknot. Several times he'd enjoyed the site of those locks spread across his pillow. But that had been in moments where Angie was happy or horny. Right now, she was about as far from happy and horny as a person could be.

"Morning," he tried.

"I don't need you tagging along!"

"Never said you did."

"But you thought it." Her finger was in his face, a long-nailed muzzle aimed between his eyes. "No sign of you volunteering, then the moment I put my hand up, you had to come, too. You don't think I'll make it without you? I'm some dumb blonde who can't handle herself?"

"I know first-hand you can handle yourself." Her eyes widened, but he cut her off. "In a skirmish. I meant in a skirmish."

"I *don't* need you."

"No, but Jimmy does."

She blinked and pulled back. "Jimmy."

"Yeah. Jimmy. That's why I stepped up." *You lying bastard*, he thought. "That poor kid is a mental case. And his men*tor* doesn't know his ass from his elbow."

"…Oh." She shoved hands in pockets. "I thought … But why didn't you stand up before I did? When Jimmy did?"

He shrugged. "Gettin' slow in my middle age."

"Yeah, right."

"Anyhoo, Woodsy only wants three, so you could drop out. Stay back and defend the farm."

"You're doing it again, you bloody chauvinist."

"What chauvinist? I said *defend the place*. Didn't you hear me say that? I'm saying they need your abilities and hardness here."

"You said four is better. I'm going on that mission."

"Fine. Of course you are."

"In fact, I can keep an eye on Jimmy myself. So maybe we don't need *you*. Woodsy wants three."

"Or we could talk Jimmy into staying here."

"In which case, there'd be no need for you to go."

Goddamnit.

An old frustration burned beneath his skin. It was a face off. She'd outflanked him, left him nowhere to run. So many relationships—so very many relationships—had come to their end this same way. Only this wasn't a relationship. Was it? Not with a capital R, surely.

74

They had a *working* relationship, getting crap done. And occasionally he invited her to his tent, or she turned up of her own volition. But it wasn't a big R relationship. So there was no reason for him to feel outflanked. No reason at all for déjà vu.

"Well?" she said, the word like a single-syllable kick in the balls. "You gonna stand there staring into space or you gonna reply?"

"I got your reply, Angie."

"Oh, nice."

"Listen, I get you don't want to spend a week-long road trip with me. But it's not really up to you."

"Nope. It's up to the Council. And they might still decide you're of more use here."

"You're telling them that?"

"I'll tell Heng. Sure."

"Then you and Heng can kiss—"

"You live here?" She'd stepped in close again, but he refused to retreat. There was apple skin in her teeth and her breath smelled like fish. But with her blood up and her hair up, she was damned beautiful. "You live here, you listen to the Council."

Quietly he said, "Maybe I don't want to live here anymore."

"What!"

Wrong move. "Or maybe I need a vacation. And this trip is just what the doctor ordered."

She was staring at—no, staring *into* him. God, he hated that. As if she'd found the video of last night's conversation with Claire and was replaying it.

He finally took that step back. "And why am I explaining myself to you?"

Her hands were on her hips now. He almost said something about her stance being a little cliché, but over the past three years he'd gotten better at resisting suicidal acts.

Like walking into a field of claymores?

She leaned in and with fish breath she said, "You come on this trip, you treat me like an equal. And you do not tell me what to do."

Her long legs carried her away, and fast.

"Good talk!" he called after her.

She flipped the bird over her shoulder.

Real good talk.

He backed the Land Rover into the garage beside the small fire tanker-truck that Dave One had arrived in. There was no sign of either Dave here this morning. By the time he'd loaded some tools and checked fluid levels and battery charge, Woodsy had appeared at his side.

"Yes, officer?" Elliot asked him, wiping grit and grease on a rag.

"License and registration?" Woodsy joked, trying for affability and charm.

Elliot wrung the rag between his fingers while working hard on swallowing his pride. Claire had told him to cooperate. Woodsy might be an asshole, but that had also been several people's diagnosis of Elliot over the years, girlfriends especially. The last thing that Angie would tolerate, and Jimmy would benefit from, would be spending a week caught between two alpha males engaged in a piss-fight.

He tried for small talk: "That's not what you guys said over here, was it? I mean, that's what American cops said."

"No, we said something different." Woodsy shrugged, losing interest in that topic. "Look, I didn't mean to imply I don't want you along. I'm thinking more people uses more fuel. The Rover's not huge and the passenger seats could hold more cargo if..."

"... if Jimmy stayed back. Sure. I agree."

"Jimmy?"

"Yeah, Jimmy. You said we need three. You, me and Angie. We're older and more experienced than the kid. We're better off without him."

"He's tougher than you think."

"Oh, trust me. First time I met him, he'd just stabbed one of his abductors to death, so I know he's tough. But he's erratic, undisciplined and untrained."

He expected Woodsy to wind up again. To claim Elliot was loading the mission two against one. Presuming he knew about Elliot and Angie. Instead, Woodsy dug deep for more charm, patting Elliot's shoulder and glancing around in conspiratorial fashion. "It's important for Jimmy to come. The kid kind of looks up to me. I'm like a father figure to him."

"A father figure."

"Sure. Like you were to Lewis."

Were.

Unaware of the gaff, Woodsy kept talking while he opened one of the firetruck's cargo bags and rummaged. "Jimmy is all right. He's starting to come good. He's not the coolest guy around, but he does what I tell him. He's good at climbing and skinny enough to worm his way through cracks you and I can't. And this trip will give him that experience he needs."

"Kim took Jimmy scouting a few months back, before you arrived. The kid fell off a ladder. A month before that he set a campfire in the back paddock and it took ten of us to put out the blaze it started."

Woodsy pulled an eighteen-inch "hooligan bar" from the fire truck. He brandished the fancy crowbar and affected a wry grin. "Well, he's not the sharpest tool in the shed, but he'll never get sharper if we don't keep honing him."

"As I said, I think he should—"

"He's coming, Elliot. My mission. My choice."

"That so? It's your mission? Not our mission?"

"All right, I shouldn't have said that. Let's not measure penises here. We can both lead it. I'll listen to your ideas. I'll value them."

"Angie's, too?"

Woodsy's frown was there and gone a moment later, but Elliot had seen the assumption, the lack of respect for her. He didn't know her like Elliot did. Why she would think Elliot didn't respect her ability and her courage and her smarts, Elliot didn't know. Because he most certainly did. And Woodsy would get a hell of a shock when he saw her in action for himself.

"Angie's, too. Of course. But I know where the meds are. I know how to get in. so I'll have to lead some of the time, of course."

"And Jimmy will follow your lead?"

"He'll follow all of us. But best we stay on the same page so he doesn't get confused." His pat on Elliot's shoulder was meant as a period to end the discussion.

He weighed the hooligan bar again and nodded. "This will do nicely if the faculty doors aren't powered. Emergency services used these babies in car crashes and house fires to—"

"I know what's it for," Elliot growled.

"Fair enough. Course you do. We'll also need a cordless tire inflator and a jump start kit."

Elliot pointed his chin at the 4-wheel-drive's cargo space. "Got 'em."

"Good man. Great minds, eh? Well, I'm off to the barn to put some supplies aside. If you like, you can back the car over there ..."

Elliot watched him go. He had lead in his gut and a headache shelling the inside of his skull. "Sir yes sir," he muttered. Then frowned, focusing on someone he hadn't noticed until then.

Krystal stood in the middle of the driving yard with rain plastering her thin raincoat to her shoulders and an umbrella keeping her long hair dry. The teenager had one of those old paper-cone face masks Elliot used to see a lot around South East Asia. Woodsy offered her a wave as he passed fifteen feet to her right. She copied it, then turned anxious eyes back on Elliot. How long had she been standing there? How much had she heard? And why wasn't she with Lewis?

He stepped to the edge of the cement floor, of the shelter. "You okay?"

He'd rarely spoken to the girl. She'd come in a year ago, quickly pulled into Lewis's orbit—a good thing all round, for her and for The Downs. Her closeness to Lewis had prevented her addition to Elliot's regular contact list, but she never seemed angry toward him.

He'd always thought her intelligent and kind. Like Lewis himself.

She ventured closer. "If it's a bad time...? It is, isn't it? Sorry."

"No, no. Just finished up here. But you're supposed to be in quarantine."

"Figured I'd be safe around you. You've been away a few days."

"Yeah, but I've been round others for twelve hours or more since I got back."

"Oh."

"It'll be okay. I haven't been that close to them. Come in here out of the rain, but don't touch anything and keep that mask on." *In case I'm sick and don't know it yet.* "So. What up?"

A few steps closer, to the edge of the cover. Elliot backed off to give her room. She said, "It's Lewis."

"Lewis?" Last thing he expected her to say. He went back to the engine cover on the car, shut it.

She came on in, both hands on the umbrella, shoulders hunched. "He...he's mad at me. And I dunno what to do about it."

He's mad at you?

"You're asking me what to do about it? Like I'd know."

She winced. "I kinda wanted to ask you about that, too."

"So, ask."

"Well," she started. She shook the umbrella and folded it. "What is it between you two?"

"He never said?"

"Uh-uh. And everyone else seems to respect you, so you can't be a bad guy. He won't talk about it."

"Pretty simple. I lied to him. I did a stupid thing there. Or maybe the right thing. I thought it was at the time. These days I have no idea."

"What did you lie about?"

"I lied about Alyssa. I'm not proud of this." *I also lied about executing a pedophile named Jock, but that's another story.* "When I came across Lewis ... He tell you *anything* about us?"

"Some other people did. I know how you met. What you did for him."

"What we did for each other. He helped me, too: when I hurt my ankle, when I hit a blocked road." *When I'd forgotten how to laugh.* "Anyway. The story is that when I first came across him, I'd already been at his home. He and she had been taken from there by bikers." Krystal was nodding. She knew this part. He skipped ahead. "I started out taking Lewis to his grandparents. I was sure his sister was alive somewhere with those bikers, but I didn't tell him. I told him she was dead."

"Oh. Why'd you do that?"

"Because A, even if we could attack a compound full of armed psychopaths, I didn't know where the hell they actually were at that time. And B, if I told Lewis, he'd get it in his head to go find them and then he'd die. Or he'd miraculously kill them all and then live with the guilt for the rest of his life."

That was his story. He'd told it. The truth and nothing but. He waited for her verdict.

"I think you did the right thing," she said. "He was a lot younger. He definitely would have died."

Elliot nodded slowly, letting out a breath he hadn't realized he'd been holding. "That's the way I saw it. I had one job: get him somewhere safe. But it's obviously not the way he sees it."

"But you got him somewhere safe—and then you went and got *her*. I don't get why he's angry at you."

Elliot scratched at his forehead for a while, trying to put it into words. He said, "Maybe it's a guy thing. We all hope we can do everything for ourselves and feel insulted when someone else does it for us."

A man don't need help from no one, no way. Like the hypocrite Uncle John was, he'd said those wise words while making Elliot wash his truck.

"Or maybe he just hated being lied to," he added, chasing John's ghost from his head.

"Men," she sighed with a roll of her shoulders.

Elliot asked her, "What's he mad at you for?"

"He wanted to go on the mission. I said he had to help me look after the kids. He feels like I guilt tripped him."

"Well, if you did, it achieved a great result."

"I didn't guilt trip him. It was true. Plus …"

"I get it. And I agree. Lewis can be tough, trust me, but he's not born to be a fighter the way I am. Or Sturgis is. Or Angie. Krystal, he'll get over it. He obviously loves you. And if you keep him focused on how he's needed here, he'll forget about going on the trip in no time." He wondered where the hell that sage piece of advice had come from.

"Thanks," she said and her eyes were misty.

Not wanting to deal with a crying young lady, he said, "You want anything while we're out there? Anything besides medication?"

"Oh, anything coke would be great, thanks. If you have time."

Coke? He remembered then, the slang word Downs young people used to mean "cool" and, more specifically, anything good from the old world that was no longer available.

That's what Alyssa had meant when she said the word last night.

He said, "And at the risk of repeating myself, aren't you meant to be helping him with those kids?"

Above her mask, her eyes widened in one of those don't-be-mad-at-me teenage expressions. "Yeah."

"Well, you can't just go in and out of quarantine." He put on a mock parade ground voice. "Soldier, you need to get your ass back there and support your squad mate."

"Okay, sir." She started off, then spun and gave him a thumbs-up. "You're a nice man, Elliot."

His laugh was genuine this time, surprised. "Not me, sister."

"Yeah. You are. See ya when you're back."

And, raising her umbrella, she skipped off into the rain.

Elliot left the Rover then and headed for the armory with the smile lingering on his face, and the lead in his gut melting away.

"Good talk," he said.

PART TWO

ROAD TRIP

7

The roads between Settlers Downs and Birns River Bridge were in good shape, despite being without maintenance for years. Four times Woodsy had to slow and ease around tree debris, and once he braked hard to avoid a wallaby the size of a small child. But most of their journey's first leg passed uneventfully.

Elliot, riding shotgun, kept his ears closed to Woodsy's effervescent prattling and his eyes on their surroundings.

Their rugged, unpopulated surroundings.

There really had been a lot of wilderness in Tasmania even before the Collapse. The island-state was the size of Ohio or West Virginia, but it had been far less populated than those US states. Its towns had been mainly small ones, dotting a map that was almost entirely forest and farms.

Being so small and having decent highways, it would have taken him two or three hours in the old days to get Lewis from Harrietsville where he'd found him to The Downs, from the midlands to the east coast. And his subsequent trip to Inglebourne across the eastern mountain ranges to find Alyssa would have been even closer. Both those trips had taken decidedly longer, and it hadn't just been the need to avoid roving packs of deaders: roads were often clogged with old accidents and abandoned vehicles, the human detritus of last-ditch stands against packs of undead where people looked now like old roadkill, fallen trees there was no one to clear, animals grown bold and sunning themselves in the open...

As if to prove the truth of that last thought, a mob of kangaroos watched the Land Rover from the verge, unconcerned.

Woodsy said, "Some great barbecue right there."

Elliot ignored him and turned his mind to the last time he'd traveled in this particular Land Rover. Their only big raid beyond their territory two winters back had meant dragging this Rover plus a pickup over the range of mountains past Birns River. But while today they'd be turning left through the relatively low foothills, that raid had taken them into the mountains proper, to the modest hospital at St Mary's. And to prove that there were people still about and with smarts to boot, there'd been a group sheltering in it. Twenty-odd survivors, nineteen of whom had taken one look at two vehicles full of people with guns and scattered into the town's side streets and the local bush. A wise thing to do. He wondered if any of them had returned to the small hospital afterwards—returned and cursed those strangers with the guns for looting a full third of their shit. Only one of them had heeded Claire's call—Nance the farmer—too old and too proud to run. Nance had convinced them to leave more supplies and equipment than they'd intended. If this current mission was unsuccessful, Nance might end up bedding down on one of those same hospital cots, only this time in the community's Infirmary.

"We should have brought the pickup," he groused. They'd welded a flat iron plate to the front of the former fencer's utility, angled and fixed with low clearance from the road to muscle through car pileups and scrape aside fallen branches. There were sure to be more blockages once they got up into the real hills past Birns River Bridge.

Woodsy took the next curve a little harder than Elliot thought wise—and there ahead were the ten-cabin motor inn and the gas station opposite that meant they were a kilometre and a half from the town. From Jock's town. When the man's face swam up into his mind's eye wearing the leer that had been its final living expression, Elliot didn't try to stem the rest of that memory, of shooting the man in the throat, of watching him thrash and bleed and choke.

Some deaths were meant to happen.

Some kills were good kills.

"This'd be so much easier on a bike," Woodsy muttered as he slowed to a stop on a Birns River Bridge backstreet and pulled at the handbrake.

"Noisier, too," Elliot said and climbed out into a misty rain to clear the way ahead, leaving the rifle, unholstering the SIG. He'd thrown two lawn chairs off the asphalt one-handed before Angie and Jimmy joined him to clear the rest of the crap blocking the street. Bad weather, he hoped, had been behind most of the mess.

It was haphazard enough, and Settlers Downs had suffered through one hell of a storm two months back; no doubt that had caused the gum tree debris they'd encountered along the way here. But it certainly had not caused the Main Street blockade of furniture and car bodies they'd tried to detour by taking this street.

He pointed to Jimmy's holstered Glock. "We'll work. You cover us. Watch the houses."

Expressionless, Jimmy pulled his piece and moved along the gutter, head turning.

"This is Vikes, you think?" Angie asked, her eyes darting around. Pigeons cooed from some sheltered roost nearby. Magpies called to each other. A wind chime tinkled. Rain pattered on the debris.

"Could be. Not much of a roadblock. They probably left a lot of this outside the houses while looting." He launched a deck chair toward a cottage front yard. "Storm did the rest."

"But the main road …" She lifted a canvas picnic umbrella and took it to the sidewalk. Water ran off it in rivulets.

He holstered the SIG and passed her, carrying a plastic outdoor table over his head. "Sure, Vikes. Or some other group. Might be an ambush. Might be demarcating territory." He dropped his load on the grass verge and returned for a long plastic planter box.

A minute later, they had cleared enough for the car to pass. They bundled into the Rover as Woodsy drew up alongside them. Angie took the shotgun seat before Elliot could.

"Hustle," Elliot told Woodsy, checking both ends of the street before climbing into the back. "I hate choke points."

He kept his rifle between his thigh and the door, his SIG out and ready, his free hand on the electric window control. Any moment, he fully expected enemy fire and cursed himself for not thinking this through better and for not forcing Woodsy out of the driver's seat. But they made it down the short lane and around the corner without interference, pointing them back at the bridge the town was named for.

The narrow steel-stone-and-concrete span ahead was clear. Wisely, Woodsy pressed the pedal down to get across it quick, the suspension bouncing them around over the haphazard bridge paving. The cargo space rattled with the cooler boxes and instant cold packs they'd brought to transport medication.

"Might be trolls under here," Jimmy murmured beside him.

"What?"

The eighteen-year-old shrugged and turned his face to the water, abruptly sullen.

Jesus, Mary and Joseph, what's wrong with this kid?

On the other side, the road turned them up onto the wooded hills Elliot and Lewis had once walked across. He twisted around to get a glimpse of Jock's expensive house standing back on the river bluff overlooking waterway and township. Seconds later it was lost behind the folds of the land and the thickening forest, as the car climbed.

"What are you looking at?" Woodsy asked him.

Straightening, Elliot caught the man's eyes in the mirror. "Wondering why whoever blocked the main road and the parkland left the bridge open."

"Would've been easier just to block that," Angie agreed.

"Perhaps no traffic comes from this direction," Woodsy said. "Or they use the bridge themselves."

Elliot grunted, not wanting to admit that sounded reasonable. Jimmy still had his Glock out and on his lap, pointing at the door. His finger was within the trigger guard. "Holster that," Elliot told him.

Jimmy considered the pistol a few seconds before asking the back of Woodsy's head if he should.

"Yes, son," said Woodsy.

So Jimmy did.

"Jesus, Mary, Joseph, kid," Elliot muttered. He shifted his rifle into a better position against the door.

The Rover bristled with weapons, but fortunately all except Jimmy knew how to secure them and still have them ready for trouble. Elliot had outfitted himself, Jimmy and Woodsy, allocating weapons he'd looted from a Druids motel-safehouse three years earlier. For Woodsy, a USAS12 shotgun to compliment his own police-issue Smith & Wesson .40 caliber semi-automatic. A Glock 17 for Jimmy—the big ass knife the teenager had found for himself made Elliot more nervous than the handguns, given Jimmy's history. For himself, he'd taken the Steyr-AUG and suppressor, along with his trusty SIG P226 and Shrade lockblade. He'd given himself a Druid-owned M9 bayonet to replace the machete he'd lost, and put a 30-06 rifle in the back of the SUV as a spare long gun.

Angie had already been there in the armory when Elliot had arrived; to her favored sawn-off double barrel, she'd added a modified Glock 18 along with two "CMAGs". The magazines were huge by comparison to the pistol, twin-drum assemblies boasting one hundred rounds. She loaded one into the Glock and kept the spare in the shoulder satchel carrying her shottie. The mags were heavy, but she'd be glad of them in a firefight. All the Glocks boasted biker-fashioned suppressors—the Death Druids had had a penchant for them—and Angie had wondered aloud if she'd get a chance to use the full-auto option on the Glock 18.

"Not if the option is running like hell," Elliot had told her. Watching the trees as they flowed past his window now, he thought that there would probably be a day where she did use that full-auto option. The one thing history said to the future was that there would always be skirmishes, and always be wars.

The car crested a rise, nosing down into a shallow dip before hitting a new upslope. Downshifting and slowing to take a tight curve, Woodsy caught Elliot's eye in the mirror and said, "Tell me about the Vikes. You're the only one who met one?"

"Only one to speak with them," Angie corrected. "A few of us have seen them, me included, but always at a distance."

"Yeah," Elliot explained. "Once they shouted threats at—"

"I heard that part," Woodsy interrupted, changing up to third and swerving around forest debris even while accelerating. "They shouted obscenities at Dave One when he was scouting solo. But why didn't they shoot him? What kind of weapons do they have? As good as ours?"

"Probably zero guns," Angie said before Elliot could answer. "Bows and arrows, slings and spears is all we've seen. The guy Elliot talked to had a sword, I shit you not. Makes sense for freaks who style themselves on Vikings, I guess." She shook her head. "They're dickheads. They're like cosplayers, but cosplayers that might kill you."

"Maybe they would, maybe they wouldn't," Elliot said. "I'm not keen to run into them again, but when Dave stumbled onto them, they were skinning a wallaby. Probably just protecting their meat."

"There's wallabies everywhere," she snorted. "Why worry about him stealing theirs?"

"Because their brains are Swiss cheese," he told her and turned his attention to Woodsy. "Look, I had a brief conversation across a creek bed one time, when we surprised each other. It was an amicable six minutes. Completely different to Dave's experience. For the first six *seconds*, I was concerned he had buddies in the bushes, flanking me. But then the wind blew the smoke from his cigarette my way. Not standard tobacco."

"Whacky tobacky."

"Exactly. The guy was spaced. And pretty stupid to be wandering the bush in that condition."

"They're potheads?"

"He was. No doubt goes with their, er, philosophy. In six minutes, he asked no questions about us except where I got my accent. And that, *I* shit you not, was a serious question. He was impressed with me being a

foreigner. Then he asked me how I liked Australia."
Elliot grunted a laugh.

"What did the bloke tell you about them?"

"That they are a peace-loving people if other people leave them alone, a force to be reckoned with if other people don't. Most, he said, knew each other from before the world ended. And they liked to live off the land, like their, haha, ancestors."

"Right. And you don't think they're all leftover Maggot Riders or Satans."

"Satans?" Angie asked.

"Satans of the South. Another bikie gang."

"Oh, yeah." She scratched the back of her neck. "I vaguely remember seeing them on *Sixty Minutes*."

"They're not bikers," Elliot said.

He glanced at Jimmy, but the kid was concentrating on a sign they were passing. *Blueberry Barn - Crepes, Pancakes, Berries, Local Cider.*

Elliot thought, *God, I'd love some pancakes.*

Only good things happened when a person dug into a short stack.

The only times—the *only* times—that Uncle John had been okay to be around had been on the last Saturday mornings of the month. That was when John's monthly paycheck meant a trip to town and a huge pancake breakfast that had always filled a young Elliot to the point of bursting. There'd been syrup, there'd been coffee, there'd been ice-cream, berries. Whatever the hell he'd wanted on those mornings. An hour or two of relief from John's temper before the man's irritability had set back in on the drive back home.

Just thinking about them, he could taste them. He could smell them.

"Yeah, they're not bikers," Angie was saying. "I've seen them three times when they didn't see me. They do the whole TV Viking thing. Bare chests. Tattoos. Heads shaved on one side with hair flipped over the other way. They're just idiots who've …" She echoed Elliot's earlier laugh. "… who aren't really taking the whole end-of-the-world thing seriously."

"Well, they don't sound too dangerous then," Woodsy said. "Potheads aren't usually violent."

"Guy I talked to was chilled," Elliot said, "but anyone is violent when they need to be. And who's to say that ganja is the only thing they're using? His last words to me were, 'You stay your side of this creek and we'll stay on ours'."

"Shit," said Woodsy. "Well, at least we've got better weapons."

For now, Elliot thought. Sure, The Downs had a reasonable stock of firearms for a place like Tasmania, between the rifles and shotguns that had belonged to its former owners and the weapons looted from the Druids. What they *didn't* have was a whole lot of ammo. Bullets and shells counted in the low hundreds, not the tens of thousands that Elliot would've liked. Conservation of ammunition was an explicit virtue in the community. In all the years since bringing in Alyssa, Jimmy and Claire, Elliot had fired nineteen rounds. Nineteen. Fifteen had been into the heads of deaders in the early days. Two had been over the heads of strangers threatening him—assholes from Nine Mile River the first time, then a disheveled crazy in a southern beachside hamlet. The last two rounds had gone into a kangaroo he wanted for meat. He'd personally supervised the use of seventy-seven 9 mm, .22 and shotgun rounds in training some basic weapons skills to others. Others had used a few rounds in their scouting—Angie, Rit, the Daves, Shaz and Tania, Sturgis—but only a few.

Hopefully, as he'd said to Angie in the armory, they wouldn't need to fire one shot on this mission.

He jumped as a crunching sound came out of the door-speakers. A moment later there followed the clang of a guitar chord and thump of a kick drum.

Woodsy withdrew his hand from the stereo to slap the steering wheel. "Love this song!"

Elliot realized the crunching sound effect was meant to be marching boots, an army.

A single punk rock riff later, Angie asked, "What is this shit?"

"Holidays in the Sun." Woodsy checked her reaction and pretended shock. "You never heard this? Never heard of the Sex Pistols? You're kidding me. Elliot, what do they teach young people in school, mate?"

"Quit the music lesson and turn it down," Elliot growled.

Woodsy reached over and lowered the volume a single notch, twisting around to grin at Elliot. "A great road trip needs great driving music."

"It needs a great driver," Angie said and turned the music lower herself. "Next safe space to pull over, it's my turn."

"Little missy, I was a highway patrol driver when you were toilet training."

"Don't care, you're—watch out!"

Elliot slammed forward as Woodsy braked and hit something simultaneously. He got one arm up in time to brace against Angie's seat, then fell back as the car slewed to a stop.

Everyone bailed. The blacktop behind the car was littered with debris chewed off the eucalyptus branch Woodsy had run over. A length of wood the thickness of Elliot's thigh poked from beneath either side if the car. Round the front of the vehicle, Angie began swearing a blue streak.

Inspecting the damage as she had done, Elliot joined in the cussing for a moment before confronting Woodsy. "Both front tires? Marvelous work for a pro driver. And how many spares we carrying?"

"One," Angie said unnecessarily. She was on her back now, head under the front of the car. "Axle's okay though, thank God." She wriggled out and dusted herself off.

Jimmy was watching the trees around them, Glock back in his hands. Like all of them, his breath was clouding in the chill September air.

Woodsy stood scowling at the tires and scratching his gut.

"Happy?" Elliot asked him.

"Fair go, mate. Coulda happened to anyone."

"Anyone not watching where they were going." Elliot went to the driver's door, leaned in and turned and pulled the key out. *Holidays in the Sun* cut off instantly.

"I love that song," said Jimmy without a skerrick of emotion.

"Woodsy, looks like you're going to be busy extracting gum tree from car and getting that first spare on."

"Where are we getting the second tire?" Angie asked, staring uphill in the direction they were headed.

"Blueberry Barn."

She turned. "What?"

Elliot went to the tailgate and opened it, rummaged around. "Back a ways there was a restaurant with a few SUVs in the lot. Jimmy and I can bring one back and we'll cannibalize two of the wheels."

"Tires'll be flat," Woodsy said, but Elliot brandished the tire compressor before handing it off to Jimmy. He pulled out the jumpstart kit and left the gate down while going around to retrieve his Steyr.

Eying the kit, Angie nodded approvingly. "Better than pushing a tire uphill all that way."

"You know it. You okay here?"

He expected her to argue, to demand that she come, but she was too smart for that.

"Am I okay to sit here on a log," she said, "while Woodsy works his arse off and you two lug those kits all the way down to the 'Blueberry Barn'? Absolutely, I'm okay here."

Patting her double barrel, she smiled, the first time he'd seen her smile in weeks. Smiling suited her, he thought. The sudden tingle in his gut agreed with his thought.

Elliot returned her smile for a moment then followed Jimmy who had already started downhill.

8

"That is so goddamned weird."

They'd walked half a klick and Elliot still couldn't work out why the woods on either side of the narrow mountain highway were so vastly different. The forest to his left was all pine, a colorless sight all the way to the top of the slope. The view to his right and downslope, however, was ablaze with color and rich with entirely different vegetation.

How can they be so completely different? It was as if he stood literally between two worlds.

The scent of the pines reached him on the breeze and his gut clenched with melancholy nostalgia, as the smell transported him back to one of the best hiking trails he'd ever tried. He'd hiked and camped among ponderosa pines up along the western slopes of the Ochoco Mountains, alone and at peace for a week. These Tasmanian pines were not ponderosas, but they looked a lot like them. They smelled like them. The ground was dusty and bare beneath them as it had been that summer.

And on the other side of the road, a vastly different ecology. A steep valley choked with plants, some of which he now knew well: tea-trees, flat pea and mint bush, eucalypts, wattles and ferns. Flowers burst in yellows and blues and reds and purples down there. Underbrush filled in all the spaces, hiding the soil.

So much life.

Too much life, Jimmy must have decided. The young man froze, dropping into a crouch, his eyes on that forest beyond the road's lip.

Elliot took a knee too, weapon up. He heard nothing to cause alarm: the *pip-pip* of some small bird, the deep buzz of a large bush insect in flight nearby, the thumping of his own pulse, the breeze sighing in the trees. He duckwalked closer. "What'd you hear?"

Jimmy said nothing, then a moment later shrugged and started off again, his Glock down by his thigh.

"Good talk," Elliot said. He jogged a little to catch up. "Hey, kid. Pretty sure I've told you a few times over the past couple years. Keep your booger hook off the bang switch."

"What?"

"Your Glock. Keep your finger off the trigger. Keep it outside the guard." Since the Glock's safety was part of the trigger, the most secure way to carry it was in a position where an accidental clenching of the fist wouldn't discharge it.

Jimmy glanced down and up, didn't break stride. Elliot craned his neck to check for a change. Sure enough, the finger was outside the guard now. "Better," he said. "It's dangerous to carry it the way you were."

Jimmy did look at him now. A glance, nothing more. "Why?"

"Why? Because I've seen someone shoot himself in the foot carrying it the same way you were."

"I know what I'm doing," Jimmy grumbled.

Elliot thought a moment. How had he gotten through to Lewis on matters like this? Actually, the question was better phrased as how had he *not* gotten through to Lewis in the early days? Whatever that answer was, Elliot should really do the opposite. So he tried starting with a compliment. "Well, that's good you know what you're doing. You're definitely a smart guy. I'm interested, though, in *how* you know what you're doing." Jimmy picked up the pace to create a little distance. Elliot added, "I'm not doubting you, kid. I just wanna know where you're getting your confidence from? Who taught you?"

"Taught myself. And Woodsy did. A bit."

Elliot frowned. "Woodsy taught you to use the Glock?"

A grunt.

Shit.

"Well. Okay. But remember to keep your finger off the trigger unless you're in a live situation."

A shrug.

"Kid. I got some experience in this, you know. I ran teams. I trained warriors." *Well, a little bit.* "We're on a hazardous trip here. We need to be good at what we do. Keep ourselves safe. Keep our ... our mates safe."

"I know that."

"Okay. And I know you can use a knife." He'd seen first-hand the results of Jimmy's knifework when he'd gone in to set Jimmy free. The young man had been handcuffed to a bunk bed during a protracted firefight between the Death Druids, who'd used him as a sex slave, and their apparently arch enemies the Maggot Riders. Jimmy had used the confusion to get a knife off the biker sheltering in the room with him and stabbed the man repeatedly. His captor didn't have the keys for the cuffs. Fortunately for him—and for Claire who'd also been trapped in the room—Elliot had come along after the fact and found the keys that had set him free.

A flinch from Jimmy at the knife reference, but no other reaction. Did he think about that, about his days with the Druids? Did he have nightmares and flashbacks and doubts like Elliot did? Elliot could ask him, of course, but he doubted he'd get much out of him. And he could well understand that. Those things were almost impossible to talk about.

"How about if you don't have a blade?" he asked him instead, staying on track. "What if you're in a situation and your Glock fails? Or out of ammo?"

Jimmy shrugged. "I run or duck."

"Good options, I agree. Sometimes the best options. Let's say you get caught in a crowd of deaders—"

"All gone."

Elliot thought of Bess, his dog. "Nope. Bastards are around still. But okay, let's say you wander into a supermarket you think is safe and there's living people there. Who want to kill you."

"I run," Jimmy repeated, tone dull.

Elliot repressed a sigh. "In this scenario you're cornered."

"Shit," said Jimmy. A little frustration crept into his tone; Elliot couldn't tell if it was because he was picturing it in his head or tired of Elliot's perseverance.

"Damn right, shit. You must've been in that situation at some time. Chased. Or crowded. Early on in the Collapse. People or pusbags. What did you do? How'd you fight?"

"I ... I didn't fight people. Real people. Just dead ones. A little."

"What with?"

"My step-father's steering lock."

Elliot pictured him trying to crack skulls with that foot-long length of steel and said, "Good. Nice. A blunt-force weapon like that is a great option. So you got your steering lock, or a two-by-four or even your pistol butt. You're attacked by deaders or, okay, by some angry living sonofabitch. How do you hit them? Where?"

"Anywhere."

"Where?"

"Head, arms, guts."

"Not guts. Hard to get to through their defenses. Won't cause enough shock. The head's good though. Arms are good, depending on where. So where *would* you hit them exactly?"

Jimmy tapped his bicep with his Glock, making Elliot glad the kid had shifted his finger.

"The muscle? How about their legs?" he asked, a suspicion growing. Jimmy tapped his thigh, the side of it. "Woodsy taught you this already, didn't he? To use a police baton?"

A nod.

"And cops were taught to go for big muscle groups." It was their standard procedure. "That's why they had to hit rioters over and over and over. Because those muscles take the shock of the weapon, they cushion it. Takes a while to hurt someone bad enough to put them down. But us? These days? We need to take someone out with one or two strikes max. Jimmy, you hearing me?"

"Sure."

"One thing I want you to remember. Like a mantra. Blades like flesh, impact weapons like bone."

"Uh?"

"You have a blade, you slash muscles or their gut if you can reach it. You have a stick or a bat, you hit their bones."

"So ... their head, like I said?"

Better. The kid was actually listening now. Maybe even interested. They neared a sign with symbols for an eating place five hundred metres ahead. So Elliot made the most of the time they had left before they'd reach it.

"The head is good if you can reach past their arms. If they're defending themselves with arms up, break a finger or wrist so you'll at least shock them. Another thing you can try is pretend to go for their groin. That's called a feint, pretending like that. Then you hit them upside the head when their hands drop to cover their nuts. Man, you manage to hit someone in the head and they'll stop thinking for a second or two. Then you do not pause. If they've been stunned, you smack a knee or an ankle or a collar bone. Breaking any bone is gonna shock them bad and might be enough to stop them.

When you hit, you hit hard. You incapacitate them and you move on to the next target."

"Fancy shit," Jimmy murmured, but he sounded thoughtful.

"Not fancy. Targeted. Hell, *clumsy* is fine as long as you hit bone. You don't need to be Bruce Lee."

Jimmy looked up at the blue sign displaying the distance to the restaurant, and then over at Elliot. "Who?"

"Christ, kid. Don't say that." He hurried past him to take point. "You make me feel old."

There turned out to be plenty of sinister-seeming shadows and cupboards in the Blueberry Barn, but no people or drybones. After a thorough and agonizingly slow recon of the restaurant and the two outbuildings, Elliot finally marched back up to one of the cars in the lot, and crow-called Jimmy in from the bush across the highway. There was evidence of looting along with some vandalism: perhaps survivors were still holed up in these secluded hills.

Graffiti-spray marred the exterior walls of the restaurant and its signs. As if a pack of wolves had passed through, pissing on things to mark their territory. Perhaps these taggers—like the old-world ones—were so unsure of their own existence they needed to leave something tangible to prove it. One message scribed in the unsteady writing of a spray can novice said, *Bastards your all Dead*—Elliot figured the odds were good that whoever those bastards were to the writer, they *were* dead. Another said simply *MINE*—a word which, he noticed now, had been scratched over and over into the sides of all the cars with a nail or knife blade.

While Jimmy came down from the road, Elliot knelt by one of the SUVs, picked up a wayward screw and scratched his name into a compote of engine oil and dust on the ground. *See it's true. I'm real. I was here.*

There'd been some cans of pre-mixed bourbon-and-cola inside. He'd brought one out and now he cracked it open and sipped—then spat it out. Flat. And chemical-tasting. "Not coke," he said. "Not coke at all." He tossed the can.

When Jimmy was close, Elliot tapped the deflated tire beside him. "I'll cover you while you air these up. Then you cover me while I jump it."

Jimmy dumped the jumpstart kit and tire inflator three yards from the car, staring downhill. "I want those first."

"Huh?"

Jimmy pointed out past the gravel lot to where the ground leveled off and a path started. A faded sign showed a cartoon blueberry with a goofy grin and stick-limbs. "Pick me, pick me!" the idiot blueberry was saying in kindergarten font. One of its arms extended like Jimmy's toward what used to be berry gardens running either side of the path. Row-stakes showed above a briar patch of weeds.

"It's all long dead," Elliot told Jimmy. "Now help me here."

"Might be some," said Jimmy, already moving. "Berries even grow in the wild you know."

"It's too early in the season."

"I'm checking."

"Kid—"

"I didn't have breakfast." He was a third of the way there now.

"Sonofa … Get your damn berries. Just hurry it up. And I *mean* hurry."

Jimmy's shuffle turned into a childlike skip.

"It's the cartoon blueberry," Elliot muttered. "Goddamn marketing assholes." Louder he said, "Be careful!"

Jimmy had reached the sign now. The word *MINE* had been painted in one of corner of that too. Well, if there were any berries in that patch, they were Jimmy's now.

Elliot sucked in cold mountain air. The season was wrong. There'd be no damned berries. The kid was wasting time. If Woodsy hadn't brought him, this would go so much smoother. In fact, if Elliot had just come with Angie, this would already be going better.

"Screw it," he said, laying the rifle on the SUV roof. He picked up the inflator.

The tire valve cap was on tight: he had to twist it hard. When it came off finally, his hand slipped and banged up against the bottom of the mudguard, scraping skin.

He gasped, fell on his ass and sucked at the blood welling on the side of his finger. "Fucking Woodsy fuckhead—"

Noise!

The crunch of boots on gravel.

The thuds of a heavy person running.

Elliot dropped the inflator, scrambled to his feet and snatched up the rifle. He stepped out from between the parked cars into open space.

The man barreling toward him was big—really big. Obese-big. Taller than Elliot by half a head. Maybe two-fifty pounds. Probably more.

Elliot took aim, then let the muzzle dip: he *should* drop the guy and quickly, but there was something off about him. Not deader-off, more like...

Scav-rat.

No weapons. Grimy cargo shorts and an unbuttoned khaki shirt, but no shoes. A shiny scalp with wild tufts of grey and brown sprouting along the sides. Eyes wide and white. Face and beard dappled with muck. Spittle sprayed from his mouth as he barked, "Mine!" over and over.

"Goddamnit." With a sympathy that went against his training, he safetied the weapon, took one hand off it to wave at the guy. "Not here to hurt you," he said. "Leaving soon."

The big man didn't slow, thirty feet away now. If anything, Elliot's attempt at pacification seemed to anger him more, his already reddened face contorting and puckering. "Mine!" he screamed.

Now he was close enough that Elliot could read the name *Greg* embroidered on his shirt pocket below the Blueberry Barn logo.

"Oh, man," Elliot muttered and braced himself, both hands back on his rifle.

As Greg lunged across the final gap between them, Elliot ducked low, dodged right and downhill. He brought the Steyr's butt around and into Greg's left

109

calf. The leg buckled, pitching the man sideways onto shoulder and hip where he skidded a metre across the gravel. Elliot lay down the rifle. He leapt forward as the big man found his knees, got his right arm over the man's shoulder and around his throat, hooked the inside of his elbow across the guy's adam's apple, his fist against the guy's opposite shoulder.

"Not yours!" Greg grated.

Elliot clasped his right hand with his left, pressing his left arm into the man's head. Greg bucked. Elliot hung on. The big man smelled like roadkill. Sweat from his hair soaked into Elliot's shirt. His neck was thick and Elliot had to press hard to find the carotid.

"Mine," the guy grunted, trying to get to his feet, trying to get an arm over to swipe at Elliot. "Mi—" With blood flow to brain interrupted, he faded quick. Started going limp.

Then Jimmy cried out.

Surprised, Elliot's grip slackened slightly, enough for Greg to get a breath, get some blood to his brain, shift and throw Elliot's grip off a little more.

Elliot maneuvered, trying for his original textbook position, then looked downhill to the berry patches. "Jesus!"

Jimmy too was down on the edge of a garden bed. He faced out, but he'd fallen into a tangle of anti-bird netting. Across the path, a tiny drybones dragged its carcass toward his feet, jaw snapping. It wore a dark blue sundress with yellow flowers. Her filthy hair was tied back with a yellow ribbon. In contrast to the dress, the ribbon was clean, fresh. A rope had been tied around her waist, but Elliot couldn't see what the other end was tethered to.

Your Glock, he willed Jimmy, fighting to get his grip tight on the squirming Greg.

"Babies," the big man mumbled. "Homes."

Holding a garden stake for balance, Jimmy got his pistol out with a shaky hand, aimed it—

Greg cried, "No!"

—and Jimmy dropped it in the netting. He fumbled around for it.

This time Greg's "No!" was a scream.

The big man surged upright, shaking himself like a wet dog, dislodging Elliot. He swung a log-like arm around so that Elliot had to block it with both of his. The blow was hard, toppling Elliot on the uneven ground. He rolled over once and came up ready to defend himself. But Greg had forgotten him, careening down the parking lot toward the gardens, arms wheeling. His cry became, "Katie! Katie! My Katie!"

This time, Elliot didn't hesitate. His SIG came free of its holster and he steadied himself with a shoulder against one of the parked cars. But he didn't need to kill the poor bastard. The guy had big legs; Elliot was certain of the shot. Hit a leg, contain him, and treat the wound later. He closed one eye.

But it was Jimmy who fired. Three rounds. Greg fell face first, slid, then rolled a couple times. He came to rest face down and unmoving.

Elliot hurried forward in a crouch, wary in case Jimmy fired indiscriminately. He was halfway to the berry patches when Jimmy put two rounds into the undead child.

"Holy Christ," he whispered and moved in on the fallen Greg. As he reached his side, the man spasmed once.

No more movement.

Nothing.

Greg's head was turned sideways.

Elliot stooped and put a hand to the man's neck.

No pulse.

Eyes vacant.

"I'm so sorry, Greg."

A thump made him look up. He straightened. Jimmy was out of the netting. He had a garden stake out of the ground, hitting the deader's head over and over until there was nothing there but a spreading stain on the path with hair and a yellow ribbon clumped within it.

Chest heaving, gut clenched tight, Elliot studied Jimmy. The kid finally tossed the stake and marched up the path again. His Glock was in its holster. He plucked a weed from the side of his pants. "Shit, that was close," he called.

"Close?" Elliot replied. Then louder: "Close!" Jimmy froze. Elliot pointed to the dead man beside him. "I had this. I *had* this. He did not have to die. But you hadda go pick breakfast from an empty berry patch! You couldn't watch your back for deaders!" Blood was seeping out from under Greg's body. One of Jimmy's shots had hit the heart. Jimmy was looking at Elliot, not at the man he'd killed. "Goddamnit, I wish I'd brought Lewis. Lewis would never have—!" He cut himself off.

Pointless.

Jimmy's face had clouded, had colored. He had an adolescent pout going, had closed himself off. Wrapping his arms around his chest, he dropped his gaze and made his way back up the lot toward the SUV. Elliot put out an arm to stop him and the kid dodged it easily.

"That's your last chance with that Glock," Elliot told him. "Strike three."

"Piss off," Jimmy replied.

"I'm pissed off all right. I am real pissed off."

His own finger was still dribbling blood from his earlier wound, he realized; he couldn't feel it. He pressed the finger hard against his pants to stop the bleeding as he followed Jimmy up the lot again.

Jimmy picked up the inflator and got to work doing what he should have done in the first place. Staying extra-vigilant, Elliot popped the hood and got the starter kit in position and busied himself with work. The tire-inflating went fine, but the SUV took a little coaxing to start—partly due to old fuel.

Thirty-two minutes after he'd first arrived, Elliot was climbing behind the wheel.

Standing outside the open passenger door, Jimmy said, "I think I'll just run."

"What?" He was gonna *run* back to the others?

"If I'm outa bullets. I'll run away."

"Oh. Truly, Jimmy, not the right time for this talk."

Jimmy clammed up again and took his seat. He put his face to the side window. Past him, Elliot could see the stumpy shape of a Tasmanian devil venturing out of the underbrush. It checked uphill and down, then scurried across to start pulling at the dead man's body.

"The circle of life," Elliot muttered and pulled the car out of the lot.

A withdrawn and sullen teenager sitting beside him felt like déjà vu. It was Lewis at his most traumatized all over again. No, not Lewis. As Elliot had said without thinking, Lewis wouldn't have caused Greg's death. Jimmy was erratic and unreadable in a different way. His childish desire for something he couldn't have— and his subsequent carelessness—had gotten that man killed. And almost gotten Jimmy bitten.

Death Druids did a real number on you, kid, didn't they?

Elliot said, "From now on, Jimmy, you do exactly what I tell you. You keep your eyes open, your ears open. Concentrate. Be circumspect: that means you keep your head on a swivel, checking around you all the time. You read me?"

Jimmy gave no indication that he had.

"I meant what I said about the Glock."

Elliot sighed. The kid wasn't listening. Perhaps he couldn't.

"All right, Jimmy. If the safest thing for you to do is run when we're in serious trouble, then okay, you run. You find your way back home if we haven't established some other fallback location already."

Further silence. Jimmy didn't shift at all.

"You can find your way home okay?"

"… No."

My God, this day just keeps getting better.

"Well. Get Woodsy to show you on a map. Find a way to memorize it. You have to work crap like that out."

More silence. This time, Elliot gave in to it. He really couldn't be bothered anymore.

Minutes later, they were pulling up near a sweaty and dirty Woodsy and an impatient Angie.

"I'll just run," Jimmy said and climbed out. He darted over to greet Woodsy with a handshake. Rather than get immediately to work unhooking another tire, Woodsy peppered the young man with questions about the "mission", nodding and shoulder-patting over the young man's short responses. There was a loud clang as Woodsy's tire iron slipped from his hand. Jimmy stooped for it at the same time as Woodsy did; they knocked heads, then offered synchronized apologies.

"Holy shit," Angie said as Elliot got out.

"Holy shit, what?"

"We're teamed up with two of the Three Stooges."

Jimmy had his Glock out again and was pointing back down the highway with it as he explained something to Woodsy.

"Put that away!" Elliot barked. To Angie, he said, "Yeah. The dumbest two."

"Any trouble?"

"You could say that." Elliot scratched the back of his neck. "One claymore. One … scav-rat."

"Oh."

"I nearly contained the guy without … without damage. Then Jimmy got sloppy, enraged the fella. Then shot him dead." An oversimplification, but Elliot couldn't find the energy for the long version.

"Jimmy killed him?"

"Yep."

"Shit."

"Yep."

Her expression softened. Just a little. She asked, "You okay?"

"Sure."

"Really?"

He nodded, took a deep breath, let it out slow. "I am. Thanks. But it's real bad us being out here."

"Agreed. But do we have a choice?" She brushed past him—the brief contact was not unpleasant, he thought—and turned the ignition key enough to light up the dash. "Still got half a tank of petrol."

"It's been sitting in there for three years, but seems fine now it's turned over a little. You thinking to keep it, the car?"

"When Mr. Talkfest and his sidekick are ready to do some actual work, they put this one's spare on our Rover and then you and I follow them in this."

You and I. He liked the sound of that.

Claire's face came into his mind's eye, smiling a smug smile. The Council member was The Downs's maternal figure and ever keen to matchmake, especially when it came to him and Angie. But there couldn't be anything permanent between them? Could there? No, he didn't have something like that in him.

Nor does she.

Still, he'd read somewhere that a single man's fantasies in their forties might turn to settling down. Perhaps, after all, there was some sense in that.

Especially if it was with someone as resourceful and—yes—and as pretty as her.

"What are you thinking about?" Angie asked him and he blinked himself back to the here-and-now. Her expression was curious, her focus intense. What the hell expression must he have been wearing while he imagined that scenario?

"Nothing," he said.

She snorted. "That's original for a man. And probably correct." She brushed by again, headed for the Rover. "Hey, don't you two dickheads worry about it. Keep on chatting and waste all the daylight. It's not like we're in a fucking hurry or anything."

Elliot blew out a breath and watched her with butterflies in his gut.

Why couldn't he have undertaken this mission just with her?

9

Even when they left the mountains behind, progress remained slow. Roads were in poor shape, covered in litter and occasionally blocked by an auto wreck or two. Weeds and three years of rainfall conspired to break up the blacktop in places. Here and there, bodies lay on the road or up on the verges. None of them moved. Some weren't much more than piles of clothing and bones after years of serving as food for local wildlife.

Elliot and Angie's car followed Woodsy and Jimmy's. Coming out of a place called Campbell Town, Woodsy pulled over beside a lorry. Parked sideways, the small truck blocked half the highway. His arm appeared out of his window, pointing at the blue spray-painted message on the lorry's side:

> *35 km to security prosperity community*
> *We're taking the world back*

Elliot stuck his own arm out his window and waved Woodsy on. "Man's stopping in the middle of a goddamned chokepoint."

Angie replied, "Anyone would think we were out sightseeing." As their car neared the lorry, she pointed. "See the other tag?"

Elliot took a second look. A smaller scrawl of red paint spelled *bullshit* in a different hand. Elliot accelerated, overtaking Woodsy as they left the town, taking point.

"Bullshit all right."

"Security, prosperity, community," said Angie. "You're not buying that?"

"If you had those things, would you advertise them?"

"Well, we *do* have them. And we don't advertise them, do we?" She huffed a laugh. "Anyone advertising something wants something else in return." She shifted in her seat, looking back at the lorry. "You know, I saw this TV show once where they did something like that…"

Despite the potential danger they might be in, the next half hour passed in what Elliot found to be pleasant conversation. Angie became chatty; she could be an entertaining raconteur when she wanted to be. They discussed old pop culture, potential choke points ahead on the road and contingency plans for ambush, weird and cool and beautiful things they'd seen while scouting over the years. Angie told Elliot how much she'd loved Tasmania in the old days—and things about her life she'd never mentioned before: illegal midnight dives for abalone with friends, bush walks in forests millennia-old, trail bike rides through national parks while evading park rangers, the lively night-life of her university, the generosity of neighbors in the

Hobart street she was born and grew up in. He risked long glances at her while she spoke; Christ, he was attracted to her. And not just because she was reality-TV pretty, athletic, or blonde. It was more that Angie—whatever her mood—was fiercely and unrelentingly *alive*. Indomitable.

He ventured a couple of jokes. She didn't laugh at them. But neither did she sneer or *tsk*. Well, that was progress.

Knowing him to be well-traveled due to his military service and private contractor work, she asked him what was the best place he'd ever visited.

"Settlers Downs," he said, surprising both of them. After a moment, he added, "Yeah. I think it's The Downs."

For whatever reason, that killed the conversation.

At twenty-five kilometres out of Campbell Town on an open patch of highway with clear lines of sight across farms to each side, she told him to pull over.

"I'll drive," she said. "You watch."

Five kilometres past the town of Ross, the roads were cleared of car bodies, branches, human and animal remains. Large boutique farms with rundown manor-style houses appeared to their left, native forest remaining to their right.

And coming over a hill two kilometres further, Angie suddenly veered off road, nosing the car down a farm driveway and behind a screen of conifers.

"Did you see that?" she breathed, cutting the engine and cracking her door as Woodsy pulled in behind her.

"Couldn't exactly miss it," Elliot said and exited the vehicle.

"See the wall?" Woodsy asked as they met midway between the vehicles.

Elliot ignored him and tapped Jimmy's shoulder before the young man could wander back down the driveway. "Up in the hedge there. Guard the vehicles."

Jimmy frowned at him, but darted into the conifers that lined the driveway.

Angie started moving, too. "You boys take a looksee. I'll be scouting the bush across the highway."

Leaving the shotgun in the cabin, Woodsy opened the Rover's tailgate and grabbed the spare 30-06 rifle. Elliot snatched at the field glasses before he could get them, then locked gazes with the other man. "You're by the gatepost, I'm over the road by the sign. Don't stand on the roadway like you're target practice for anyone on that wall."

Woodsy's mouth opened, but Elliot was away before the argument could start. At the curb, he crouched low and scooted across the tarmac, avoiding a clear profile. He took a place by another of the *security prosperity community* signs. There'd been two more along the way, marking off the distances at thirty then twenty kilometres. This version was a sturdily erected three-by-two metre billboard; the signwriting was more carefully finished, using brushes rather than spray guns. And no one had added *bullshit* to it. He got down in the dirt and gravel beside it, lay down his Steyr and raised the glasses.

The road dropped gently before them into a straight run through a flat valley. The land below was mainly cleared of mature trees, but choked with towering grasses and saplings. Most of a kilometre away, giant power pylons marched across the valley between them and the edges of a hamlet beyond. More notably, behind those pylons, someone had built the wall to protect that hamlet.

Through the field glasses, the barrier appeared as a rust-colored bank of shipping containers and what looked like flood control barriers, all of it three to four metres high. In places, barbed and razor wire had been strung along the front of the containers as an extra deterrent. He couldn't see a single deader stuck in there anywhere.

"One hell of a building project," he murmured. The ingredients were spoils from the decaying city of Hobart, perhaps.

He could see no movement among the dozen buildings in the hamlet beyond the wall. And no patrols at the—

"Wait."

He pulled the glasses back to the left.

"Smart."

They'd built a sniper's nest up on one of the pylons, a box made of iron sheeting with a good view of valley and highway. He watched it awhile: maybe that was two heads bobbing around in there, maybe that was a fuzz of cigarette smoke or camp stove smoke, but the glasses weren't good enough.

When he glanced across the asphalt, Woodsy signaled a query. Elliot motioned him to stay put and alert. One more time, he scanned the wall, the land beyond, and the sniper's nest. This time he was sure he caught movement—enough to confirm the shapes were heads and they were alive. Better, he saw zero indication anyone was paying attention to him. No glint of glass, of a scope or binoculars. The forest to his right was raucous with bird song. A flock of black cockatoos were out near the pylons, making the worst of it. Unless those sentries were alert to frequent traffic—which there wouldn't be—they hadn't heard the cars and they were bored, distracted and probably playing cards.

"Not so smart."

He gave a low whistle of inquiry. A few seconds later, Angie answered it with a crow's caw: *all clear*. So far.

He sat on his heels behind the sign, one hand tapping his holstered SIG.

That wall. That big bastard of a wall. Possibly miles long, surrounding that tiny town and its outlying areas. The ends disappeared where bushland curved around to obscure them. The facility they were seeking was south and west of here, and Elliot could only hope the wall wasn't that extensive. From the section he could see, a *lot* of people took considerable time to build it: the flood barrier blocks and shipping containers would have taken cranes or loaders, and presumably transport from Hobart ports, requiring further manpower to guard the vehicle operators from deaders or dangerous humans. He used the field glasses again. That gate was made of shipping container doors with a lock-area between it and another similar gate beyond.

Elliot had difficulty picturing a community large enough to build this. It was three years and ten months since that day when his old life had ended along with everyone else's—and his new life had started, along with far fewer of everyone else's. He'd been in Hobart then. Not a big city. Not even middle-sized. Way less than a million people. Most of them would have turned, been killed *by* the turned, starved, or died from injury and illness. It hadn't seemed like there was anyone left alive when he'd made it out of there, but there must have been. Thousands might have fled to remote locations like this—or lived here already and perhaps welcomed that influx of refugees coming to them. And in these places, no doubt further tragedy had befallen many, based on his own early experiences. Other Downs' residents—and Birdy, poor Birdy—had reported the arrival of mainland refugees to the north of Tasmania where there had followed a Hurricane Katrina pro forma of murder and abuse. And then, unlike Katrina, there followed more outbreaks of the undead. This had apparently been the genesis of that massive tide of deaders that came south and east in search of prey. The tide Birdy had saved him and Lewis from by landing her plane to warn them.

Birdy. He sighed at the thought of the pilot's name again and the memory of her small and finely featured face. The sigh was partially in relief that the images of her death stayed where he'd buried them. It was fine to remember her name. It was *important* to remember her name. She was a comrade. She was a hero.

Sometimes he had wondered why he had outlived so many people who deserved to live more than he did. Perhaps part of his role in life was to remember them, the fallen, the brave, the innocent. In remembering them, surely he kept a part of them alive: Da Cruz and Crouch in Libya; Holbeck, Rogers, Fayed and Álvarez in Jordan; Radler, Eames, McGovern in Syria; Tommy Harrison; the chef at the resort south of Hobart whose name he'd never gotten before the poor noble bastard got bit. And Birdy.

And when he bought it one day, who would remain to remember him? Who would bother?

Would Lewis?

Would Angie?

He shook it off and got his focus back on the wall.

Had local people built this wall? Were the builders from overseas? Military? Civilian? A mixture? Friendly or unfriendly? It couldn't have been outlaw bikers, the Druids, the Maggot Riders or the Satans of the South. The dead tide had killed many of them and he was pretty sure those left had taken each other out after that, around the time he was extracting Claire and Jimmy and Alyssa.

Okay. So flood barriers notwithstanding, these could be ordinary folk but resourceful. And guarded. Like us. Like Barnabas Island and Nine Mile River.

"Only there must a lot more of them than us."

He gave Angie a different crow call—*regroup*—and moved across to Woodsy.

The motorcycle cop grinned. "Holy shit, huh?"

"That we agree on."

"We're going around?"

"Hell yes we're going around."

"Not worth knocking on the front door? Might be good people. There *must* be more good people left than us."

"Helluva risk."

"I could go alone."

"You want to go alone?"

Woodsy thought about it. "Nope."

"We'll go around. Your facility was secret, right?"

"Very."

"Let's hope these builders thought it was a worthless site if they saw it. And let's hope they left it outside wherever these walls extend to."

Woodsy made a face. "Bloody sorry I didn't travel up this way before I found Settlers Downs. Wish I'd known about these walls. Woulda taken us a different way."

"We'll leave the spare car here," Elliot told him. "Less noise and trouble in one vehicle." He pointed as Angie scuttled across the road to join them. "And she's driving."

When they got back to the car, Woodsy was chuckling.

"What's so funny?" Elliot asked.

"Whoever built that humongous wall knew their Bible and has a bloody good sense of humor." He waved Jimmy down from the conifer hedge. "Bloody good commitment to the joke, too."

"What're you talking about?" Angie asked.

"The little town down the road behind it? One of the oldest in Tassie. Small. Historic. Know what it's called?"

They all shook their heads.

Woodsy laughed again. "Jericho."

10

Woodsy was no longer laughing when the fifth road they tried was also blocked by the wall. Angie stopped the moment it came into sight, then reversed for twenty metres, did a U-turn and drove slowly a little ways further along the narrow dirt track until she reached another of the signs. There, she let the Rover idle. Its fuel needle sat just under half. They had the spare cans in back, and the fuel in the SUV they'd left on the main highway was good. But gas—or *petrol* in Australia—was not an infinite resource; they couldn't afford much more screwing around. Daylight was also ebbing.

"This one had a gate," she told them in case they hadn't seen. "But I didn't see anyone." No one had been visible at any of the last three locations and there'd been no gate at any of them.

"Who the hell made this damned thing?" Woodsy complained. "It shouldn't be here." He had the map across the rear seat between him and Jimmy, running his fingers over it as if the explanation could be found there. But they all knew that this was the final road they

PETE ALDIN

could take to unpopulated Gum Hill where the facility had been built.

"Okay, I'm driving again," said Woodsy, as if a change of driver would help them find a way in.

"And I'm riding shotgun," Jimmy said.

"You're not," Elliot told both of them. In his peripheral vision, Jimmy slumped. Woodsy swore and made a meal of folding the map. Elliot touched Angie's arm. "Remember that homestead back a ways? The one with the accommodation sign out front?"

"Yep. Sounds good." She put the car in gear and as she pulled out, she indicated the *Welcome* sign nailed to a telegraph pole. "Come into my parlor said the spider to the fly."

"All things considered," said Elliot, "I'd rather be the spider."

Paratarra Forge Homestead turned out to be a two-story building dating from the early twentieth century.

No one had presumably been there in a while since the drybones that lay in the driveway *had* been there a while. Atrophied muscles managed to turn its head a little toward the sound of the Land Rover; its limbs shifted weakly. Angie took great delight in lining up the head with the front tire on her side.

"Score!"

She hid the car behind the main house. Inspection showed them that the property's main business had been farrier work. Its metal-forging equipment had been stripped away, probably by the people behind those walls. A water tower out in one of the fields

128

would make a decent sniper's nest—its access platform proved to be dry, now the rains had passed. The homestead boasted six upstairs guest rooms with original mattresses; although they'd been relieved of pillows, sheets and blankets, they were clean and dry, free from animal droppings, grit or mildew.

"Score," Angie repeated, though less enthusiastically.

With Jimmy the first to head up to the nest, the others dragged chairs to a downstairs bay window, catching the last daylight and considering the area map.

"A fucking wall," Angie growled. "We've gone back to the Middle Ages."

"Bronze Age," Elliot corrected. "That's when walled city-states started. Ur. Babylon. Indus Valley, too, I think, 3000 BC, or maybe it was earlier." Upon noticing her raised eyebrow, he explained, "Too much Discovery Channel."

"So there was another Jericho back then in Bible times?" she said. "With walls?"

"Sure. Ask Chuckles here. He saw the funny side earlier."

Unperturbed, Woodsy replied, "Aussies love irony, Elliot. You should know that by now. And yes, Angie, like I said, it's mentioned in the Bible and probably existed in the ninth century BCE. Historians now call it Before Common Era, Elliot, not Before Christ. I watched Discovery Channel, too." He got up, put his hands on his hips and stretched road-cramps from his back. "We have a real setback here."

Angie said, "And this was your idea. So what's your next idea, genius? How do we get in?"

Elliot smiled. God, it felt good when her ire was turned on someone else. Especially this dipshit.

Woodsy put one boot up on the coffee table with the map and commenced a hamstring stretch. "Buggered if I know. I'm not sure we should now."

"Why the fuck not?" she said.

"Well, it's breaking and entering, now, isn't it? Now that we know the area's occupied. Theft."

"We're scouting," said Elliot. "And if we do end up *stealing*—" He made air quotes with his fingers. "—it's coz we have people we want to keep alive."

Angie leaned closer to catch Woodsy's eye. "That *was* your reason for this trip, wasn't it? Keeping our people alive? This whole damn thing was your idea."

Woodsy scowled and concentrated on his stretch.

Elliot shifted the map away from the mud dripping off Woodsy's foot and opened the flask he'd brought from the car. The sweet scent of mutton broth wafted from inside. He'd cleaned four mugs in the homestead's commercial kitchen and he now filled three, leaving enough in the thermos for Jimmy. "Got another question for our fearless leader. Or a cluster of questions." Yeah, it'd be a cluster of them; he'd been thinking about this for hours.

"Shoot," Woodsy grunted as he swapped legs. The new boot came close to toppling Angie's soup. She pulled the mug away with a curse.

"First. It never bothered me earlier. But it should have. This facility full of super-meds was out here in the ass-end of nowhere. Nothing around but farms and farriers and forests. Why not Hobart?" He sipped at his broth: it was cold now, but it tasted like heaven.

Woodsy's voice strained as he leaned into the stretch. "Hobart's kind of at the bottom right corner of our state, you might remember?"

"Sure. Wasn't most of the population living there or else up along the north coast? Seems dumb to have a storehouse of super-meds outside those urban centers and away from your two main airports."

"Maybe," Woodsy conceded. "No one ever accused politicians of being smart. But the facility was first built in 1986. Height of the Cold War. Our illustrious state government of the time was shit-scared of the Russians or Chinese nuking any big city centers." He removed his boot and leaned his sizeable backside on the window sash. "So they built it far enough away from Hobart and Launceston to survive nuclear attack, but close enough to Hobart to service us in a few hours if needed. Travel times back then were pretty quick."

"A lot of holes in that plan."

"As I said, politicians and smart aren't always a connect." He reached for his mug and settled back. "It probably wasn't full of super-antivirals back then, but it would have had medical supplies and maybe food *et cetera*. All successive governments kept it running because we moved out of the Cold War era into the global terrorism era. And whadda ya know? One of those dumb politicians was actually right about us needing something like this."

"Okay, so next question."

"Shoot."

"I will if you don't stop saying that."

Angie snorted, but managed to keep from smiling. *Close but no cigar, Elliot.*

"Next question is a yes or no question. They, the authorities, gave motorcycle cop Terry Wood, the codes to this facility?"

The first signs of discomfort appeared in the lines of Woodsy's face. "The codes for the medical part of the facility. God knows what's in the rest of it."

Ah, deflection. We're getting somewhere.

"Right. And you haven't answered why they gave those codes to a traffic cop. But we'll return to that soon, because now we come to my favorite question: if you knew about this place, why haven't you been here before? Since civilization collapsed?"

The sudden flush in Woodsy's cheeks was obvious, even bathed as they were in the orange light of sunset. He averted his gaze and sipped broth, thinking.

Elliot waggled his brows at Angie. *Good questions, huh?*

The gaze she returned him was steely rather than impressed. "And you couldn't have thought of these questions back home?" she asked.

Elliot stopped waggling his brows and gulped his own broth instead.

Woodsy eased himself into a chair and cleared his throat. "The answer to how I know about the facility is a bit, er, embarrassing. See, I was a high-ranking officer for a long time."

"Riiight," Angie said slowly, putting down her mug. "I thought you looked familiar when you first turned up. I remember your name now, from the news."

Now that's *fascinating.*

"How high?" Elliot asked.

She said, "I remember his name, not his rank."
Woodsy didn't respond.

"How high?" Elliot pressed.

"Pretty high."

"And you did something bad, didn't you?"

"No. I was accused of it. And in those days, that's all it took. One good thing about the apocalypse was losing all the bloody HR departments. Bastards."

"But your superiors spanked your hairy ass? Demoted you to traffic cop? You fell a long way, Constable."

"Sergeant."

"Whatever. What'd you do, you bad boy?"

Angie was nodding, interested.

Woodsy's jaws worked. "I didn't."

"What were you accused of?"

"My business."

"Ours, I'd say."

Angie *mmm*-ed agreement.

"Nope. It's not. It doesn't affect anyone here. It was a ... It was political and bureaucratic bullshit, that's all. Happened in a different world at a different time. And it wasn't true. It's meaningless now."

"Even so—"

"I'm not telling you!"

The moment hung in the air, time thickening around it.

Finally, Woodsy spoke again, voice shaking as he got it under control. "And the other question. As I've told everyone, my group were stuck in Cairns Bay down south for a long time. Scavenging, fishing, avoiding zombies and trigger-happy farmers. Took a long time for the undead to die off enough for us to find a way out of there. I've told you all this."

"Tell us again," said Angie.

"And answer the question," Elliot added.

"Short of it is: when we finally left, we'd had bad experiences with other survivors, so we figured those dangerous kinds of people would have gone inland. More resources. So those of us left kept to the coast to search for somewhere safe. I have told you all this. The answer to the bloody question is we'd lost people, and when it was just three of us left, I wasn't risking a trip into the midlands if other unsavory types had taken up residence there."

"But you figured it's safe now? Six months after your journey started? With you, Jimmy and one other person, you could attempt the midlands now? Not that Angie doesn't make a helluva difference, I'll grant you that."

"Don't patronize me."

Woodsy swished his mug. "Well, the truth is, there's more at stake now. Isn't there? There's a community of forty-seven good adults and little children, whose health and safety might depend on this mission. Prior to that, I had no compelling reason to risk the last few lives we had left. I want to do what I can for The Settlers. I'm a cop. Protecting society is what I do." He sipped soup, checked their reactions over the lip of the mug.

Angie nodded to herself and stood, started for the kitchen. "Fair enough. We need those meds and that's all I care about. Except that this broth needs more salt and pepper."

Woodsy gave Elliot a tight smile and turned to the window. Elliot's grip tightened so hard around his mug, he expected it to shatter. Woodsy had dragged them hundreds of kilometres on a fool's errand. Seconds earlier, Angie had been on Elliot's side and ready to take Woodsy to task for the holes in his story, for his deceptiveness. Now she'd turned full circle to accepting the man's flawed and dangerous mission again, as well as his patchy story. She was willing to put herself in harm's way for a man they barely knew while dismissing Elliot's reservations with a curt *Fair enough.*

For a short time that afternoon, she'd made pleasant conversation with him. She'd shared a little of her history. A couple of times, she'd touched him casually and accepted the same from him. He'd been regaining the ground he'd lost with her over his volunteering to come along. And then he'd blown it with one patronizing—yes, she was right about that—one patronizing comment.

See, Claire. This is why I don't do Relationships.

At the window, the dying sunlight lit up Woodsy's profile in a messianic glow.

Right then, if Elliot had been scripting it, a sniper round would have hit the lying prick mid-forehead.

11

"No way in hell," Angie said. For emphasis, she kicked a piece of litter across the homestead drying yard at Elliot. Steam blew from her nostrils, a product of the early morning chill rather than some cartoonish measure of how mad she was.

The sun had appeared an hour earlier in a largely cloudless sky without making much impact on the crisp spring air. When they'd stepped outside for this "discussion", they'd brought their coats with them. Wearing hers, Angie looked more like a ski bunny than a warrior, but Elliot knew first-hand that this was an illusion. However, there was no way he was letting her inside those walls. If Woodsy was going to get someone killed, it wasn't going to be her.

"I promise you," he said, "the decision is not in deference to your femaleness."

Oh, that was smooth.

From the kitchen came the clicks and clacks of Jimmy and Woodsy cleaning and checking weapons. Jimmy seemed more sober and focused around weapons now; perhaps the scare had gotten through to him. And he and Woodsy both seemed happy to let Elliot and

Angie talk this through without getting involved. About the wisest thing either of them had ever done, Elliot figured.

"I'm going over that wall," she said.

"I think you should stay with the vehicle. Here's—"

"I'm going in!"

"—why I think that. A, someone has to."

"Yeah, but not me."

"B, I have a lot of covert mission experience."

"Here we go. Big hero. Hero's gonna leave the girl behind because girls can't do hero stuff."

He could have responded that he'd served with plenty of heroic women in the military. He could have mentioned Birdy. But he decided to stay on message, keep moving forward. "C, Woodsy knows how to get into the actual facility."

"Which he could tell me and then he could stay here with the car."

"And if things change, he might be the only one with enough background knowledge to adapt our plans." He dropped his voice. "I hate to admit it, but we need him." She pressed her lips together and didn't reply. "D, Jimmy is a skinny runt who can crawl and climb places Woodsy and I can't."

"And fat Angie can't?"

"Did I say you were fat?"

"Exactly. I'm not. I'm almost as slim as Jimmy."

Unwittingly his eyes traced her figure before he brought them under control.

Different shape though.

The momentary scrutiny hadn't escaped her notice, but she didn't comment on it. She asked, "There's an E?"

"There is."

"E?"

He dropped his voice again. "I trust you protecting the vehicle a lot more than either of them. And F…" He was suddenly out of points.

Into the silence, she muttered, "I can think of a phrase beginning with F."

"Classy," he replied.

"I'm the car's bodyguard then?"

He attempted some humor. "And getaway driver."

She didn't find it funny. She said, "Arsehole."

And he said, "I get that a lot."

She took them down the road they'd tried yesterday and then down what appeared to be a narrow park ranger access trail. A kilometre and a half from the wall, she turned the Rover around and the three men got out. Elliot watched it crawl away and thought of all the APCs and helos that had left his various squads and platoons in other drop zones over the years.

"You thinking you'll never see her again?" Woodsy asked.

"I wasn't."

"Oh. Sorry. It's just you two make such a good pair …"

"*What?*"

"Nothing," said Woodsy and added unnecessarily, "It's this way."

Halfway to their destination, Woodsy was puffing and Elliot pushed past him to take the lead. Jimmy kept up a flow of whispered gibberish, talking to himself;

three times Elliot had to make a slashing gesture to get him to stop. They met no resistance along the way, the only signs of life in the damp bushland the squawking and cheeping of birds, the chirrup of insects and the occasional rustle of some small animal in underbrush. This did not mean that death could not suddenly erupt from all that innocence—in thick woodlands, rival human factions and drybones were not the only dangers. More than a few times, Elliot and other scouts had been troubled by tiger snakes, feral dogs and feral cats. The latter were arguably the worst: mean as bobcats and grown as large, the creatures were descended from domestic cats who'd reverted to the wild. They were not easily chased off. Elliot kept his weapon up.

The three men halted at the edge of a firebreak plowed around the wall by some form of earthmoving equipment. Flood barriers, steel sheeting and wooden braces faced them across a gap of thirty metres. No one could be seen along the wall, though a nest of planking had been piled on a shipping container two hundred metres to their left for lookouts. Elliot wondered if the circling flock of cockatoos were the same ones as yesterday—and wished they'd shut the hell up so he could hear better. He kept catching the bass note of *something* in the vicinity, but it was too low to define.

"You can climb that, son?" Woodsy asked Jimmy, who nodded gravely.

"Better idea first," Elliot said.

They followed his outstretched arm toward the whitish line in the wall off to their right.

"A crack?" Woodsy asked.

PETE ALDIN

Elliot raised the field glasses. "Yep. A join, poorly done. So, how fast are you, Jimmy?"

"Real fast," the kid boasted.

Kid. Elliot had never thought of Lewis that way, even when Lewis had been five years younger than Jimmy was now. But Jimmy seemed immature—even by Lewis's original standards. His abuse at the hands of those Druids had badly damaged him. Elliot again regretted him coming.

"All right then, listen up. You're gonna run fast to the wall." He pointed directly across the firebreak, the shortest route to cover. "You get there, you stop still. You listen carefully. If you hear voices on the other side, you break off and get right back here."

Jimmy had his Glock in both hands, studying the grip.

"You listening?"

"Yeah."

"What I say?"

Jimmy's expression soured. "Run there. Listen. Run back if I hear talking."

"Okay."

Jimmy looked at Woodsy who nodded. "Elliot's right."

"What if there's no talking?" Jimmy asked.

"Then you quietly make your way to that crack in the wall. Take a good look. Then reverse the process."

Jimmy frowned.

Woodsy explained patiently, "Get back here the way you came."

"Oh." He made to stand, but Elliot caught his arm.

"Holster your weapon."

140

"*Huh?*"

"You're not shooting anyone unless there's a lot of trouble. And if that happens, we'll be shooting before you are. Your job is stealth."

Jimmy holstered the Glock. "Can I go now?"

Elliot removed his hand.

The kid was as fast as a rabbit across the open ground. Elliot had rarely seen him doing anything besides gardening, fruit picking or laundry. Or flicking through comic books. He had to admit there was some physical grace at work here; the kid could have made a solid athlete.

In another life.

Jimmy did as he'd been told. To the letter. At the join between sections, he spied on the terrain beyond. He didn't stay for long, on the move again after thirty seconds. When he was back, he said, "Old crops. Looks like they had corn which is all dead and folded over now. No people."

"No people?" Woodsy asked.

"None."

"Deaders? Drybones?" asked Elliot

Jimmy shook his head. "There's more bush across like a road or a path. Dirt. And it looks like something drove down it not so long ago."

"How can you tell?"

"It's muddy. There's fresh tire tracks."

Still a working brain in there. Nice.

Woodsy patted the kid's shoulder. "Buildings?"

"Couldn't see any. Just bush like this." He gestured around them.

141

"What's on the other side of the wall itself?" Elliot asked him. "This section in front of us? Are there ladders? A walkway?"

Jimmy scrunched up his face. "I think there was a ladder back this way a bit. Yeah, there was." He pointed to a spot about halfway to his spyhole. "Couldn't see what it led to."

Woodsy had the regional map out, folded over inside its protective plastic. Elliot reached out and angled it his way. They'd sketched their idea of the wall across it in pencil last night, based on what they'd seen each time they'd approached: the wall, they thought, was uneven in direction, possibly following geological contours. Beyond it the map was largely bare apart from the narrow blue markings of creeks, a handful of roadways, the hamlet of Jericho and another larger town they thought might also be contained within the far southern boundary called Pankhurst. A medical symbol indicated a clinic or hospital. A school was marked there, too. Nothing but a regional name had been marked for the place where Woodsy said the facility lay. Elliot tapped a spot the map said was the exact middle of nothing.

"We're here?"

Woodsy said, "Yes. And headed there." He tapped the folded page's diagonally opposite corner. "Four kilometres."

"Four and a half," Elliot corrected. "As the crow flies. Like I said at breakfast, best we meet this creek here and follow it. Adds a couple more kilometres to the trip, but keeps us near potential cover and off any roads." He pointed to Jimmy. "You're over first. When you give us the all clear, we'll follow."

Watching Woodsy climb a wall, Elliot thought as the young man sprinted away. *This'll be fun.*

Inside the wall, the terrain was familiar Tasmanian midlands. A patchwork of low rolling hills denuded of trees and green with winter grasses, contrasted with squared-off swathes of thick bushland. Paddocks and woods, paddocks and woods. Crisscrossed here and there with low wire fences, brooks or dirt access tracks.

On their way to the creek shown on the map, they kept to the shadows cast along a dirt road by lines of pine and gum trees. Woodsy was breathing heavily within ten minutes. Jimmy had swung out deeper into the bush, but the occasional crack of a twig indicated he was keeping pace. Elliot could have gone faster, but rushing this would be stupid. And he had Woodsy to think of. Eventually he made out the chug of a generator north of their heading—this was making the bass note he'd been trying to identify earlier. So there was fuel around. And people. A half-kilometre out from the creek, Elliot stopped to examine footprints in the soft soil; they seemed recent and made by heavy boots. Near them, an empty juice bottle had been shoved into a bush and was swarmed with ants. Further along he found desiccated corn cobs, perhaps months-old. A minute later, just as Jimmy was rejoining the older men, the rumble of a quad or motorbike made them all freeze and duck. But it was distant and soon faded.

A narrow bridge came into view at a dip in the road—the creek. Elliot almost left the cover of the trees before he registered movement ahead.

Christ.

"Hold," he hissed and dropped into a crouch, the others behind him.

A woman had shuffled onto the bridge, one leg dragging beneath her long skirt as she moved.

Woodsy's shotgun rose.

Realizing the woman wasn't a deader, Elliot pushed the shotgun back down.

Moments later two more women joined the first, and then a teenage girl, all climbing up from the creek bank. Each had water in plastic jugs. The quartet trudged away from Elliot's position, crossing the bridge to place the jugs on a trolley he hadn't noticed until then. With their scrawny appearance and shabby clothing, their cowed posture, their lack of energy, Elliot would have made all of them as deaders if sighting them at a greater distance. The women's matted hair fell in tangled, greasy locks. Their t-shirts and sweaters hung loose on their frames. They did not speak that he could see or hear, merely walked slowly away with heads bowed.

"Follow 'em?"

Woodsy's murmured question shook Elliot out of deep thought.

"Hell, no."

"They look like they need our help."

Elliot gave him a hard stare. "That occurred to me, too, Mother Theresa. It also occurred to me that it's off-mission. We're here for one reason only. And for all we know, they're as crazy as scav-rats and they'll attack us if we try and help them."

"I guess."

"We wait another five minutes. If no one else comes up from the creek, I go first then signal that it's safe for you to follow. Capisce?"

"Sure."

"Sure," Jimmy echoed.

Goddamn moral choices, Elliot complained to himself as he waited. Those women might need help, but they might also lead him to an unpleasant situation where he put him and his team in greater danger. In a way, he'd tried to help that poor bastard at the Blueberry Barn and it hadn't worked out.

No, I'm right. My duty is to The Downs. That's it. Anything else is unimportant.

A grey shape bounded from cover nearby and headed for better cover across the road. A rabbit. Nothing to warrant this fresh spike of adrenaline. God, he hated being out here doing this. Had he seriously been considering leaving Settlers Downs to live like this full-time?

Five minutes later, he made a dash for the creek with the Steyr up and ready.

His dive watch read 11:13 when he allowed them to rest for the first time. Panting hard, Woodsy collapsed onto the creek bank. Jimmy immediately scampered up it to watch their surroundings. Past his position, the ground kept rising into a scrub-covered ridge. Preferring water from their canteens to that of the shallow stream, the two men also chewed dried fish and fruit.

Clouds had closed over the sky, keeping the September sun at bay and the day cool. But all three men had stripped down to t-shirts, stuffing their sweaters in their packs.

"Bloody pooped, I am," Woodsy wheezed.

Elliot shifted closer, kept his voice low while he recalled the map in his head and overlaid their current position on it. "I'm thinking of a change in plans. We leave the stream and head over the ridge there. Still lots of cover, but quicker, and the high ground gives us perspective."

Woodsy looked about to argue, then slumped. "Agreed." Red-faced, thin hair plastered to his scalp, shirt soaked, he didn't look like he had the short climb in him. But Elliot knew he did. He'd come this far without collapsing. He'd kept up. The shotgun's strap was tight across his chest, crossing the strap of a shoulder satchel; he hadn't taken either off, nor asked for relief from them. And that was a relief to Elliot.

The only thing to be concerned about was whether or not Woodsy had it in him to take a life.

"We didn't discuss facility guards in detail," Elliot said and sipped again before replacing his canteen's lid.

"Because we won't know till we get there."

"But you *have* been there."

"Yeah, mate, once. I drew you the diagram at brekky."

"And I remember it." Elliot used a stick to draw a bare-bones sketch of the facility's two ingress points. "You say this one is probably least guarded."

"Because it's an underground garage. And the door's powered, so all they do is close it and leave it."

"Right, but it might still be guarded. At least that side, that side of the building will. And here's my question. So we're clear: you're committed to killing them? Living people? Possibly former comrades."

"I'm not okay with it, but I'm committed, yes. I've had to do it before."

"Even though the signs all invited people into a happy community?"

"From my experience, Settlers Downs is in the minority, Elliot."

"Mine, too."

"Those women back there—"

"Forget them."

"Can I make another point, then?"

Something rattled bushes upslope from Jimmy and Elliot put his hand up, shutting Woodsy up. A moment later, a parrot burst into flight from the trees and Elliot relaxed a notch.

Goddamned wildlife.

"What point?" he asked, eyes still on that scrub up there.

"I'm starting to wonder if the facility will be guarded at all. There's a shitload of land within these walls, but we've hardly seen anybody. There were crops. And a vehicle."

"Two sentries at the northernmost gate. Four women back there."

"You said forget them."

"What's your goddamn point?"

PETE ALDIN

"Well, the women were malnourished and grubby. What if whoever built these walls was actually only a handful of people? Or they all died off? We don't know much about the other factions out there, but we do know that a lot of people died in the Collapse. Most people. Maybe there's not enough here to cover the whole place comfortably. Not too many sentries on the walls. And if no one who came here could get into the facility—entirely possible—they'd have long since given up interest in it."

"Or there might be plenty of them sheltered in small interior compounds with enough weapons to be unconcerned about people climbing their walls. And some of them are guarding their highly valuable facility." If he could be sure it was safe, Elliot might have suggested returning to that northern gate and offering to trade some sheep or cattle. They'd seen no sign of livestock since entering. Perhaps a disease had wiped them out in this part of the country. Perhaps the deaders had. "If they're all so malnourished, it could be that the original wall-builders either died off or returned to Hobart. Could be, the people here now are basically scav-rats."

"Squatters."

"Exactly."

More noise made Elliot glance up. Just Jimmy sliding back down to them.

Woodsy said, "We could be raiding an empty facility. The builders might have taken the medical supplies back to Hobart. Shit."

Perhaps Jimmy had caught something in their body language. He asked, "We going home?"

148

Elliot shook his head. "Too close to leave now. We have to know." He brushed an early season bush fly from his Steyr. "And if it is guarded, well, then we know the good shit's still inside. You ready to climb that hill?"

12

The building was a windowless box, a single floor showing above ground, fifty meters by twenty. Heavy-duty chain link surrounded it. The facility was much as he'd pictured it from Woodsy's breakfast-time diagram and road trip descriptions.

Leaving the other men hidden in thick bushland, Elliot reconned three of the four sides. The fourth side faced a dirt access road he wasn't going to venture onto. The six-car parking lot out front was empty. Mid-building, a single entry door faced the road. A cement driveway ran around one side to the back right-hand corner and the only other entranceway: a steel roller door high and wide enough to admit a lorry; a ramp led down below ground. The roller door seemed to be stuck three-quarters of the way up, leaving the way clear for incursion. Perhaps raiders or ex-government people had left it that way as they ran off with the resources from inside. A lone white van sat idle on the lush lawn at the back of the building. Judging from the height of the grass around its tires and the missing left front wheel, it hadn't moved in a while. Thankfully, he encountered no drybones.

He returned to crouch with the others among the trees, keeping his voice low.

"No sign of movement or habitation. Front gates are wide open, a lot of weeds on the dirt road out front. Front door is closed and it's exposed, so we'll be entering via the rear roller door as discussed. That's our only option, right?"

"Door inside will be easier to open than the front door," Woodsy said.

Elliot pointed through the thick screen of vegetation. "Camera on each corner. No light to indicate they're on, but that means nothing. We're doing this for our people, so risks are part and parcel. If someone has time to sit and watch those cameras 24/7, then we'll deal with whatever comes. If we're doing this, we're doing this. But. One last time—" He looked toward the open roller door. "—you're *convinced* there are antivirals in there?"

"I'm convinced there *were* before the crisis happened. Nothing left in any hospital will be any good. This is our best bet."

"I prefer intel to bets. What's under the building down that ramp, for example?"

Woodsy shrugged. "Loading dock?"

"Great. Going in blind. Say your prayers, boys." His companions shifted uncomfortably. "First step: you keep an eye out while I cut us a hole in that fence. From there, it's a brisk walk in formation across the grass. We go direct to the loading dock entry. Any contact at any time, we get back to the fence hole, back to this point, then we get the hell out of here. If we make the ramp without contact, the real fun begins."

"Fun?" said Woodsy.

"You ever cleared a room, rescued a hostage?" he asked Woodsy.

"I was *at* a hostage situation. Once. Twenty years ago. Domestic situation. I didn't go in, though."

"Others went in?"

"Yes."

"They kill the guy, the hostage taker?"

"No. Pepper-sprayed him and detained him without firing a shot."

"Right. Because for most cops in Britain or Australia, excessive force means you guys lose your jobs and pensions. And you're trained to protect people from harm, even bad guys. If you're coming in with me, you need to forget that. We're following three principles: we move methodically, we move decisively, we take immediate violent action when meeting resistance. Immediate violent action. No second guessing. This is you, too, Jimmy."

"You yelled at me for shooting that guy."

Elliot ran a hand over his face. "This is a different situation."

"How?"

"It … it just is. Now concentrate. Hear what I'm saying and do what you're told. If either one of you sees a person holding something and facing us, you put them down. You put them *down*, you get me?"

"Yes."

"Yeah."

Woodsy didn't look happy about it; Jimmy showed zero emotion at all, eyes on his Glock.

"You didn't kill that Vike you spoke to at the creek that time," Woodsy said.

Elliot shook his head. "Again, a different situation. This isn't meeting a neutral party in the open or on our terms. This is close quarters combat. This is ingress, incursion. We do it this way or we don't do it."

Woodsy nodded again. "Okay."

"That ramp entry is on the corner of the building, so presumably the space at the bottom opens up to the left, spreading beneath the ground floor. Woodsy, you and I are going to do what's called slicing the pie. At the bottom of the ramp, I'll move left and you'll move right. There's an imaginary line from the bottom of the ramp across to the far diagonal corner. Anything to the right of that line is yours and to the left is mine. We are responsible for our own slice. You getting this?"

"I'm not an idiot."

"Good to know. When we leave the ramp, you'll follow your wall to the closest corner while sweeping your slice, and at that corner you will stay until I reach mine to the left. When we both signal clear, we advance along the side walls, clearing obstacles as we go. Obstacles might be cars, pallets, trash cans, pillars."

They all flinched as two birds speared through the canopy above, one chasing the other, squawking. It went on a while and Elliot slow-breathed, scanning the bush again. Sound like that could mask the approach of hostiles.

When the birds had moved out of the immediate area, Elliot continued, "If the next obstacle is on your side of the room, I pause while you clear it. Then we move on together. You pause while I clear them on my side. We move *together.* We reach the next entryway to get into the building interior. I'll take up a cover position while you either input the code or use that hooligan bar."

Jostling the twelve-pound fire department pry-bar in his pack, Woodsy said, "What if the hooligan doesn't work?"

"You'll apply the shotgun to hinges or locks. That doesn't work, we'll makeshift a battering ram."

"What if *that* doesn't work?" asked Jimmy.

"Then we wasted our goddamn time, didn't we?"

"Let's get on with this," Woodsy said, wiping sweat from his brow. "We still have to get out of here before dark."

"Two more things first, because I don't plan to die today. One, neither of you sweeps a weapon across my position or each other's. You have your zone, you stick to it."

"Have we swept our weapons across you yet?" Woodsy grumped.

"We haven't had a situation where you really needed them yet. Two, when we pass that fence, we're walking in a triangle. We're walking in a hurry, but a careful hurry. Jimmy, can you walk backwards without falling over?"

"Yeah."

"Right. Woodsy and I will be shoulder to shoulder. You'll be right at our backs as we cross that yard. Again, Woodsy watches right, me left. Oh, and three: as I said, Jimmy will be on that ramp when we reach it, lying down, facing *out.* Jimmy, you will *not* look back into the garage once you're there. You will keep watching outwards."

"Wouldn't we be better with Jimmy in there with us?" Woodsy said.

"You gotta argue every point? Do what I say and we all live."

Maybe.

"Fine," said Woodsy. "Then I'll repeat *my* point. Let's get on with it."

Elliot took the cutters from his pack, left the pack where it was and moved to the fence.

PART THREE

THE KILLING FLOOR

13

It didn't go as planned.

Inside the building was white and grey.

All of it.

The room they'd entered off the garage.

The stairwell to the level below the garage.

This corridor.

The air was flat. Filtered. All Elliot could smell was his own body odor. And Woodsy's.

He followed at Woodsy's heels while the former cop hissed curses. Elliot had a few of his own going.

It was far warmer inside the building than outside; even without his sweater, Woodsy had a triangle of sweat darkening the back of his t-shirt. Elliot could feel the same on his; with his weapons missing from his belt, he felt as good as naked.

The corridor ended in a T.

The man walking three metres back from Elliot said, "Left."

Woodsy turned left. Elliot followed with a backwards glance; he'd have about a second to turn and brace himself to catch the man trailing them off guard—

"I wouldn't," the man said.

Elliot swore and gave up that idea.

The branch corridor stretched ahead for thirty metres. There were several doors along each side. Woodsy drew level with the third on the right.

"Stop," the man ordered. "Open it."

Woodsy did.

"Inside."

Elliot turned to face the leader of their black-clad and helmeted captors. Another man and one woman flanked their leader. All held short-barreled assault rifles, wore black ballistic vests. They'd hidden their eyes behind tinted assault goggles.

"I said inside," the leader repeated. He was barrel-bodied with a couple of inches on Elliot. There was no urgency in his tone. No irritation at the delay. The command was matter-of-fact.

"We're not your enemy," Elliot tried. That provoked a slight smile on the clean-shaven face beneath the goggles. For a moment, Elliot flashed back to The Guy in Al-Kasrah. He hadn't thought about that asshole in years. He said, again, "We're not enemies. We're people like you. We need—"

"Don't care. Get in the room."

When Elliot turned around again, Woodsy was already inside. With a growl of frustration, Elliot went in, too.

A lunch room. Empty counters and sink, a rectangular table, six kitchen chairs. Counters on two sides. An empty cork bulletin board glued to one wall. The door closed behind them. There was no lock, but at least one armed guard would stay out there. No windows, since they were maybe twenty-five feet underground.

Woodsy slumped into one of the seats.

Elliot opened cupboards and drawers.

When he'd checked the last drawer, he slammed it as hard as he could. Not a knife, spoon, plate or glass to be found.

"Elliot."

No microwave or kettle to strip the cord from. "We could break a chair. Use the leg. Or," he reopened the drawer, leaning over to study the steel tracks it ran on. "Help me pull this out."

"Elliot!"

"What?"

Woodsy pointed to the ceiling opposite the door. The dark lens of a tiny camera glared at them.

Elliot reared back and slammed the sole of his boot into the drawer, then whirled and kicked a chair across the room. "Sonofa*bitch*!"

"SERPs." Woodsy smoothed his thin hair down. "Bastards."

"SERPs." Elliot stood there, clenching and unclenching his fists, filling his lungs with air, needing intel, needing grounding. This whole damn trip had been a mistake. And he'd known it; he'd felt it in his gut the whole time. "What are SERPs? Counter terrorism?"

"Counter-any-bloody-thing the government was afraid of. Counter-protest, counter-gangs, counter-terrorism." Woodsy checked his palm as if expecting to see color had come out of his hair. Then he slapped the table. "I was a good cop, you know. In my younger days. Then I got into management. Found out what the force was really full of and really for. Everything was about keeping the world the way the politicians wanted it. Not the way normal people needed it." He tapped a rhythm on the table for a while, then seemed to realize again he'd been lost in a memory. And that Elliot was awaiting more information. "SERP stood for Special Emergency Response Police. But these mongrels were never true cops. Too full of themselves. Most were army rejects who didn't make the cut for the SAS. Others were the type who thought policing was about batons or bullets first, discussions later. And that guy running them? That bloke is one true narcissist. I mean it. He's—"

The door opened then. Elliot guessed he'd find out what Woodsy didn't like first-hand.

Several "SERPs" crowded outside the doorway. Their helmets were missing this time.

A smirking cop with Indian features entered the tearoom first. His breast-badge read DA SILVA. *Sri Lankan then,* thought Elliot—he'd spent time in South East Asia right before the Collapse; Sri Lanka had inherited many Portuguese names during the Colonial era. Da Silva was a little shorter than Elliot but much *much* bigger, bulked with muscle. He'd be stronger in a clinch, slower in hand to hand. The man was hard as nails, there was no doubting that.

A female SERP entered next. ERIKSON. Her posture marked her as one of those who'd ambushed them in the garage and marched Elliot and Woodsy down here. Her close-cropped blonde hair reminded Elliot of Angie's when he'd first met her; her dead eyes did not. Something about the way she held herself—the bunched-up muscles of her forearms below her black shirtsleeves or the cruel curl of her lips—told Elliot she was perfectly capable of hurting him if he gave her cause. She'd also be perfectly okay with doing it.

Below their necks, every other part of the two SERPs' bodies were covered by either black hard-shell or tough flexible clothing the same color. Da Silva moved to one corner, covering his prisoners with a yellow taser, his cocky smile lifting his cheeks and revealing clean white teeth. Erikson remained by the door, holding her Smith & Wesson .40 cal semi-automatic in a relaxed grip by her side, finger on the guard. Her other hand rested on her holstered taser. Neither one was close enough for Elliot to tackle since he was backed up against a wall beside the sink.

Their leader came in next. He, too, had lost the helmet and neck-guard. Also his dark glasses. He stood at the table beaming down at Woodsy. His shoulders had rounded with late middle age, his cheeks and forehead wrinkling, a small paunch pressing against his shirt. But his face was rugged, 1950s-movie-star-handsome. Thick black hair showed white at the roots, overdue for its next dye-job. The .40 cal in his holster was clipped in, and he wore no armor over his shirt. With two subordinates in the room, he obviously didn't feel like he'd need those defenses. His glasses had put little dents either side of his aristocrat's nose.

And the ring and pinky fingers of his left hand were completely gone.

But the man looked *ready* the way the woman Erikson looked ready. A star-shaped scar marred the skin above his left eyebrow. And his hands—what was left of them—were big: broad with thick fingers and knobby knuckles. Brawler's hands.

Following at his heels came a fifty-something civilian woman ... *Civilian.* It was curious that Elliot's mind reverted to categories like this under stress. She remained in the doorway with slumped shoulders and wary eyes, a notepad and pen clutched to her blouse. Her plain grey business slacks had seen too many washes. Her hands and face were horribly pockmarked and there was something wrong with her right eye, the random flutters of its lids like the flickering of a bad neon.

Elliot caught movement out in the corridor past her, shadows. More cops, no doubt.

"Kyle," the leader said. He wore no name tag, so Elliot would take his word for it. His sidearm might be holstered, but he had not left himself completely defenseless, tapping Elliot's confiscated Shrade lockblade on his thigh. He added, "Surname, not first name. I'm telling *you* that," he said to Elliot, "because *he* already knows me. Dontcha, Terry?"

Woodsy's head had drooped when Kyle entered and he didn't acknowledge him now.

Kyle pointed the blade at him. "Terence Matthew Woods. Never thought I'd use that name or see that face again." The knife tracked toward Elliot. "And you are?"

"Wondering where the kid is."

"Hah! Nicely done. He's quick, Jason," he told Da Silva with the taser. "Do you mean Jimmy? Jimmy Schaefer, former resident of Huonville, eighteen years old last December? He's currently a resident of another room one floor up and he's answering our questions to the best of his ability. Unfortunately, the best of his ability isn't proving very useful to us." He tapped the scars on his other hand with the blade. "None too bright. Hopefully you're brighter, my friend."

These last twenty-four hours, several things had made Elliot wonder just how messed up Jimmy really was. Perhaps the kid was good at playing that part. Maybe that was something he'd learned while a slave to the Druids. He said, "He's just a kid."

"Sure. And I asked you a question. Your *name,* sir?"

"Elliot."

"First name or last?"

"Does it matter?"

A smile leaked across Kyle's features. "S'pose not. American?"

"Sure."

"Occupation?"

"Survival."

"Before that."

"Truck driver."

"Logging? Freight? Garbage?"

"Sure."

"Sure. A truck driver. And I'm Father Christmas. What do you reckon he was, Jason?"

Da Silva narrowed his eyes in scrutiny. "Private security. Cop. Something like that."

"I agree. Handles weapons like a pro. Had a system for clearing the parking bay. Watches his choke points. Yeah, 'something like that'."

"*You're* cops," Elliot said. "Hopefully that means you're good guys."

"We're the authorities here, that's for certain."

"And we're just people. Citizens."

"Oh, Jimmy Schaefer is just a people-citizen. Not you, though. Not Woodsy here." He turned to the policewoman, Erikson. "You remember Woodsy?"

"Sure do." Her smile was grotesque, a mannequin trying on human expression.

"Assistant Commissioner Terry Woods was right on track to be our next *Deputy* Police Commissioner. And maybe from there, he'd get the top job."

"Not a highway cop then?" Elliot asked.

Kyle laughed. "He tell you that? No. Not a highway cop for about fifteen years. Thing was, Assistant Commissioner Woods was a very naughty bloke and they were about to fire him. Possibly charge him. The story broke a week before the outbreak happened." He put on a newsreader's voice. "Assistant Police Commissioner's cocaine and prostitute habit uncovered. More details after this commercial." He waggled those eyebrows again, then feigned seriousness. "But. A day or two before he was gonna resign or get fired or get arrested, the toxies came along and prevented it. New headline: End of the world lets Police Bigwig off the hook." His grin was back. "Is that not a great story, Elliot?"

Elliot said nothing. Woodsy's chin was pressed onto his clasped hands. Despite the heat, he was trembling slightly.

Kyle continued, "Technically, he's still our Assistant Police Commissioner. How about you, Glenda?" he asked the civilian woman behind him. "Remember Woodsy?"

She gulped an affirmative. Neither she nor Woodsy made eye contact. She glanced at Elliot though. It was quick: he saw fear there, and he saw pity.

Ah, shit.

"Glenda used to be our state Attorney-General and Minister for Justice. Before you broke into our facility and we locked you in the garage, Glenda and I were conducting inventory downstairs. Inventory of ... Oh, that's right! The items we were counting were the items you came here to *steal*, weren't they? No need to explain them to you then. So, Glenda and her daughter were amongst the people we evacuated from parliament during the outbreak. Girl fell and hit her head. She's a bit brain-damaged these days, unfortunately. A bit ... *special*. But we take care of her. Because we like Glenda. She's educated. In return, Glenda and the other politicians we saved take care of us. A small price they pay for retaining a relatively affluent lifestyle."

Erikson's face had returned to stone, but Da Silva let out a small snicker at whatever joke Kyle was making.

Woodsy cleared his throat. "You...you're rebuilding society here?"

Kyle sighed wearily. He was still standing between the table and the open door. He pulled out a chair and jiggled it. "Glenda. Guess we're chatting a little before business."

Tentatively she sat, kept the notebook to her chest.

"Write down anything they say you think is important." Kyle pulled another chair, sat between her and Kyle. He commenced cleaning a fingernail with

Elliot's knife and asked Da Silva, "Am I good cop or bad cop this time?"

Da Silva grinned. "You're good, I'm bad, Erikson's indifferent."

"Thought it was your turn for indifference."

"I need the practice being bad."

"Right-e-o, then. I'll make some chit chat to put them at ease, then you come in with the threats if and when the time's right."

Elliot had thought Glenda to be wound as tight as she could be, but she hunkered deeper into her kitchen chair. The notebook crackled in her grip.

Kyle changed fingernails. "And Erikson shoots 'em if they try anything a taser can't handle."

Erikson murmured, "Absolutely." She took out her taser. A weapon in each hand now.

"This is unnecessary," Woodsy started, but Kyle raised the hand with the knife.

"It's hospitality, Assistant Commissioner. You asked a question; I'll answer it. Yes, we're rebuilding society here. This facility is a cornerstone of that. What's a society without medicine? And that's what you came here for, right? The drugs?"

"The man does like his drugs," said Da Silva.

Woodsy dropped his head again.

"That was a little unkind, Jason."

"My bad."

Kyle leaned across the table. "It's okay, Terry. What else would ya be here for, if not the meds? You're not the first. Been a couple of others who knew about it."

"You … you made it here first? You got your whole team here?" Woodsy mumbled.

Kyle waved the blade in a *naughty-naughty* gesture. "Trying to get information? Work out our numbers? I won't be telling you that. Even though whatever you discover wouldn't do you much good. Lemme ask Elliot-slash-Mister-Elliot a question now. You drove around our entire perimeter, I think. A thirty-six kilometre barrier is pretty impressive, huh? In this day and age?"

Elliot eyed the blade hungrily. His right palm itched. Kyle was out of reach, as were his two armed cronies. Elliot tried to sound defeated, cooperative. "We came in from the south, took—"

"You entered from the *west*. But you must have checked out a few other approaches first, a man like you. Unless Woodsy's been by here in the last eighteen months, he wouldn't have known about the wall. So, yeah, maybe you originally came up from the far south. More likely it was down from the north. Midland Highway would make the most sense. It *was* north, yes? And you have a vehicle outside somewhere don't you?"

Elliot's heart lurched. If they had seen Angie. If she hadn't left the vicinity of the wall. If they knew where she was …

Kyle continued, "You have other people waiting?"

Elliot let out a small sigh of relief. People. Plural. No, they didn't have eyes on Angie.

"What, now you've lost your tongue?" Kyle said. "Really, Elliot? All right, I'll offer you info as a trade and maybe you'll have the manners to reciprocate. Ask me something, anything. Except—" he tapped the table with the lockblade "—our numbers."

Behind his back, Elliot flexed his hands, keeping them limber. "We saw people earlier. Malnourished and dirty. What's their story?"

"Their story. Well, *that's* an old story when times are tough. We can't all be the bosses, can we? And we can't all be workers. You think Glenda and Jason here built that wall? Planted our crops? Shit, no. They've got more important stuff to do. And before you go all bleeding heart on us, our little peasants are luckier than most. I'm damned sure you've seen worse out there. Jimmy certainly acts like he has. Don't write any of this down, Glenda."

Glenda hadn't moved a muscle in the last minute, and she hadn't moved her pen.

"Not gonna bore you with the tale of the wall, but it's a good story isn't it, Jason, our story?"

"I reckon it'd make an awesome movie," Da Silva said.

Kyle laughed. "You're meant to be bad cop, not stand-up comedian cop."

"Oops."

Still grinning, Kyle continued, "I'll tell you this much. There was a BAFFLE flood barrier business near Richmond. Global warming created some real niche manufacturing businesses, didn't it? The BAFFLE people had eighteen hundred of those big-arse barrier blocks sitting in their warehouse and on their trucks, enough to cover almost eight kilometres of ground." He gave Elliot a thumbs-up. "God, they're easy to transport and erect. You ever come across 'em, Elliot? No? Oh, I'm sure you did. Maybe you did a little disaster relief? Well, trust me, if you ever do, get some of these buggers, they're awesome. Kept out the last of the walking toxies. And if anyone comes here from overseas and sniffs around, well, hopefully it'll slow them down, too. At least we'd have something between us and them. She ain't the Great Wall of China, but she'll do.

"Now," he leaned forward again and tapped the blade again. "Let's come back to the question you asked. The people you saw might not have their plates piled high every night, but they do have food. Dry beds. Clothing. No gangs assaulting them, no rapists assaulting them, both of which are very much against our laws. And this segues nicely with my next line of inquiry for you. You blokes look well dressed and well fed."

"Especially Woodsy," Da Silva added. "Tubby bugger."

Kyle nodded. "Indeed. You're well-armed, too. A SIG Sauer P226, a Steyr-AUG assault rifle, Glocks, an assault shotgun, for Chrissake? The Glocks and the Steyr are old biker weapons, I reckon. Yessiree, something tells this old detective you three blokes have a pretty sweet setup somewhere. And that's all I want to know. Where you came from. Where your camp is. Your compound. Did you team up with some of those Maggot Riders? Or the Satans of the South? Did ya take a few out and steal their weapons for your own base? I'd really like to visit with your people and learn more about them."

He waited ten seconds.

"See, competition is bad for us. It makes life more dangerous and complicated than we want it to be. On the other hand, new people coming to join *us* are good for our society, good for keeping things ticking over. So. I ask again. Elliot? Where's your camp? Where's home? Woodsy? Home? No comment, really?"

The chair scraped across the floor as he stood. Glenda flinched. "Jason, we're close to bad cop time."

"Looking forward to it."

He held a hand out to Glenda. "Pen and paper, love."

The paper rattled as she passed the notebook and pen across. Kyle dumped them in front of Woodsy.

"Draw a map, Terry. Nearby towns and landmarks. Diagram of your compound or whatever you live in."

Woodsy didn't budge.

The three SERPs were completely focused on Kyle and Woodsy. Muscles buzzing, Elliot inched around in Da Silva's direction. He got a half-metre closer without being noticed.

Maybe an opportunity would come.

Maybe he could make his own.

Maybe he and Woodsy were dead already.

Kyle's tone had turned grim. "We tried the easy way. Jimmy was the easy way. But he's a retard. He genuinely doesn't know where he lives, or the way back. You two do."

Voice a whisper, Woodsy asked, "What did you do to him?"

Kyle continued without breaking rhythm. "I know it's called Settlers Downs. And it's near the coast. Might be east, might be north. Once again, Jimmy wasn't real clear on that. I can't find a place with that name on any maps and there's no internet anymore. So you're my next option. Not him." The knife winked at Elliot just as he was about to take another surreptitious step sideways. "Coz Elliot's a pro. A real life hard-ass. But you're a weak-willed, selfish, sad-sack of crap. So be your true self, Woodsy; be that sack of crap. Get it over with and draw us the map."

There followed another pause, a little longer than ten seconds this time. Then very quietly, Kyle said, "Glenda, you can leave now."

She did. Fast. Knocking over her chair in her haste.

Elliot risked another little step in the ruckus of her leaving—and Da Silva caught it. He lifted an index finger and wagged it at Elliot then pointed back to the spot where Elliot had been a minute earlier. Returning to that space, Elliot's mind reeled. There had to be something he could do. There had to be an angle.

Another cop was out in the hallway, as Elliot had suspected. The square-jawed, marble-eyed thug leaned in once Glenda's footsteps had vanished along the corridor. Instead of the MCX rifle Elliot expected, he carried a shallow plastic box, his sidearm holstered like Kyle's.

Kyle had lost most of his sense of theater now. But he did say, "Bad cop time, Jase. And I feel like playing it."

"No worries."

Without taking his eyes from Elliot, Kyle beckoned the thug—nameplate MILLER—from the doorway. Miller dumped the tray on the table, got behind Woodsy who twisted in his seat to keep him in view. The little tray contained cotton gauze and something that looked like a big epipen. Da Silva's focus shifted to Woodsy and he started to move his way.

173

And Elliot acted, lunging for the chair he'd kicked aside earlier. He had it in his hands, turning and almost ready to release it across the table at Da Silva and Kyle when Erikson's taser hit him.

Pain!

Muscles frozen, he hit the floor hard on thigh and shoulder, the chair slamming harmlessly into a table leg.

The electrical charge felt like it lasted an eternity and then he was free of it, stiff as a board on the linoleum, groaning through clenched teeth.

"Don't do that again," someone said from far away. Or maybe that's what they said. The voice sounded delayed. His muscles everywhere burned as if they'd been on a twenty-mile run with a full pack. Elliot tried to get up again, got into a seated position and had to stop there. Wires trailed between his gut and the yellow unit in Erikson's hand. The taser's barbed darts were still hooked in his skin.

"Happy to do it again if you like," she deadpanned.

"Stay on the floor, mate," said Da Silva.

Elliot wanted to reply; he had the requisite curses in mind. But the words wouldn't travel as far as his lips.

He must have blanked for a second or two, because people had shifted places. Da Silva and Miller were now pinning a squirming Woodsy to his chair. Da Silva wrapped the crook of one elbow around Woodsy's throat and used his other hand to pull his prisoner's right arm down and back, locking it against him. Miller wrestled Woodsy's free arm onto the table and anchored it there, his weight on it.

"Now that little *fracas* is over," Kyle said, "let's get back to business." He stuck his left hand in Woodsy's face, angling it for a good view of the scar tissue that replaced two fingers. "See this? A toxie bit the tips of these fingers. Just a nip. Just enough to turn me if I let it. We'd found out from experience that if you get bitten, you can prevent the spread of the toxin by amputating the extremity. Which is tough luck if they bite your arse … ha, or your neck. So, what I did was I killed the bitch who bit me and then I cut off my own fingers. To save my life. Seems to have worked."

"Seems a logical conclusion," Da Silva agreed.

"Having experienced it, I know the pain is survivable. Even for you." Kyle grabbed Woodsy's flailing left hand in his own, flattening and stretching it. "Last chance, Terry. Where's your settlement?"

"Okay, look!" Woodsy was sweating so hard his hair was soaked. Droplets ran down his face. "Listen. There's an island. Full of people. I can direct you."

Idiot, Elliot thought. *They'll pass near The Downs to get to Barnabas.*

Kyle scoffed. "We're already on an island."

"No, a smaller one, I mean. Fifty people over there. More, probably. Plenty for you."

Kyle made a *nice-try* face. "But they're not *your* people. And you won't have good information on them."

"I do. I swear."

"Terry. We're not exactly an amphibious bunch here. Let's try it again. Your place?"

Woodsy blinked sweat from his eyes. "Not the island then. There's other groups. We'll help you defeat them and then—"

"Don't need your help. Just the information about your group."

"Okay, *okay*. You let me and … and the boy go. We'll bring you back six people. Healthy people."

Yellow bastard.

"Hah! That's more like the Terry we know and love. Terry the dealmaker. Terry the bloody politician. The weasel never changes its spots does it? Selfish to the end. You'd probably keep that deal, knowing you. Problem is, I now suspect there's a *lot* more than six people back home. So, for the final time, answer my damn question or I'm performing surgery on your hand with Elliot's knife."

"But … listen … we can …"

Kyle said, "Enough."

"*Wait!*"

Miller shifted to get a better hold on his prisoner, his shoulder and vest obscuring Woodsy's face. All Elliot saw now of Woodsy was the bucking of his shoulders. The thrashing of his legs beneath the table. Elliot didn't see the lockblade's work but the crunch was godawful—the sound followed immediately by Woodsy's bellow and then the other men yelling at him to shut up.

Elliot didn't realize he'd lifted his butt off the floor until Erikson raised the taser meaningfully. He'd never pull the barbed darts out quickly enough: plenty of opportunity for her to press that trigger and hold it there.

He sank back as Kyle shouted his question again and received no answer beyond Woodsy's subdued moans. The chair had shifted in the struggle, giving

Elliot a new view of Woodsy's ashen face, his twitching cheek, the dribble of blood from his lip where he'd bitten it. Their eyes met for a moment before Woodsy's slid back to watch Kyle rummaging in the tray.

Leaving the knife there, Kyle's right hand came out holding gauze. "Can't have you bleeding to death. Hold still while I soak … that's it … now …" He took something else from the tray with his left hand.

Elliot heard a soft electrical crackle and sizzle, quickly drowned out by fresh yowling from Woodsy.

"Hold still, you big baby, I haven't got it all! There we go …"

He held the implement up for Elliot see before flicking it into the tray. What had looked like an injector was an electrical cauterizer. The sulfur-and-copper stink of burnt skin and blood vessels hit Elliot's nasal passages like smelling salts, sobering him instantly, slapping away the grogginess he'd suffered since the tasing.

"Stop this, you bastards," he growled, but no one responded.

"Once more, Terry," Kyle said. "*Terry*! Focus here. The location of your settlement or the next joint comes off." Woodsy spat in his face and Kyle's cheeks flushed with anger. "I wasn't enjoying this. But now—"

The knife crunched through bone.

Terry shouted all the things he wanted to do to Kyle, acts that Elliot would have loved to assist with.

But neither one of them was going to get that chance.

Elliot had heard enough stories of CIA assholes putting hapless Muslims through this same thing.

And none of those poor people—innocent or guilty—ever found their way out of it.

But they weren't Ranger-trained and bred. I should be able to do something.

The process of maiming-pressure-cauterization cycled twice more.

Elliot felt impotence. He felt shame.

Do something!

But he couldn't. He wanted to twist that handgun from Erikson's grip and shoot all of them. Or at least put one in Woodsy to stop him giving away Settlers Downs. And, yes, to spare the poor bastard more trauma. But Elliot's muscles shook with the aftereffects of electrocution. It would take longer to recover than the time they had. And Erikson—with her finger on her taser's trigger—was too alert.

Kyle shouted. The crack of a slap filled the room. Elliot's head jerked up in time to see Woodsy's do the same. He'd passed out, but Kyle wasn't letting him get away with that. The SERP leader held up the bloody knife—blood was all over the table now, and over Kyle's hands—and shouted, "You seriously want more of this? You stupid, *stupid* prick!" He threw the knife out the door to bang against the corridor wall, then sighed, rolling his shoulders, looking at Miller. "Get the kit. Fix his hand properly."

His men let go of Woodsy. Their victim slid off his chair and into the fetal position beneath the table, sobbing.

Miller stomped from the room while Da Silva indicated Elliot. "Him next?"

Kyle dabbed at his hands with spare gauze. "If Woodsy won't talk, there's no way he will."

"Want the kid then?"

"Yeah, go get him."

Before the bandages went on, Elliot saw that three of Woodsy's fingers had lost their first joint. Miller treated Woodsy's wounds with antiseptic and bandaged them. Neither Erikson nor Elliot had moved from their spots. Like a well-trained guard dog, Erikson hadn't once taken her eyes off him. But she did direct him to take the taser darts out of his flesh. He slid them out as careful as possible, but still their barbed ends tore a little skin. As Erikson tossed the weapon out the door for later maintenance, Elliot bunched his t-shirt over the wounds and pressed them there to stop the bleeding. He winced: there was a little blistering around the twin holes.

Erikson winked at him and showed him the Smith & Wesson.

The reprieve from further tasing did not mean mercy; it meant they were saving him for some other fate.

Woodsy had dragged himself out from beneath the table to let Miller treat his hand, but hadn't made it any further: he sagged by his chair, clothes stained by his own blood and by sweat, face white. To his credit, he hadn't soiled himself.

By the time Da Silva guided Jimmy into the room, Kyle had washed his hands and helped Miller clear the torture and the first aid kits out of the room. Then they'd returned to stand either side of the door.

Jimmy didn't look much better than Woodsy. His left cheek was cut. Also his lip. His t-shirt had red stains from the facial wounds and was torn at one shoulder. He'd been crying.

At the sight of his young friend's condition, Woodsy whispered, "I'll kill you all" and Elliot snarled wordlessly.

Kyle didn't so much as glance their way. He said, "Hold him."

Da Silva went to grab the kid by the shoulders. But Jimmy dropped, slipping through Da Silva's gloved fingers to curl in a ball at his feet. Da Silva laughed in surprise. Jimmy's arms were over his head. Whether this was habit born of his earlier treatment by SERPs or by Death Druids, Elliot didn't know. He *did* know he wanted to badly harm whoever had caused the kid to react like this.

Da Silva clamped a boot onto Jimmy's ribs, holding him in place. He gestured for his boss to continue.

Kyle said, "Pay attention, Terry. Listen very carefully. You're going to tell me where your camp is."

"Maggots," Woodsy whispered.

"All right then. Don't say I didn't try to be nice. Jason, the boy's useless to us. Take him outside and shoot him in the head."

Jimmy whimpered.

"What!" Woodsy gasped. He struggled to stand, but slipped. His chair skidded away.

This time, Kyle did look to Elliot. "You two want to save this boy's life, you know what to do." When there was no response, he waved a hand. "Jason."

Da Silva had a thrashing Jimmy to the doorway before Woodsy coughed, "Wait!"

Da Silva did.

The look of hope on Jimmy's face soured when Elliot said what he had to. "Woodsy, you can't."

"I have to."

"You don't. It's three of us. Only three of us."

"I'll tell you," Woodsy said to Kyle.

"Be strong, man!" Elliot shouted.

But the fight had left Terence Woods. "I'll tell you," he repeated softly.

"How about that?" Kyle asked his team. "Success at last."

Da Silva chuckled. "You'll really *really* tell us, Mr. Woods? Truly ruly?"

"Yes."

"You'll show us on a map?" said Kyle.

"Yes."

"You won't lie and try to stall for time."

"No."

"You'll give us accurate numbers?"

"… Okay."

Da Silva dumped Jimmy in the chair that Kyle had occupied earlier. Slapped the back of his head.

Jimmy slumped forward with his arms over his head again.

Then Da Silva and Miller half-carried and half-dragged Woodsy from the room.

Kyle went into the hall, held the door for Erikson, leaned in again. "Don't be mad at Woodsy, Elliot. He's not our kind of man. Someone will be back for you later. There's water in the tap. Drink it. Lots of it." He started pulling the door shut. "You'll need it."

14

Erikson was right outside, or maybe the regular chuffs of fabric on the other side of the wall were coming from the brutish Miller. The SERPs weren't taking chances with an unlocked door.

The tiny dark eye of the camera warned him off action. Even if he could use a chair or drawer or some part of them, the hostiles would be ready. He slumped against a wall and tried to think. Nothing came to him. Unless one of these assholes made a mistake, there were no plays to make.

It took some time for Jimmy to move. In a single moment, he went from catatonic to manic, jumping to his feet, pacing a while, before drinking from the tap as Kyle had suggested. Wiping his mouth, he said, "You wanted them to kill me."

Maybe if he got his bootlaces off under the table where the camera couldn't see, tied them together. Miller had a collar on his armor, but Elliot might get a garrote over the top. He realized belatedly that Jimmy had said something. "What?"

"You wanted them to kill me."

"No way, Cochise."

"You did."

"I didn't want the rest of our people getting in the same trouble as us."

Jimmy huffed and dropped back onto his chair. For a half minute, he whispered to himself and then he asked, "What's happening to Woodsy?"

How the hell did Elliot know? "They might kill him. After he gives them the info." Jimmy put his hands in his oily hair, his elbows on the table. Elliot continued, "Or they might take him with them when he shows them where we live. They can use him as bait to get our people to drop their guard."

Or maybe—just maybe—Woodsy would lie and buy them all some time.

For all the good that would do in the end. How in Christ was he going to get out of this room, this building?

They'd taken his dive watch; he felt an hour creep past as Jimmy muttered and smoothed his hair and worried at the splint on his fingers, and Elliot fought the urge to turn over tables and chairs.

What was Angie thinking now, doing now? They'd been inside the walls for over twelve hours. Would she have left? Would she wait?

"What will they do to us?"

It took a moment to recognize the question wasn't rhetorical. Elliot said, "You and I are fit and strong. They'll make us work for them."

If we're lucky.

It was the most likely reason Kyle had left Elliot his fingers and toes, elbows and knees.

Another hour slid by. And then footsteps, voices. The door swung out and two stubby SIG MCX barrels poked in at them.

"Stay where you are," Miller rumbled unnecessarily. He and Erikson flanked the door and Da Silva entered, tossing two sets of handcuffs onto a kitchen counter.

"Sorry to keep you. Put these on."

"Where's Kyle?" Elliot asked, unmoving.

"On his way to your place." His brows rose in triumph. "Put the cuffs on."

Jimmy slid from his chair and complied. But Elliot said, "Why?"

"Why? So you don't try anything and get yourself killed. We need you."

Yeah. Need you to not leak your brains on our floor when we shoot you.

"Told you," Elliot said to Jimmy and joined him at the counter.

The trio of cops marched them up the stairwell to ground level and out the main entrance. All the interior security stations had been wide open, unattended and the front doors whirred shut and locked electronically behind them. In the fresh air, another two cops waited in the parking lot beside a white panel van with police lights and markings.

"Never seen a divvy van?" Miller explained, "You ride in the back."

The night sky was clear, the air cold. Jimmy had started shivering the moment they stepped outside. Elliot was shivering by the time they reached the "divvy" van. They'd both already stripped down to t-shirts when captured. No one had offered them anything warmer from their packs.

Those packs were long gone, along with their weapons.

Both squeezed inside the back of the vehicle which was as white inside as out, with two hard plastic benches along the sides. No handholds. No windows besides one fore and one aft, shuttered from the outside. The interior light was on, allowing Elliot a clear view of Jimmy's terrified face as the door locked behind them.

"It's okay, kid. Follow my lead. We'll get through this."

Jimmy showed no sign of understanding this.

They traveled reasonably slow for fifteen minutes. Elliot had expected a rough ride, but it was smooth: he doubted the car had exceeded fifteen miles an hour at any time. When they stopped, another vehicle's door slammed outside before the divvy van's occupants got out to join whoever else was out there. Several minutes' conversation followed. Elliot smelled cigarettes. Another car's brakes squealed nearby. More doors slammed. More voices joined the group.

There came a clatter at their door and it swung out. Streetlights glowed around an asphalt lot. A white building showed past the line of six cops armed with cattle prods, tasers or MCXs. Elliot exited first, and turned a full circle, taking in the sights before a powered-down cattle prod jabbed him in the back.

"That way," said Erikson.

They were in the parking lot of the small regional hospital Elliot had seen on the map. This was Pankhurst, then. Across and down the street were homes, what looked like a library, a small school, six stores, a park. Every third streetlight worked. There were cars in the lot: sedans, SUVs, utes, station wagons. And an armored truck, a variation on the old BearCat. Another BearCat was out in the street. The trucks looked extra bulky around the wheels—tire protection? Sure: the SERPS had frankensteined both vehicles: plates welded over tires with a few inches clearance above the asphalt, more plates attached to the fronts to form cow-catchers. Had Kyle taken one of these behemoths to Settlers Downs? Had he taken two? How many could tiny Tasmania have had?

"Keep up!" Miller barked and Jimmy staggered, catching up to Elliot's shoulder. The six cops fanned out, sheep-dogging them toward the end of the hospital building.

"Not going inside?" Elliot asked. "No checkups? Shots?"

A cop said, "I wouldn't say 'shot' if I was you." Others cackled.

Elliot faked a laugh of his own. "Good one. But seriously, if you want Jimmy to work well, you'll need to set that finger. Da Silva said you had a surgeon and nurses."

"Shut up, dickhead."

"Kid's got one good hand," drawled Miller. "All he needs."

Some more cackling.

They'd reached the end of the building. Herded, Elliot turned the corner, expecting some kind of corral where they kept their workers—and heard the sound coming from the far side of the building, around that next corner. Crowd burble. Not a large crowd—thirty or forty. And though the paths were unlit down this edge of the property, light bloomed from around that corner.

Erikson pointed. Elliot tried to control his breathing and continued on. But the low thrum of anxiety that had buzzed in his chest since they'd been caught now flared into something wilder.

They came around the corner into an outdoor lunch and recreation area. Well-lit by portable floods. Small squares of overgrown lawn. Picnic tables and bench seats, all pushed back now, because someone had dragged in bleachers. Two sets of them, six rows high and wide enough for ten people per row. They were about one third full. Most of the people up there wore police utility belts. A few were civvies, warmly dressed but without visible weapons. One of those was Glenda; no sign of a daughter. She didn't look at him. On the left front row shivered six skinny workers—

Peasants, he heard in Kyle's voice.

He and Jimmy received a drunken cheer from a few of the cops seated—Elliot now noted bottles passing around. Erikson and Miller poked them in the back to get them moving again. Jimmy started muttering nonsense, fretful, picking up on the mood if not the intention.

And what was that intention?

Either we're watching the entertainment, or we're it. The presence of a stage attested to that.

He thought of it as a stage because there was an audience. But really, from this angle, from the side of it, it was a box. Constructed from the same mishmash of wood and steel panels as some of the Jericho walls had been. Presumably the box would be open at the front, open to the spectators.

Elliot caught a whiff of rotting meat, of old blood. His heart rate was already elevated; the stink set it to racing.

Da Silva awaited them where the path rounded the front of the box. His thumbs tucked into his belt. Chest puffed out. Grinning. Elliot imagined smashing those teeth with a rifle-butt.

Da Silva jerked his head toward the box, the stage.

Elliot moved no closer to it. "Jimmy is a good worker," he said. "Obedient. Fit."

The big SERP dropped his shoulders, stepped over to speak quietly. "Mate, he probably is. And we could do with the both of you. But the truth is, the Boss doesn't trust you. And neither do I. He's a whacko, and you, you have an unpleasant look in your eye. Constantly. Plus, from what Woodsy told us, we'll soon have another thirty-odd adults to replace you. So …" He stepped back and gestured to the box. "This."

"He's a kid," Elliot tried.

"Ya never know," Da Silva replied. "Give it a chance. This might turn out okay for him."

"Winners is grinners," Miller said.

Da Silva added: "And winners get dinners." It was obviously something they'd said before. Obviously something they'd done before. Which made what was happening systemic, routine. Evil.

Da Silva said, "Elliot and Jimmy, you trespassed on our land, broke into our facility. We don't have courts or prisons anymore. This is kind of it. So…" He took another step back, gestured again. "If you please."

Elliot took Jimmy's elbow and led him reluctantly around the front of the box. "I gotcha, Cochise," he told him. The kid's eyes were glued to the crowd of laughing, jeering cops. He made a little whimpering sound. But Elliot was only interested in the stage. Three solid walls ten feet high and smooth on the inside. The floor…

Shit shit shit.

The floor was a grate, thirty feet by thirty. The kind that might cover a sewer pit or drain. Which might have explained the smell—except for the rust-colored stains that weren't rust, and a couple of clumps of hair and skin. A patch where Elliot first trod was a little sticky. The space beneath the grating caught some of the floodlight beams, illuminating it to the floor about six feet down. It shimmered, slick with puddles from recent rains—or perhaps a hosing down—though the grate was dry. Its bars were three inches wide, just wide enough to get a foothold on, but they were going to make movement precarious. On the back wall of the box, two weapons lay across a shelf made of thick nails driven into one of the wooden panels. A yellow plastic t-ball bat—a kid's toy—and a foam-dart gun, a toy.

Holy Christ, these people are insane.

Prodded by real gun barrels, Elliot pulled Jimmy fully onto the grate, helped him pick his way to the middle and then stopped him. The bars were just wide enough to balance on if they were careful, the gaps between them wider, eight inches by eight.

"What's going on, Elliot?" Jimmy whispered.

Out on the path, Da Silva was raising his hands for the crowd to cool off.

"We're about to find out," Elliot replied, and only hoped it'd be deaders they'd be fighting and not each other. There was no way he was killing this boy. He'd choose suicide-by-cop before he chose that. "Stick near me and do as I say."

"I ... I dunno what to do."

"We've got this. You've got the juice to do this, kid. Just damn-well stick close."

As the crowd began to still, a lone voice, a female voice, coarse, hoarse, called out, "I'll have the taller one! What's left of him!" Half the crowd laughed. Not the civilians. Nor the poor workers on the front row.

"All right folks," Da Silva boomed. Obviously Kyle had provided thorough mentoring in the art of theatricals. "All right. My turn to talk. Ladies. Gentlemen. The rest of you. Welcome to Night Court."

Some cheers.

"Tonight's proceedings will be a little different. As you can see." He favored Elliot with a brief grin and wink before continuing. "Our regular surviving prosecutor is taking a night off with the Boss's permission. Lucky bugger. So we have two sets of defendants tonight. For the benefit of the two behind me, either of whom might survive this, I will elucidate."

Some *Ooo's* at the fancy word.

"Defendants One and Two there were caught breaking into Jericho and—even worse—breaking into the medicinal reserve."

A chorus of *naughty naughty* and *shame* from the crowd.

"We've interviewed them and find them to be complete and utter arseholes. And thus, their fate will be decided by the Night Court."

He shifted attention to the hapless people on the front row, who cowered under his gaze. Elliot noticed now a cop was seated either side of these six, each with an electrified cattle prod, powered on ... and that there were more trash-weapons on the concrete path in front of them: a garbage can lid; a child-sized plastic garden chair; half a broom, its handle snapped; a vacuum cleaner pipe and head. His stomach churned, bile in his spit.

Da Silva called, "Defendants Three, Four, Five and Six! Please stand!"

Four of the workers got to unsteady feet, one of them kicked off his chair by the audience member behind him. Two men, two women. The women clutched each other's hands, pressed together at the shoulder. A man and woman remained on the bench, wringing their hands.

"You four are accused of stealing food from the warehouses and of planning an escape. Ironic. One set of defendants wanting in. One wanting out." A ripple of obliging laughter among the crowd. "Well, we can't have either. Hence tonight's proceedings.

"You two—" He pointed at the pair on the bench. "—are our court reporters and will report what you see back to the other workers. Then everyone will stay up to date on what happens when you break the law.

"And you four—" he indicated the others "—need to get your arses onto the arena. Now."

Trembling, the four citizens selected weapons from the path. Elliot moved a couple of grid squares toward the back wall, then paused when Jimmy didn't follow him.

"Kid," he barked. "On me."

Jimmy took one backward step without taking his eyes off the people joining them on the grid—for a heart-lurching moment, Elliot thought the kid would slip and make himself an easy target. But his footing was as sure as a mountain goat's. Elliot glanced toward the toy gun and bat, more interested in the nails they lay on. Jimmy could have the bat. The other defendants were picking their footing onto the edge of the grid, taking their time. If he could worry at a nail, get it out ...

Unnecessarily now—for the idea was clear—Da Silva called, "Last one standing becomes our new 'prosecutor'. They get a good meal, a shower and a comfy bed. So let's see some spirit, defendants."

"Last one ...?" Jimmy looked to Elliot.

"Nothing to fear from me, Cochise," Elliot told him. Forgetting about the mock-weapons behind him and the nails holding them, he chose a more useful option. He unbuckled his belt and pulled it out through the loops. He let his empty SIG holster and bayonet-sheath drop, heard them splash in a shallow puddle six feet below his boots, the sound a bleak reminder of what he'd lost. Winding a part of the belt around his fingers, he left the buckle to dangle loose with a good twelve inches of leather free to swing. He told Jimmy, "We're in this together. Let's find a way to the path. We can hurt a couple of these cops before they take us down."

Jimmy swallowed and faced front.

To even get close to those bleachers of cops, they had to get through four innocent citizens who were carefully finding their footing on the steel gridwork. Innocent or not, like Elliot, they would be more inclined to hurt strangers before hurting friends. They had no reason to pity him. Or the kid.

Da Silva moved to the seat between the remaining workers on the front row, called out again. "Any of you leave without my say-so—any of you—and it's this." He held up a pistol.

Sonofabitch. So much for that idea.

"Jury!" called a spectator and another mimicked her.

"What's that?" Da Silva put hand to ear in panto-mime.

"Jury!" called some others.

"Oh, yes, how could I forget?" He called louder and into the pit, "Release the jury!"

Locks clanked in the hollow space beneath Elliot's feet; steel doors scraped open. A strong waft of rot carried his way. Lit by the spotlights above, ten or more undead people staggered into the pit.

And they looked a helluva lot fresher than the ones that killed his dog.

15

"Go get the bat, Jimmy! You remember what I told you at the Blueberry Barn about working with a stick?"

Jimmy wasn't listening, fixated on the movement below him, he dodged aside and landed safely two bars over while a blackened hand stretched up through the floor where he'd just been.

The two male workers took a few careful steps forward. The one to Elliot's right held the trash can lid, the other the vacuum pipe. The women just stood together on the first row of squares, cowering, clutching at each other with the hands not holding weapons. On a better day, Elliot might reason with them, talk them into rushing the cops with him and getting at least one of them. But this was not a better day. This was a FUBAR day. One of the worst in an endless stream of them.

"Jimmy! Listen to me! You remember what I taught you about fighting with a stick?"

Jimmy's head snapped up and around, then back toward the two men. The floor sprouted dirty hands and forearms now, the deaders reaching, clawing, clutching before withdrawing to try again elsewhere as they tracked the moveable feast above them. The man with the pipe was forced to jump aside, mimicking Jimmy. His landing was not as graceful and he had to bob down to regain balance.

"Get the goddamn *bat*," Elliot snapped and added, "Elbows, head, hands", hoping the oncoming men wouldn't register it above the roar of the crowd and the snarling of the infected. He whipped the belt buckle at a set of fingers that grazed his boot, but the blow didn't strike hard enough to break anything. He moved two squares over. "Jimmy!"

The man with the trash can lid shifted back and forth between two squares, sidestepping a persistent zombie below him. His frantic dance drew raucous comments from members of the crowd. And Elliot was doing the same damn thing, skipping left to avoid the one hunting him, marking time—*wasting* time. His blood pounded in his ears. He was about to call to Jimmy again when a gunshot rang out.

Da Silva had fired into the air. Now he shouted at the women stalled in their starting position. "Move forward or the next round is in your heads!"

"Jesus," Elliot breathed as the women lost their footing. One of them had tried to obey Da Silva. The other had stayed frozen. The result was the first falling and pulling her friend with her. They sprawled awkwardly across the floor, gasping, limbs disappearing through the gaps, faces contorting with pain, with terror.

Jimmy came alive then, shouting, "No!" All danger forgotten, the kid bounced across grid squares like they were stepping stones.

Elliot's shout to stop him was lost in the screams from one of the women. Pinned beneath her friend, her lip ran with blood from banging it on metal. Both her arms were down through the grating. When her friend began to roll off her, she stayed there, anchored from below, now jerking and shuddering and squealing as the deaders tore at her.

As Jimmy reached them, the other woman started up her own wailing. A leg was through the grate. She yanked it up and got to crawling back to the path, bleeding from the calf and ankle. Abrasions? Or bites?

Jimmy tried to pull the first woman up, but lost his grip and had to do a little dance of his own to stop from toppling. She kept screaming, even as she tore free, rolling over onto her back. Her arms ran red. Flesh hung ragged above her wrists like torn sleeves

The second woman made it to the path and Da Silva was up and striding toward her. Would he shoot her? Shove her back onto the grid when she came off it?

A flash of light drew Elliot's attention away. The guy with the vacuum pipe was headed for him, light glinting off the metal. Elliot tightened his grip on his belt. Blinking, sweating, the man advanced in small steps; his length of steel was probably the deadliest weapon in the game.

"Same side, man," Elliot said to him, but pointlessly. The man snarled and pressed forward. A moment later, Elliot pulled away as the pipe's end sliced the air three inches from his nose. He stepped forward to whip the belt across the man's head, catching his ear, sending him crashing to the grate. The pipe fell through, the man landing over the gap. On the balls of his feet, Elliot considered hitting the man again. He was reticent to finish him. But this was The Battle for The Downs all over again. This was the goddamned Middle East.

Take him out and get to Jimmy.

The guy had a hand out near Elliot, scrambling for purchase. Elliot stomped it, breaking fingers. The man pulled it to his chest, but didn't make a sound. Braced on three limbs, he glared death at Elliot. Elliot raised the belt—

A blur of grey-metal and a loud clunk. The trash can lid did the job before him. The man with the broken fingers slumped, stunned as his former friend side-stepped him, changing his grip on the lid as he shifted attention to Elliot. Elliot moved a couple of squares sideways, watching hands reach up and clasp the fallen man's clothing.

Jimmy screamed.

The young man had fallen across the heavily bleeding woman's legs, trying to help her again. His own left leg and arm had dipped into the space below the steel struts. Hands snatched at his clothing. Jimmy wrenched the arm back up, swearing. His sleeve was ripped, the wrist oozing red. He scrambled on hands and knees toward the front, kicking and slapping at pusbag hands, reaching the path in moments and rolling onto it near where the first woman had come to rest. Rather than shooting them, Da Silva leaned over both of them, squinted, then gestured. Four cops came to wrench the injured people upright.

Elliot stepped away from his opponent as he advanced, watching the activity off the stage with teeth grinding. He fully expected Jimmy and the woman to get tossed back onto the grid, into the waiting arms of the undead; the mere act of falling onto that uneven steel could break bones. Instead, the four cops got a hold of their arms and armpits and dragged them down the path away from the arena.

What!

He got it then. They'd been bitten. The SERPs would let them turn, put them in their "jury".

"Wait!" he yelled. But nobody heard him.

The guy with the metal lid came in close. Elliot feinted at his head, reversed the swing of his belt as he put the lid up to shield himself, sliced at the guy's knee. The man cried out, faltered, wobbled as he lost balance, leaving his left side exposed. Elliot slammed his belt buckle across the guy's ear, flinging him onto hands and knees, the lid flying free as the pipe had for his former comrade.

Elliot vaulted closer to the dying woman still down on the grid near the path. She shuddered in shock as the undead pulled at her, trying to get her limbs back down within reach of their snapping jaws.

Jimmy was being dragged the opposite direction, face swiveling between the men carrying him.

"Take off his arm!" Elliot hollered at them. The two men hauling the teenager along slowed, blinking at him. Then they laughed and carried on hauling. "Above the bite! Cut it off! You got surgeons! He can still make it!"

"Shut up!" shouted a crowd member, a civilian.

Elliot's opponent had made it to his feet again, one arm cradled to his chest. The lid was firmly in the other hand. His breathing was ragged, his eyes wild. He knew the game, he knew the rules. Even damaged, he was committed. He moved between Elliot and Jimmy, got closer.

Already balanced right for it, Elliot delivered a straight kick to the guy's right knee, pulling back into a controlled stance as the leg crumpled. The guy cried out again, sprawling face down. A couple of shadows shifted below, coming for the man. Ideas flew through Elliot's mind, impulses, ways of killing this guy quickly to end his suffering—he saw the belt around the man's neck, pulling up, back and around …

But Jimmy.

Elliot's gaze locked with Da Silva's. He was about to demand they take off the kid's arm again—but the message behind the faux sympathy in Da Silva's face was plain. There'd be no surgery for Jimmy.

"Sonofa*bitch*!" Elliot roared and hopscotched across the rows of square to the path, tinnitus building, squealing, his vision going white around the edges, rage burning in his gut and pressing against the insides of his temples—and then he was off the gridwork, his feet on concrete, vaguely aware of cheers and applause. He was raising his belt, gunning for Da Silva, legs pumping—

A moment's disorientation. The crowd and spotlights swung around. His back was to the concrete. And he was spasming, convulsing. Confusion. Then the pain: a thousand burning needles. The second taser of the night hurt just as bad as the first had.

Somehow, he got enough control of his head to turn it, to turn it the way they'd taken the woman. And Jimmy. The kid was down, too, dragging along the ground, each foot in the hands of a black-clad cop. He thrashed, might've been yelling—Elliot couldn't hear anything beyond the roaring of his own agony. But the young man's face was turned his way, his mouth open, his bitten hand stretching toward Elliot. The same way the boy in the Al-Kasrah market had held out his hand toward parents who could never come for him, would never save him.

White mist and white noise closed around Elliot. As abruptly as the pain had come, it departed. Everything "Now" was gone and there was nothing but white static, dust and cordite, the ringing of tinnitus.

And the guilt.

Always the guilt.

16

The concrete path was cold, hard, rough. It should have hurt his back, his head.

Elliot was beyond hurt.

The time he lay there—watched over by a sneering Erikson—was indeterminate. Everything moved at breakneck speed around him. As if in time-lapse, the crowd ebbed and shifted and flowed, some leaving, many more milling while finishing drinks and talking over micro-events from the "trial".

"Did you see that...?"

"How funny was it when ...?"

"Man, I'd hate to be ..."

"Next time, we totally should ..."

A chinking sound was Erikson kicking Elliot's belt away out of reach. Perhaps some fragmented part of his mind had commanded one of his hands to reach for it. He didn't know.

Then in the cloud of noise, he heard Miller discussing with a woman how long it'd take "the kid and the chick" to turn.

"I'll put a bottle of Captain Morgan's on one hour."

"From now? Bottle of scotch says closer to two."

"Where'd you take them?" Elliot's own voice sounded flat and metallic in his ears, like he was playing the game he and Tommy Harrison had played as kids, putting a can to their bottom lips, attempting robot voices and then army radio ones. "Where's Jimmy?"

Only Erikson caught it. She said, "Waitin' to join the jury." She reached out and slapped someone's arm. "How long I gotta stand here? Been a long day, mate."

The man turned, separated from the mob. Da Silva. "Can ya walk?" he asked Elliot. "Are ya right?"

Elliot closed his eyes to shut him out. The longer he lay here, the longer he rested, the more "right" he became. The more *ready* he became. Despite the cold night air and the hard concrete. Despite the second tasing.

"He's faking it," Erikson said. A boot kicked his glute. Not hard. Exploratory. But it should have hurt. He barely felt it. She said, "Get up."

Da Silva made a musing sound. "Two tasings. I think he cracked his head on the ground, too."

He hadn't, not that he could feel anyway. Elliot didn't feel concussed, he didn't feel injured. He just felt ready to kill bad people.

"I'm not standing here all night," Erikson complained.

"All right, ya big sook. Go get your baby sleep. I'll take care of it."

A scrunch of her boots turning on the pavement, retreating.

Da Silva called two names that Elliot forgot the moment he heard them. More scrunching and scuffing on the path nearby. "Put him away for the night."

"Rooster's not gonna like company," one said. The woman who'd been betting with Miller. "Gonna be interesting having two prosecutors for a while."

"True. Rooster's even less sociable than this prick is. So put him in the ice room."

Elliot kept the frown from his face, hearing that. A night in a freezer was not acceptable. Then the penny dropped: *ice* was what Aussies called crystal meth. There was a hospital right there, right behind the stage where these mouth-breathing toilet stains had just murdered five people. The ice room would be where they kept meth addicts in full freak-out in the old days.

"And his dinner?" Another voice Elliot didn't recognize, male this time.

"Make it breakfast." Da Silva's voice was already receding into the background buzz of other conversations, the clink of bottles and glasses. "Glenda can make it."

"Up ya get, buddy," said the male voice. Another prodding boot.

Elliot opened his eyes slow, blinking, then rolled onto hands and knees, got himself up on his feet in stages. He hoped he appeared less steady than he felt. Because he certainly felt steady—detached, but steady. On autopilot, he moved with them—a man and woman whose nametags he wasn't the slightest bit interested in. Elliot was an observer, watching on as two SERPs marched a former Army Ranger and PMC into the hospital proper. Moving. Across moist lawn. Through powered sliding doors. Along squeaky hospital floors, under low emergency lighting. Following signs toward the emergency department on the far end.

A slide show of death played in the peripheral vision of his mind's eye. His treacherous memory spewed up sights and sounds and stinks of violence— some from minutes ago, some from years ago—mixing it up, keeping him guessing about what and who would pop up next. Despite it, Elliot did not lose himself. His cold, dark rage kept the past at bay, kept it *over there* on his internal screen, rather than letting that past swallow him yet again.

His rage did another thing: it drew strength and focus from his past. From his ... his *trauma*, as the army psych had called it. Elliot the observer was in control. Elliot, the operator. Aware of hospital smells and the sounds of his captors' boots on linoleum. Noting each component of the two cops' relaxed and incompetent behavior ...

They bracketed him, the female behind, the male in front. Confident in their armor, their weapons, their location. And careless with fatigue, weary from another long day of psychopathy.

The woman whistled quietly, some pop tune from when the world had had the luxury of happiness. Her rifle was in front of her. But he'd seen the safety was on. And her dominant hand kept going to her hair, brushing it from her eyes. Or rubbing her neck. Her combat knife was sheathed on her chest plate, not on her belt. Her sidearm was clipped firmly in its holster.

The man had slung his MCX behind him like an idiot. A kid playing at soldier. An arrogant buffoon. The stumpy rifle lay against his lower back and ass, the strap loose across his left shoulder, under his right armpit. Elliot wasn't going to get enough control to take a shot with it. But he wouldn't need to. The idiot had a hand on his sidearm, but his holster was also clipped securely across the grip. He yawned frequently. And he'd bumped his shoulder against the doorframe when they'd entered the building; tired, ready for bed, sleep chemicals flooding his brain.

There were no sleep chemicals in Elliot's brain.

The woman was drifting a little behind now. One of her boots squeaked against the polished floor as she stumbled in her tiredness. She swore and laughed to herself. Elliot turned his head, side vision catching just how far she'd drifted back. He passed a fire extinguisher and counted the seconds between his passing and hers.

One one-thousand. Two one-thousand. Three one-thousand. Four one-thousand. Five one-thousand. Six one-thousand. Seven one-thousand.

That was plenty of time. That next corner would be the perfect opportunity.

They turned it and Elliot closed the distance between him and the leading cop.

He took firm hold of the rifle, snatching it back and twisting it hard and counter-clockwise. The strap yanked the guy's right arm up and pinned his hand tight against his neck. Elliot kept twisting, swinging the cop around to face the direction they'd come. The man's free hand went to the strap as he started choking. Elliot felt the trachea give under the pressure. One last twist. Then Elliot tugged the rifle hard. Speed, leverage with the strap, the rifle's weight, Elliot's weight—these conspired to snap the man's neck.

Five seconds' work. Done.

In the sixth second, Elliot was vaulting the falling corpse to meet the female cop as she rounded the corner, her eyebrows raised in query over the noise. Her eyebrows dropped. Her dominant hand went to her rifle as she saw him coming. Exactly what he wanted. He wrapped his arms around hers in a bear hug. His first headbutt broke her nose. The second headbutt ensured the shock set in good. As she crumpled, he let her go, one hand going to her rifle to keep it from swinging up. He followed her body down to the floor and kneeled on her hip, drew her knife. Her eyes had rolled up and she made little sounds like queries as blood poured from the shattered nose. A throat slash would paint him red, so with one hand pressing her head to the floor, he struck her twice in the temple with the knife's pommel. She went slack. He hit her a third time, then felt for a pulse. Weak for a few seconds. Then none. He waited a little longer to make sure. From where he knelt, Elliot paused, listening. No other sounds in the hospital at all. And yes, the woman was dead.

He straightened, considered the bodies a moment. The two of them were complicit, they were—

Murderers. Slavers.

No better than ISIS and all the other petty warlord psychopaths. No better than the Death Druids. No better than Jock.

Blood from her nose stippled his left hand. He wiped it on his pants before dragging the woman's MCX off her corpse. Listening again: the distant sound of a car engine, nothing close.

Her rifle went on the floor for the moment, her handgun into his waistband.

Pausing every ten seconds to listen, it took a full minute and a half to strip the items he wanted from them both: armor-vests, the male's MCX and belt with handgun, their ammo pockets and knife-sheaths. He put on the vest and the belt. Slung the woman's rifle over his back and tightened the strap hard against himself. Stuffed the spare magazines for both her weapons into pockets. Got her sidearm holster off her belt and added it onto his new belt, put her pistol in it.

It took him a while to realize he was standing there now. Just standing there. Swaying on the balls of his feet. Clenching and unclenching fists. Repeating his new inventory over and over like a mantra.

Two .40 cal handguns, four spare mags. Two assault rifles, six spare mags. Two flashbangs, one can pepper spray, one combat knife.

Get yourself a vehicle.

Two .40 cal handguns, four spare mags. Two assault rifles, six spare mags. Two flashbangs, one can pepper spray, one combat knife.

Get yourself a vehicle.

Except he wasn't getting any closer to a vehicle. He was standing there in a dimly lit corridor, swaying and grunting. The slide show from earlier was still playing to the side of his mind. He could hear some of it now—McGovern asking Radler to massage his feet on the way to Al-Kasrah, the gunshot that heralded Birdy's death. Smell some of it—smoke and dust and Woodsy's cauterized flesh.

What now?

There was blood on both his hands now from the woman's nose and head wounds, a little on his boot. It was still quiet. The hospital didn't even tick with temperature changes. No air con humming. Silent as a tomb.

What now?

He could leave this godforsaken world in a blaze of glory. He was better armed than he'd been in a very long time—and carrying more ammo, too. He could find that other "prosecutor", Rooster they'd called him. Join forces—if he could work out where they stored the guy. How many SERPs could they take out tonight? All of them? Half? What would be a better option now than that?

Looking for Jimmy.

"Jimmy." He reached for a wall to stop the floor from sliding out from under him. Bile rose in his throat.

Jimmy.

The moving image was burned into his mind of Jimmy being dragged by the legs away to a room somewhere to turn.

He could go get Jimmy. Only, Elliot couldn't know where they'd put him; he and the woman probably weren't in under that grid where they stored the rest of that "jury". Besides, Jimmy would be too far gone now—the only reason for finding him would be to put a bullet through his head. If only they'd taken the arm off at the elbow fast like Kyle had done with his own fingers, the infection might not have taken. The boy would have had a chance. But how long had it been now? Fifteen minutes? Twenty? Forty? No, the kid was gone.

Gone!

Elliot kicked the male SERP's body in the chest, hard. A rib broke.

"You killed him, you prick. You killed him and those people and—"

There were *other* people, people Elliot had to help. Another choice, another option.

Settlers Downs.

Lewis. Heng. Claire. Alyssa. Kim and Rit and Chariya and Faye and ...

Angie.

His heartbeat had been calm since his second tasing wore off, even as he took out his two captors. But now it spiked.

Angie.

If they got her.

If they put her on that stage ...

She was out there somewhere. Kyle had sensed it, too. Had she stayed close? Had she returned to the fallback? By now, she may have given up on him. On him and Woodsy and Jimmy. Maybe she was on her way back home, a mile or two ahead of Kyle and his new breed of slavers.

He stooped and felt at the man's thigh pockets and then the female's. She had a key; when he dug it out, it had a logo he recognized from a couple of missions around Libya, a logo from a military vehicles manufacturer. The find gave him the smallest burst of satisfaction. He could get out of here, and a BearCat armored truck would give him as much edge as a couple of SIG MCXs did. He stood, with the key in his pocket and one of those MCXs in his hand and the other bobbing against his back, started marching down the corridor.

Jimmy was lost—*leave no man behind*; what a joke!—and Elliot had to get home.

But there'd be no home, he realized, he *admitted*, without Angie.

He tucked himself into the nook between a tree and the hospital wall as he got his night sight. The only light left burning in the town was a solitary street lamp down by the school. The moon was up, the sky clear. He felt the chill out here now as his rage abated; it seeped through the arm-holes of the vest and the thin cotton of his tee.

All of the people had left the hospital grounds. But not all of the vehicles were gone from the lot. One sedan, three station wagons, a motorbike. And out on the road, one of the BearCats. Confident in his night sight now, he left cover and strode through the lot. No movement by the Bearcat, no lightning-bug flare of a cigarette, no one waiting for their buddies to lock the prisoner away and come back. This was the SERPs' turf, a kilometre or three inside their thick walls, and they had nothing to fear.

"Until now, assholes. Until now."

The big truck was unlocked. Probably the two ex-cops he'd just killed were meant to put it away for the night. It started on the first try, the rumble gratifying, vibrating into his thighs and back and stomach wall. He stood both MCXs in the racks provided between driver and passenger seats. The clock on the dash read *3:44 a.m.*: two hours until dawn. Whoever had driven this last had left the shifter in 4X4 Low. He switched it to 2WD. Plunged the clutch to the floor, shifted into first gear. Paused for a few seconds as the temptation returned from earlier, the impulse to find the place where SERPs lay their heads, maybe run the truck through the side of the building where their beds all touched the wall.

Instead, he called up the map in his head, scanning it until he found the markings for a school and hospital close together, recalled the roads around them until he got himself oriented. He gave the truck some gas, let out the clutch, and U-turned toward the west.

If he couldn't quickly find the road to the gate near where Angie had dropped them, he would twist that drive-setting back to 4X4. And he'd drive along the wall until he found a way out. Flood barriers, armed guards? No bother. Elliot had a frankensteined armored truck and rifles of his own.

And he had someone he needed to find.

PART FOUR

OUR ROLES IN LIFE

17

The Jericho-Pankhurst region was mainly open ground, farms and woods with few roads; Elliot's first turn out of Pankhurst put him on the direct road to the gate he wanted. He fully expected people to come running from one of the buildings, rounds to ping off the ballistic glass, a chase. Nothing. As he entered farmland outside of the hamlet, he checked his mirrors compulsively for headlights. No one came for him. Mile after mile of farm fences passed by on either side.

In a little under fifteen minutes, he was cranking on the handbrake after slipping the truck into neutral. Two weary gate sentries wearing no armor stood center road with a low oil-drum fire at their backs, blinking in his headlights. Thickly bearded and clad in beanies, duffel coats, sneakers and jeans, they didn't look like SERPs. One sported a hunting bow, the other cradled a small caliber rifle. Neither was expecting an attack from *within*: one had a smile forming, perhaps hoping for early relief from his post; the other scowled, no doubt expecting a message that meant more work for him.

Standing on the running board beside the driver's seat, weapon braced in the wedge between open door and chassis, Elliot delivered a message neither expected. And took six rounds to do it.

He collected the rifle, a .22. He checked the owner's pockets, but when the first thing he found was the key to the gate's padlocks, he resisted checking further for extra .22 rounds, more interested in getting that gate open and getting away from anyone he might have alerted.

More interested in finding Angie.

As dawn thought about breaking, Elliot eased the driver's door closed and slung one of the MCXs, locking the other rifles in the cab. The dirt side road he'd parked on was wet with the previous day's rains, forcing a careful pace through the gloom. There was no way he was using a flashlight when he didn't know who was around.

A rhythmic thumping sound off to his left. A small kangaroo in travel, no threat. Moments later, another following it. Crackling sticks to his right revealed an echidna, waddling around in its search for food. The only other sounds were the mocking laughter of distant kookaburras and closer, the upwards-inflected *whip-whip* call of a bird he didn't know.

He left the road, jumped a waist-high wire fence. Four hundred metres of thankfully sparse bushland later, the farrier's homestead came into sight as a blur of lighter color through the trees. The rising sun was hidden behind a panel of cloud, leaving the property corpse-pallid. He took cover by a towering gum at the wire fence separating property from forest. No lights in the house. It was fifty metres to the drying yard behind it, another thirty from the drying yard gate to the back door. If they had snipers …

He hopped this fence, followed it along the property line. The light and the hour were in his favor, making for potentially sleepy hostiles, and a dark backdrop behind his dark clothes. Closer to the drying yard fence, the paddock was broken up by a children's playhouse and a large free-standing water tank; he left the fence line to use them as cover.

The tactical part of him murmured, *They might have one man watching the rear but their attention would be on the road.*

The impatient part of him said, *This is pointless.* Woodsy might have told them about this place, but they wouldn't have anyone waiting for Elliot. Jericho wouldn't have roving radio-equipped scouts routinely patrolling the roads who'd been alerted to arrive here ahead of him.

They might give chase to their stolen truck. But they wouldn't be here ahead of him.

And yet.

And yet.

Haste was usually a mistake.

As he'd proven several times already this week.

And Angie? As unlikely as it was for SERPs to be here, it was equally unlikely she would be. There was no point raising his hopes. If Woodsy hadn't sold her out, if she hadn't been captured or killed while Elliot languished in that underground lunch room with Jimmy, she'd have left for home.

We're not back by sunset, you go.

That was the arrangement. That was the plan.

He paused at the water tank. Five metres to the low brick wall at the border of the drying yard. No sound but birds. Until a dog barked, and then another, somewhere out in the forest behind him. Wild probably. Feral. He hoped. The SERPs weren't tracking him. He hoped.

He shifted forwards, then froze as a brown blur stirred and vanished around the corner of the house. The afterimage resolved itself in his brain seconds after the thing was gone. A wallaby. The animal's presence a good sign no one was indoors. Or at least not making noise in there.

He made the gate, a squeaky-looking square of rust as high as his knee. He stepped over it.

Close now. Damn close.

The Rover was not back here where they'd parked it the first night. Angie was gone. She had to be.

And if they had her, he'd...

He'd what? Collapse and weep? Put a bullet through his skull?

The deep well of his rage had been opened by Kyle's brutality, by two close calls with the undead in a few days, by what had happened to Jimmy, by being forced to put down that man on the grid, by the imminent threat to Settlers Downs.

And if they'd hurt Angie, that would be the clincher, the straw for the camel's back. If she was gone, not headed home, but really *gone*, another hole would open. It was threatening to already, a sinkhole off to the edges of his psyche and between him and what was left in his cold reservoir of rage, a gulf labeled *why bother anymore?*

No. He had to snap out of that shit.

Don't think; act.

And act, he did. Step by quiet step, closing on that back door. Fast and silent across the yard, ducking beneath drooping clothes line, almost slipping on a peg, then a weed, barrel sweeping windows upstairs and down. If they hadn't shot at him yet, they weren't going to: no way were these guys giving him another reprieve like they had by putting him in the "court". Not after he'd taken out four of them. Next time they crossed paths, they'd be gunning for him.

He made the door, found it unlocked—like they had left it open for him. A trap? He eased it open, slipped into the narrow laundry room. The next door was wide open, flat against the wall. He moved there fast and entered the kitchen off the living room, keeping left to the hallway wall where no window could backlight him, MCX sweeping the living area.

She was sitting on the sofa in front of the bay window with a blanket over her thighs, a shottie and Glock on top of that, and her hands raised.

He shifted aim away from her. No one else was there. The room was open, it was clear. No one holding her hostage.

"What …" he started. He didn't know what words came next. He stumbled a couple of steps closer. She dropped her hands to her lap, moved the weapons to the floor and got to her feet, the blanket slipping onto her shoes. Her face was as drawn and pale as Woodsy's after his torture, her eyes puffy, the whites shot through with red. There were tremors running through her micro-expressions, aftershocks of a night of aloneness and terror. Her first step was a stumble, too, one shoe catching in the blanket. She kicked it aside, her expression twisting from blankness to anger as if that recalcitrant object were the cause of all her woes. He crossed to her, intending to comfort. But as her gaze came up, and he saw the want there, the need, and as he saw that her fear had been for *him*, and not for her, it was he whose knees buckled. And it was she who caught him.

Sometime in the past few minutes, she had sunk back onto the chair and he had come to his knees before her, his head turned into her breast. One of her hands held him beneath the shoulders while the other stroked his hair.

They couldn't stay this way. They shouldn't. There was work to do.

But Elliot couldn't break away. No tears came to him; he didn't believe he was capable of them. But his breath shuddered on the way in and out. His throat had a lump like an RPG stuck in it. No words came to his lips, and those in his mind were fragments of thought and intention and observation.

She smelled faintly of lemon-curd soap from her shower, days ago now. She smelled of sweat and fear. She smelled of life.

Eventually, she broke the tableau, pushing him gently away with hands on his ears, holding his head straight. "They're dead?"

"Jimmy. Maybe not Woodsy."

"Tell me."

He swallowed against that lump, forcing it down. "We need to move. I'll … I'll tell you on the way."

She released him, sat back and pointed to the rifle at his side. At his vest and belt and the objects on them. "That's not yours."

"Is now."

"Tell me. I need to know."

He told her. In rapid, bullet-point fashion that took all of two minutes. He felt like crap, breezing over Jimmy's fate so fast, so matter-of-fact.

"We need to move," he repeated.

"Do you know what the mind does to you when you're alone? When you're wondering?"

He was pretty sure he did know, but he gestured for her to continue, giving her a moment to vent.

"I imagined you dead. You three dead. Then getting back home and everyone there being sick and dying. I'd really be on my own. Completely on my own for the first time since…"

Her voice caught and then she caught herself. She punched herself in the thigh. She straightened her back and cleared her throat. "And that's my pity party over and done with. Next item: you really think they've gone to The Downs? It's a long way, and there's sickness there."

"I think they need bodies, they need manpower. And Woodsy just handed them thirty-plus workers. They can find some way to quarantine our people while they treat them with their meds. But they're already on their way I was told. You didn't see trucks leaving this way?"

"No."

"They would have gone from the north anyway, not this side of their ... region ... whatever it is."

"City-state."

"Yeah. City-state. Jericho."

She bent for her weapons and he stood to make room for her. "What's the plan?"

He pointed out across the bushland beyond the house. "So far it's getting in the truck I left out there and driving like hell."

"And make up the rest as we need to?"

"Yep."

"I'll grab my pack from the Rover." She prodded his vest. "Got me one of these?"

"You can have mine. And I've got doubles of these weapons in the truck for you."

"Good boy."

"I hope you won't need any of it. But I think you will."

"If they've hurt any of our—any *more* of our people—I'll help you kill every one of them whether *they're* wearing armor or not." She made for the front door but he caught her by the belt.

She rounded on him. "What?"

"I really wanna kiss you right now."

"Well, don't just talk about it," she said.

Their mouths met in a crush of passion, their hands and fingers tangling in each other's clothing. Her lips were soft and firm at the same time. She pressed against him and he wished he'd taken off the vest.

Heat—good heat—rushed up his back, his neck, his face. The lump in his throat melted away.

When they separated, he kept his hand twisted in her belt, pressed to the small of her back. He put his forehead to hers. "If we could stay like this. If we could have … this … *Us* … forever. Be normal."

"We're not normal, Elliot." She pulled back to catch his eyes. "We're nowhere near it. And for some bizarre reason, that works for me."

"Me, too," he said. "Me, too."

"Okay, so what do we do about this Kyle arsehole?" Angie asked as Elliot turned the truck back onto the main road.

An idea came to him, threads of thought converging, entwining: Kyle's potential convoy of armored trucks; one main road in and out of the area around The Downs; the Vike blockade at Birns River; Woodsy trashing both front tires of the Land Rover on that tree branch. What if they could rig a couple of bombs? IEDs had worked hellishly well in the Middle East. Well enough to stop a dozen vehicles he knew about from experience. Well enough to—

—to kill half the people in a market square including everyone else in his fire team.

Radler. Eames. McGovern.

Angie's hands wrapped around one of his. They were cool. They squeezed. He came back. Immediately. Not sweating. Not smelling copper or dust or smoke. Not hearing screams and sirens. Smelling the electric stink of the truck, Angie's sweat, and only faintly the odor of the deaders from beneath the killing floor.

"Where do you go?" she asked him. "You never talk about it. And I've never asked. But I want to know."

He squeezed her hands then let them go. Her callouses rasped across his as their fingers separated. "I'll do you a deal. We get through this, we get time for a heart-to-heart, I'll tell you." And, surprising him, he meant it. "All of it."

"Holding you to that."

"As you should." He took his foot off the gas momentarily while a wallaby bounded across his path. The BearCat's headlight missed it by inches.

"Lucky thing," she said. "Lucky and dumb. Why would it pick now to jump in front of a truck?"

"It's his world. We're the dumbasses, making it dangerous for everything else."

She waited a beat, then: "Yeah, we're the dumbasses who go out into the wilderness to find charms to give to psychologically damaged young girls so they'll be a little bit happier."

"Oh. She told you."

"She hardly speaks, you know that. No, I worked it out. All on my own." She batted her eyelids. "Ain't I clever?"

"Well, use some of that cleverness to help me figure this out."

Sobering, she straightened in her seat, staring forward. "What the hell is wrong with the human race? Seems like fighting slavers at Settlers Downs is becoming a habit. Feels like déjà vu. How'd we do this last time?"

"We used what we had."

"And we teamed up with complete strangers. With a common interest."

"You want to go get some of Jericho's ... workers?" He almost said peasants.

"No. I was just thinking. It'd be nice if we had allies. Why can't the other damn factions near us be friendly, instead of marking out territory?"

"Like you said: what's wrong with the human race?"

"Well, maybe a miracle will happen. Maybe we'll stumble across whoever wrote *bullshit* on that sign."

"Someone put barricades across the roads in Birns River Bridge."

"You're thinking of joining up with *them*? It was probably Vikes."

"I'm thinking of the barricade. It's a good idea. To beat the SERPs, we need to get them somewhere we control the conditions. Even if Kyle only took one truckload of men, there's a lot more of them than you and me."

"One truckload of men and women."

"Men includes women."

"People includes women. Staff, team members, soldiers, dumbasses—those designations include women. Men means men."

"Fine. Let's call them SERPs. Anyways, I'm considering ambushing them."

"Okay. I like that. Tell me more."

"I will. When I get the ideas straight in my head."

"Not wearing my tiger-print bra, this time, sorry."

He grinned briefly. The smile turned to scowl as he was forced to crank hard on the wheel to turn onto a connecting road; the BearCat was a real bastard to control. "I'm open to other ideas."

"Because we worked so well together the first time we met."

"Because we did."

"This is where you say, 'And because you're really clever, Angie, even if you never watched Discovery Channel.'"

He repeated it dutifully.

She pretended surprise. "Was that a compliment? I think I heard a compliment."

Stick around, he thought and brushed his knuckles across her hair. *You might hear more.*

18

On a wide stretch of flat highway, Angie stirred and said, "You're very quiet there. Planning that ambush?"

The sun was fully above the trees now. And Elliot was not thinking of solutions. Elliot was driving on autopilot. Elliot was somewhere inside his own head, thinking about the smell of cordite and of opened stomach cavities. Thinking about how distant the whump of an explosion could sound, even when it was only a couple dozen metres away from you. And he was beginning to think that he should just accept these kinds of things as *the way of the world*, as normal. There'd be more of it, that was certain—a lot more. Blood. Screaming. More unnecessary bullshit. And he'd be causing some of it, hopefully *all* of it.

"Elliot?"

He patted the automatic rifles snug in the weapons-bracket between their seats—he'd stowed the .22 in back. "I was thinking how we all get dealt our roles in life."

"Our … roles?"

"Sure. Like a movie. We get a role and then we play it out."

"Okay?"

"You asked."

"Go on."

"So, it doesn't matter whether we like them or not. We can try and pull away from them. But the Universe pulls us back into them. It won't let us off that hook."

She gave him a quizzical look. "And?"

"Well. Your role is to build community, hold it together. Like Claire." Well, she wasn't much like Claire. "Kind of."

"*And?*"

"Mine's to do the dirty work. So … you should let *me* do the dirty work." Then she wouldn't have to have the ghostly carnival of sights and sounds and stinks that he lived with all the time.

"Bullshit, Elliot." He blinked at her. She said, "Your role is to lead. Your role is to get the rest of us to help you fix this."

"Now who's talking bullshit. When I try to lead people, most times they end up dead."

"Most times? You have actual statistics on that? Look, do not start doubting yourself. And do not try and sideline me again."

"I'm not doubting myself. Trust me, I know what I'm doing when it's just me. I'm better when it's just me. And I'm not saying it's my fault people I knew died. Sometimes they had their own trouble. Sometimes they were dumb. Or as unlucky as that wallaby was lucky just now. Sometimes some other sonofabitch did it to them, like they did to Jimmy. But … you know …"

"What?"

"What if I get you killed? What if I can't stop it?"

"You already did stop it, you ... you dumbarse. You kept me out of the Death Druids' hands three years ago."

"You did that."

"You did it, too."

"It was teamwork. You worked as hard as I did."

"Exactly. And now you've walked into your own logic trap. Like we said before: we work well together. So we're gonna work together. And hell, if I die today or tomorrow, then I've already lived a few years longer than I might have—and I've certainly lived free. Some of that, sure, I did for myself. Also, you helped me. You led me. You led Lewis and Dylan and Heng. And you've led Settlers Downs from the sidelines ever since. Get used to it, dumbarse: *this* is your role in life."

"But—"

"Discussion over." She rummaged at her feet, in the box they'd taken from the back of the truck, came up with a water bottle and sealed jar of dried pears. "Breakfast?"

"Good talk," he muttered.

The thing Elliot liked most about the BearCat-analog was the frankenstein-modifications. Following the precept of *You Can Never Have Too Much of a Good Thing*, the SERPs had indeed welded plates across the tires to within a couple of inches off the ground to dissuade sniping. It meant zero off-roading, really, where uneven terrain might jam the plates into the earth, but for road driving it was smart. They must have had a heavy-duty hoist somewhere to raise it for tire changes. The plates across the front wheels were curved like cupolas to allow for turning, steering. Better, the cow catcher meant he could keep his speed up. Some of the obstacles forcing careful driving or detours on the journey to Jericho presented little challenge now. Others had already been cleared, testimony that Kyle's convoy had been along this route.

Retracing their steps through Ross and Campbell Town, he filled in more details as Angie asked about them. The wipers swished against a light rain shower.

Ten kilometres out of Campbell Town, she started oiling the knife from the ballistic vest's sheath. "What d'you think they did with Woodsy? Is he going with 'em?"

"He'll be alive. It makes sense to keep him that way. So, yeah, probably."

"He might die in friendly fire. When we start shooting."

"He knew the risk. He wanted to be a hero. He signed up for whatever came of it."

"He's one of us, Elliot."

"He's not. His big mouth has put all our people in danger." He could see her staring at him out of the corner of his eye. "I mean, the man endured getting the ends of fingers clipped off, for Christ's sake, and then *after* that's over, he goes and gives them all up. Jesus Christ."

"It was for Jimmy." Her fingers brushed his arm before returning to their work. "You wouldn't do the same if Lewis was threatened?"

He ground his teeth together. After a while, he murmured, "That's not fair."

"Not fair that I'm right? Or not fair that you can't justify hating Woodsy?"

"Sorry I brought it up."

"He's not a bad guy."

"He's a moron."

"And he cared about Jimmy like you care about Lewis." Her fingers were back on his arm. "Like a son."

"Son," he snorted. He shifted in his seat, leaning over the wheel. Goddamn, but his back was getting stiff driving this beast. It sure as hell wasn't built for long trips. "Simple arithmetic. I wouldn't have given you all up. Not even for Lewis."

"Not even for me?"

He squirmed some more, dislodging her hand from his arm. "Sorry, but no."

"You don't know that." If she was hurt she didn't sound like it. She sounded—he risked a glance—and *looked* calm.

"Let's drop it," he said. Conversations like this—where he was being asked to compare the woman to something else, or to make some kind of promise—shit, historically these were often where relationships started going south.

"Nope," she replied.

"*What!*"

"I said nope. This is a necessary conversation. It could be me one day sitting where Jimmy was sitting, with you in Woodsy's seat. Or vice versa." She sheathed the knife, dropped down in her seat enough to prop her feet on the dash. "And I get the arithmetic thing.

231

I really do. Far as I'm concerned, if they're pressuring you to put good people at risk or it's my head, you let them shoot me. Or I'll never forgive you. I can live with a lot of things on my conscience, Elliot, but not with knowing I got good people killed. And if the seats are reversed, and they want me to give up Lewis and the others or they'll shoot you, I'll let them shoot you. Got it?"

"Yeah. I got it."

"Deal?"

He settled back from hunching over the wheel. "Hundred per cent."

"Right. Good." They drove in silence a long while before she added, "But if it's a choice between adults dying and our kids dying, it's not so easy to choose. Not for me. And I know not for you. That happens, and I guess we do what we have to."

"Fair enough."

"Like Woodsy did."

"Fair enough."

"Lewis is one of our kids. And Jimmy was, too."

Damned Woodsy had put everyone in the worst situation possible, and himself along with them. He'd sacrificed everything to save Jimmy. And Jimmy got bit anyway.

Elliot slowed, ready to swerve around a plastic planter box blown onto the road, then changed his mind and sped up to plow on through, demolishing it.

"This goddamned world," he said.

19

The rain shower passed as they coasted down the mountain road toward the Birns River. Exhaustion and grief applied pressure to Elliot's temples; he wasn't certain if the buzzing in his muscles was the after-effects of adrenaline, of his tasings, or of lack of sleep. Probably all three.

"What?" Angie asked.

He realized he'd muttered a thought out loud. "Telling myself I can sleep tomorrow."

"Oh. Yeah." She yawned and flexed her hands, her arms. Then reached over to massage one of his shoulders. "Sorry. I should drive."

"Let's get through Birns River first."

At the bottom of the hill, he stopped before the bridge. "You got binoculars?"

She dug some from her pack.

The glasses didn't reveal anyone across at the shopping precinct. What they showed was a wide gap in the Main Street barricade. Something had pushed its way through from this side, shoving two car bodies clean out of the way. A big vehicle could do that in low gear, an earth-mover, or a BearCat like his.

Yeah. His fingers squeezed the steering wheel. *Mine.* He handed her the binoculars then patted the MCX on his side of the rack. *Mine also.*

"This Kyle guy did that?" Angie had the glasses to her face.

"He'll have at least one truck like this."

"Well, at least that's confirmation he's headed for our place." She kept the glasses on her lap and picked up her Glock with its big fat C-MAG. "Might finally get the chance to use you, big girl."

"Let's be careful waving guns over there." He put the truck in gear, steered it onto the bridge, crossing slowly. "If those Vikes are around, we want them to help us."

"Wait. What?"

"I've been thinking …"

"And you couldn't have thought that out loud? I think we call that conversation."

"Sorry."

"So, you've been thinking what?"

"That if they hang around this town, maybe they'll help us."

"The Vikes. How about we stick to you and me doing it?"

"Problem is I can't see you and me pulling off what I have in mind."

"Oh, you've been thinking a *lot*, haven't you? So you'll tell me about this big plan you're developing?"

"Some time." He forced a light-hearted brow waggle. "Every relationship needs suspense."

"Gimme a break."

At the junction of bridge and tarmac on the other side, Elliot put the shifter into neutral, engaged the handbrake. The PA/Siren controls were in a small panel in the center dash. He flicked the dial selector to the PA setting, adjusted the volume, hoped the SERPs weren't taking a break nearby and lifted the handset. Depressing the thumb-switch caused a squeak from the speakers set behind the front bumper. He released it, chewing his lip, and passed the handset to Angie.

"Me?"

"Not to sound sexist, but a female voice might be less threatening to any Vikes in town."

Her shoulders hunched in irritation, but she said, "Probably right."

With the handset to her chin, she thumbed the switch. "Hello, *Vikes*. Calling all *Vikes*. Any *Vikes* out there today?" Her tone made their name sound like a cuss word.

"Try saying 'Vike' a little nicer."

She scowled and tried again. "We probably look like the faction that smashed your road block. We're not. In fact, we hate those fucking people's guts because they're on their way to hurt *our* people. So we're on *our* way to kill the fucking bastards. Before they hurt our friends, preferably. If you're out there, we could use your help." She passed the handset back. "That's all I got."

"Not bad," he said and concentrated on scanning nearby windows, the park, alcoves and hideaways down along both streets.

Angie's mention of their friends brought his concerns crashing back. What the hell was happening at

The Downs? Did they have Lewis and Alyssa in their truck already? Had they—?

Cease this shit right now. The job. Mind on the job. Nothing else. Concentrate.

Angie had the glasses up again, for all the good they'd do this close in. "Damn big house up there on the hill. Maybe they're up there? Wanna go check?"

"Remember I told some of you about a guy named Jock?"

"...Yeah?"

"That's his house."

"Ah." She put the glasses on the floor. "Screw that."

"No movement," he said. "One more try?" He offered the handset.

She didn't take it. "Your turn."

"But—"

"You have a nice speaking voice."

"Goddamn liar." He hit the switch. Fumbled for words for a moment, let the switch go.

"It's not that hard," she said. "Just talk, dumbarse."

He took a breath and tried again. "I once met a guy named Spider. At a creek. Had a good talk. If Spider's there—or if he told you about me—then you know I'm no danger to you. I'm the American guy."

Angie chuckled. "I think they've worked that last part out."

He continued, "Our people are in danger from a bunch of assholes who'll one day put your people in danger, too. If you're up for helping us, and thereby helping yourselves, show yourself now. We leave in two minutes." He put the handset away and reflexively checked his watch before remembering it wasn't there; the SERPs had taken it. The dash clock read 10:44.

At 10:45, Angie said, "Well, at least you got to play with your loudspeaker toy." Then she froze, staring forward.

There were three of them.

Directly opposite and in line with the bridge, the road continued, cutting across Main Street to bisect the town. The three men had appeared from the properties down that way, forty metres past the intersection. They wore tight denims. No shirts, despite the cool weather. Tattoos covered their torsos. All were bearded and they'd shaved different areas of their scalps. The two to his left were stocky; they wore sneakers. The guy on the right was skinny, but not like the workers in Jericho: his arms and stomach and shoulders were well-defined; there simply wasn't an ounce of fat on him. Even at this distance, Elliot could see his naked feet were brown with mud. And he looked familiar, like he could have been the fella he spoke to across the creek that time.

They all had a bow slung over one shoulder and a quiver over the other. One of the stocky guys held something in his right hand.

"Is that a—?"

"Boomerang," Angie confirmed, the binoculars to her face. "Viking-wannabes carrying an indigenous Australian weapon: how do *you* spell incongruous?"

"Who is he, Zombie-killer Dundee?"

She lowered the glasses. "He's a whack-job, my dear. A nutcase. They all are. They're dressed like cosplayers and they do drugs. Let's get out of here and do this ourselves."

Elliot shook his head. "I have to try. I need more people." He cracked open the door, causing the men to flinch. Holding his empty hands high, he shouldered it open and slid out. He left one hip and shoulder in the cover of the door, painfully aware that Angie wore the ballistic vest now. Still scanning the store windows nearby, he called, "Willing to help us?"

The skinny one opened his mouth to say something but the guy with the boomerang got in first. "Help you what, exactly?"

"Ambush those pricks."

"What's in it for us?" The boomerang-wielder tapped his chest with the stick.

"Apart from protecting your people? Apart from making friends of us?"

"Nice voice, remember," Angie warned from the cabin. "Make friends and influence people."

Swallowing the quick eruption of temper back down, he called, "Half the haul if you want it. We just want our people back."

Boomerang-wielder gathered his mates into a tight huddle where they argued in harsh whispers.

"Shit, they're gonna take all day," Elliot muttered. Angie echoed his sentiment with softly spoken curses. "Leaving now," he called to them. "You in or not?"

The huddle broke up with the boomerang-carrier stomping off up the street away from them. The other two seemed to forget him instantly, venturing closer until Elliot was sure the skinny one was "Spider".

"How do we know you're safe?" Spider said. "How do we know you're not on their side?"

"Have you ever *met* those guys?" Elliot replied.

The stocky one raised his chin. "We sure have." His voice was gravelly, like someone had taken to his larynx with a broken bottle. He was older than Spider, in his early forties, Elliot's age. Parts of his cheeks were shaven, leaving a goatee flanked by wide sideburns. A pink pucker of skin on his chest spoke of an old stab wound, or bullet wound. Years old. He continued, "That's why he's asking. They're not exactly social workers."

"You lost people to them?"

"One," gravel-voice said. "In a gun fight. About a year ago."

"Wanna lose more? Because if we don't teach these sonsofbitches a lesson today, they'll only get bolder."

The men conferred some more. Then Spider smiled, revealing stubs of teeth. "Half the haul?"

"Fifty-fifty."

"Who else is in the truck?"

"Only one person. Two of you, two of us."

"You sure we can take two trucks out with just the four of us?" asked the bigger man.

"Two trucks?" Elliot patted the door. "Both like this?"

"One like that, plus a removals truck. Like for moving house."

"Only the gods know how many men they had in them," Spider added.

"Gods?" Angie snorted quietly. "Dickhead."

"We have a good chance, fellas," Elliot said, wishing he believed it. "We do this right, then yes we can take them. But you'll both have to do what I say. One hundred percent."

They looked at each other and shrugged.

"Should be fun," gravel-voice said.

Spider added, "We have our own car. I ride with you. Your friend rides with him."

"No way. You both follow us."

"Want us to trust you?"

"I—"

"I'll go with him, Elliot." Angie was busy gathering her gear, weapons and pack, shoving the field glasses in the latter.

Elliot's head snapped toward her. "The hell you will."

"Stop trying to shelter me. You want them onside, trust goes both ways."

"You said they're dickheads." He had the sense for once to keep his voice down as he said that.

She flashed a harsh smile. "Yeah, but so are you sometimes. And I've driven with *you*." She stroked her Glock. "Besides, my little friend here will look after me." She climbed out the other side.

Both men's eyebrows rose momentarily at the sight of her, but they covered their attraction quickly, switching their gaze back to Elliot and closing the distance a little more. Their weapons remained slung.

Spider said, "Why are you driving one of their trucks?"

"Where'd you get their gear?" gravel-voice added.

"I stole it all. Long story for later. Important fact is they've killed one of ours. Maybe two. And we'd rather they didn't enslave the rest of our people."

"Enslave?" The stocky man spat on the ground. "They're as bad as the fucking Death Druids were."

240

"And yet, they wear cop gear." Spider smiled his stub-toothed smile again. "Smell the irony?"

"They *are* cops," Elliot said. "Or were."

"Awesome," said gravel-voice. "All the more reason to help you. What's the plan?"

"The plan right now is to get closer to home. To our farm. Find a perfect spot for the ambush. We get that far, I'll explain the rest then."

"Haven't thought it up yet, eh?"

"Most of it I have. First step is finding that site. And the clock's running here."

"Let's party," Spider said.

"Our car's back there," gravel-voice said.

"Dandy," Angie said and followed him down the road. Whether or not she knew Elliot would still be watching her, she flipped him the bird good and slow. At this, Elliot nodded, satisfied: she could look after herself.

"How long since they broke through your barricade?" he asked Spider. Down the street, Angie got into a green Mazda hatchback with the other Vike.

"Three hours. Something like that. We were hunting roos behind those houses when we heard the noise. Scared the complete and utter shit out of us."

Three hours. Kyle had taken it slow, or he'd left later than Da Silva had claimed. Or maybe he'd had other business while he was on the road. Elliot thought of the original inhabitants of The Downs, the farmers who'd made their deal to buy protection from the Death Druids by catching others for them. Maybe there were groups out there with similar deals with the SERPs. Maybe even the Vikes—same as in the Middle

East, there was always the chance that his new allies were actually working with someone else. And wouldn't that be ironic, him and Angie having to fight their way out of the same situation twice? A return to the day they had met? Circularity.

The hatchback coughed into life, gravel-voice revving it, waking it up. Elliot looked Spider over as he did. Built like Jimmy, but harder, Spider was in his mid-twenties. He had a little buzz on, bobbing on the balls of his feet. Meth? Nerves? Every few seconds he flashed Elliot a smile. Shit, but this was risky.

Yeah. But what isn't?

"Three hours," he said aloud and Spider grunted confirmation. Kyle's delay for whatever reason might be a good thing. But a three-hour head start was still a head start; a whole lot of bad could already have gone down back home. Which, once again, Elliot could not dwell on.

The hatchback wheezed its way out into the middle of the street and crept toward them, trailing smoke.

Elliot grabbed the BearCat's frame to haul himself up. He said, "Climb in. And let's get to know each other a little more."

20

"Your name's Spider?"

"Yep. Can't remember yours. Sorry."

Sparkles, Radler's ghost said. "Elliot."

Spider offered his hand, reaching past the rifles. The move was oddly businesslike.

Elliot clasped it briefly—it was rough and gritty, the grip firm.

They were out of town now, passing between the motel and gas station. Elliot's gaze switched between the two properties, still not convinced the SERPs hadn't organized an ambush of their own. Surely, those trucks would have radio contact with Jericho. Surely, Da Silva had updated Kyle on Elliot's escape. Maybe; maybe not. It was always better to be suspicious than not to be.

The hatchback was a green blob in his side mirrors, Angie's blonde hair visible through the windshield. It left a thin wake of sickly smoke behind it. Elliot asked, "Your guy back there with Angie? What's he called?"

"Mafia."

"*Mafia?*"

"He worked for them in Melbourne. Good guy."

"Right. Wow. We have very different definitions of good."

"Don't worry, Elliot. He's reformed."

"I goddamn hope so."

Spider gave a little groan as he stretched, wiggling his bare and dirty toes. He seemed completely at ease and Elliot gave him another checking over to see if he was stoned.

"He used to break legs for a living," the Vike continued, "but after all we've been through, he's a humanitarian now. He don't wanna do that shit no more."

"But he's doing it now. He's about to, anyway."

"Well, okay, yeah. He also believes in taking care of our people. And he never liked pigs."

"Criminals rarely do."

But taking care of your people was something Elliot could relate to. As long as "Mafia" minded his business, did his job, kept his hands off Angie, he could call himself whatever stupid nickname he wanted.

Besides, everyone had a past. The guy might have turned over a new leaf.

"And your name? Spider. Your parents call you that?"

"Nah." He looked embarrassed as he admitted, "They called me Barney."

"You're kidding."

"Wish I was."

"Spider's better," Elliot agreed. "But why that name?"

"Well, Vikes give each other our names. Kind of a ceremony. They gave me mine coz I've got these long skinny arms and legs—" He stretched them all out in front of him. "—and I'm good at climbing and sneaking around and shit."

Just like Jimmy, Elliot thought, and changed the subject. "Your car back there's making a lot of smoke." It wasn't enough to telegraph their approach to anyone, but it looked truly unhealthy.

"We rigged a few for bioethanol." Spider laughed. "Be grateful you're not driving behind it, dude!"

It had quickly become clear that Elliot would have to drive slower than he'd like in order to keep the struggling little sedan close. Perhaps that was for the best: taking this slow was good, despite the desperate need he felt to get home.

"Why'd your other friend leave?" he asked Spider.

"Bourbon? Coz he's a dick. He didn't trust you."

"You do?"

"You're good people."

"And how do you know that?"

"Well…" Spider made a face, looking sheepish. He wiggled his toes some more.

"Well *what?*"

"Truth is I've checked out your compound before. Quite a lot."

Elliot tensed. "You—?"

"From the outside. I promise I never went in."

"You never went in."

"Never. You guys looked like good people."

Are you shitting me? He scoped us. We had no idea. Spider: good at sneaking around.

"Those people in that farm aren't just good people, they're the *best* people," Elliot said quietly. "You help us, I'm in your debt."

"Like you said, we gotta do something. Those pigs might come after us if they get too cocky. We can't let that happen. We can't." He stretched again, eyeing the MCXs lustfully. "Anyway, this could be fun. You're letting us use guns, right?"

Elliot chewed his cheek then said, "Guess I am."

"Sweet. Ran outa bullets two years ago." Spider slapped his knee. "Jeez, I love shooting."

"Right. Just don't shoot anyone we care about."

"Oh, no. No way." He tapped a rifle with a fingernail. "What do I need to know about these before I use one?"

"Before we get into that. Last time I met you, you were using. Convince me you're straight right now."

"Hey, trust me, mate …"

"Trust? Trust starts with honesty. And I need to know what I'm working with."

"Okay, look, we're all smokers back there, back home. Potheads. We grow our own. That's all. Just bud, that's all."

"That's all?" Elliot gave him a hard look.

"And booze, of course. What's left of it."

"That's *all*?"

Spider squirmed a little. "Well."

"Seriously, stop saying *well*."

"Sorry."

"You were saying?"

"So some of 'em—two of 'em—they do use harder stuff sometimes. Not me. Honestly."

"You seem a little wired for a pot-head."

"I'm excited, man. I'm … well … nervous."

"Fair enough. And Mafia? He use 'harder stuff'?"

"Nah. Not Mafia. Bourbon does."

"*What* harder stuff?"

"Not meth. Definitely not meth. Promise. There was three guys tried to join us in the early days and when it turned out they were meth-heads, we chased 'em away. We ..." He turned his hands over, studying them, front then back, front then back. Softly, he said, "We had to kill one of them. Stupid bastard would have killed us if we hadn't."

"Okay, I'll accept that. No meth-heads you say. So, Bourbon and this other guy—"

"Girl."

"This other girl. They use, what, smack?"

"Painkillers in the early days. We keep them for what they're meant for now, for medicine. But I think they still have a little coke left. They used to have a *lot* of that."

Elliot grunted something halfway between a laugh and a groan.

"What?" Spider said.

"Nothing. Except 'coke' is the word our young people use to mean something they liked in the old world. Something good you can't get anymore."

"Nice. Yeah, good word for it. Ya can't get any brand of colas or lemonades or mixers or anything ... and if ya do it's flat and tastes like piss so what's the point. Hardly any good stuff to be found in our territory anymore."

"Or ours, huh?"

Spider blushed, concentrated on giving his toes another wiggle.

Elliot shrugged. "So. Bourbon and the girl use coke, painkillers. What else?"

"Well."

Elliot glanced at him.

"Sorry. I'll stop saying it. Right, so there's this group up north. They took over the poppy fields and they make good shit apparently, so Bourbon and Traci trade for it sometimes."

"*Poppy fields?*"

"You didn't know Tassie had poppy fields? Oh, yeah, dude. Pharmaceutical companies grew hectares of it in the old days. This group—"

"Okay. Okay. I've heard enough for now."

What the good God? Another group? Another faction processing and dealing in opiates? That sounded like outlaw biker business. Maybe they weren't gone, after all. The other night, he'd told Claire, *Helluva lot we don't know about the world outside our region.* He'd sure been right about that.

"Let's focus on the mission to hand," he said. "But when we get through this, I wanna know everything you know about that other group."

"Sure, I can trade you that info."

"Trade me?" He supposed that was fair enough. Spider was here risking his life to help. If—*when*—they beat Kyle and took back Settlers Downs, it wouldn't hurt to trade something for decent intel. An alliance would be good; it would be what Claire would want. He said, "What kinds of things you gonna ask us for?"

"Only one thing." Spider studied his hands again. "I … I got kind of an exterior motive for coming along to help you."

"Ulterior motive," Elliot corrected him. "And what the hell would that be?"

"You take me in."

"Take you in?"

"Me. My missus. My kid."

Elliot looked him over and Spider straightened under the scrutiny. He raised his chin. "I don't smoke anymore. Don't even drink. I'm high on life now, that's all. I've been clean for a year. Ever since my missus told me she was pregnant. If Mafia can reform, so can I."

"Keep talking," said Elliot. The more Spider spoke, the more opportunity for Elliot's bullshit detector to kick in if needed.

"See, that's the reason I was scoping out your place. I only went there when I was on me own. Honest. I … the others, they're okay. They're not *bad*. But the way we live, it's not … I dunno, I just don't want my daughter growing up there. Better than nothing in a dangerous world. But if there's a chance we can come with you …"

Elliot's bullshit detector detected no bullshit. Spider appeared sincere: for the first time his calm and careless toker demeanor was slipping. His eyes had misted as he spoke.

Elliot said, "You do realize our place is up shit creek?"

"Well, what place isn't?"

"I mean, it's a *long* way up shit creek."

"Trust me, I won't be bringing 'em to your place until this crap with the bad cops is sorted. But when it is … well …"

"That word again," Elliot said, lightly this time.

"What I mean is, you folks are the kind of people my kid should grow up around."

Elliot thought about the kids at The Downs, saw them running, playing, sitting under the tutelage of Lewis and Krystal and Neil. He saw the indulgent expressions of the adults watching them play and heard mealtime conversations of people's hopes for these children's futures.

"Agreed," he said. "But hear me. I have a zero-tolerance policy on drugs. You got anything on you, *anything*, dump it out the window now. It'd be a solid gesture of good faith."

Spider patted a hip pocket. Something in there rattled inside a plastic container momentarily. He was grinning like a fool again. "Hardest stuff I've got is three aspirin and six Tic Tacs. You want a Tic Tac?" He contorted himself to dig in the pocket.

Elliot gestured for him to stop. "I'll pass."

They'd passed beyond the outer limit of Birns River Bridge now. Elliot gave the truck a little more gas. More smoke pumped from the hatchback behind them as Mafia tried to keep up. Elliot could only hope Angie's conversation with an ex-kneecapper was as reassuring as his had been with Spider.

On a three-hundred-yard straight-run of asphalt between two sweeping curves, Elliot pulled the BearCat onto the side. Ahead, the highway's curve vanished around a natural spur where elevation would be good for a sniper. Ignoring a query from Spider he grabbed both MCXs, got out and checked both ways along the road. Grunting in satisfaction, he signaled Mafia to cut his motor and went back to cut his own.

"Stretch your legs," he told Spider, "and watch the road ahead."

He joined Angie and Mafia at the end of the truck.

"I like this place." Facing back the way they'd come, the whole siding to his left—the south—was up high, fifteen to twenty feet above the roadway. The land leveled out opposite and to his right, filled with old orchards gone wild.

Angie cleared her throat. "We're going to wait here and hope they come past? Maybe going to the farm is better."

"You mentioned something about leadership," he replied evenly. "I was on the other end of a rifle from several grass-roots insurgencies. And … and an IED, too. A smaller force against a bigger, better-armed one? We have to hurt them, we have to contain them, we have to get the upper hand quick. The four of us walking back into that farm leaves too many variables."

"I don't like it here."

"Don't have to." He whistled and waved Spider to come back to them. When the skinny Vike drew near, he continued. "We have two choices, right? Go in after them, or lay an ambush."

Angie brandished her sawnoff shottie and her Glock. "I'd rather go in than wait."

Mafia nodded and grinned.

But Spider said, "Probably not the safest thing to do."

"I agree," said Elliot. "The main problem with incursion is that there's most likely six or more of them. What if there's ten? Or twenty?"

No, there wouldn't be *that* many since they needed space in their trucks for their victims. Their cattle. But it was good that Angie and the Vikes were wary.

He continued, "We'd have to sneak in the back entrance. Can't go in the front gate, which they'll be guarding. We won't know how many they have or where those individuals are. They could be in any building or any paddock. It's chaos. And we might be firing into our own people used as meat shields—or hit them for the simple reason that chaos forces mistakes." He gestured to the highway. "At least here, we'll have the hostiles contained in vehicles and we'll have more control of the situation."

Angie said, "We could hit our own people here, too."

"I got thoughts there. I'll talk you all through it. But, yeah, there's a risk. And I hate it. And it's better than the third choice we have."

"Which is let them take our people back to Jericho."

"Exactly."

Spider asked, "Couldn't you get them out after they're there? Like sneak in?"

Elliot's laugh had zero humor in it. "Sneaking in there didn't work too well for me last time."

"I've been telling Mafia," Angie said to Spider. "Entering their territory is basically how we got into this mess."

"Oh."

"Elliot hasn't told you any of that? What have you two been talking about in the truck? Oh, wait, that's right. Elliot doesn't do conversations."

"Time and place," Elliot growled.

Spider cleared his throat. "I think I should mention that she has body armor, and we ... well." He gestured to his own naked torso.

"You could start with shirts," Angie grumbled. She shifted focus to Spider's feet. "And shoes."

"Only the one vest," Elliot said. "I'm as vulnerable as you guys. If we take out more of these assholes today, there'll be plenty of body armor to go around."

"After they've been shooting at us," Spider sighed.

"I'll risk it with or without armor," Mafia said. "But what if this Kyle bloke goes in a different direction. He might take the coast road to go looking for other survivors."

Angie added, "Or he might stay at Settlers Downs for days or weeks while we're freezing our arses off out here."

"I don't think so on either count. This guy wants bodies, but he really loves his walls. He's proud of them. He feels safe behind them with his own mini-army and his little medieval setup. Out here, body armor and trucks notwithstanding, he is vulnerable. And those meds we wanted, they're back at Jericho, so he's not going to stay away any longer than he has to. Especially not when he's been around sick people he wants to treat and wants to avoid getting sick from."

"Sick people?" Spider asked.

Mafia told him, "Some of 'em have the flu or something. That's why him and her went to Jericho to get some top-shelf meds. Which we'll be getting half of—if those trucks have any with 'em. Right?"

"Right," Elliot said.

Angie kicked a stone into the closest drainage ditch. "I don't like it, but okay. Ambush, it is."

Elliot looked to the Vikes.

"As long as I get to shoot some corrupt coppers, and get some good loot, then it's all good for me," said Mafia.

More softly, Spider added, "I think your reasoning is sound."

Angie gave the skinny man a double take, then said to Elliot, "Time to give us your plan, boss man."

"We've got a box of Molotovs in the boot of our car." Mafia was grinning, eager.

Angie gave Elliot a meaningful look, one that said, *I just traveled in a car full of bombs?* She said, "And I thought the smell was a faulty muffler. Silly me."

"Ya got some free chroming," Mafia chuckled.

"Molotovs are too messy," said Elliot. "We'll just as likely burn our own people to crisps along with the hostiles."

"But—"

"Or it might kill you," he said.

"We've used 'em before," Mafia said. He let it go, but his expression had soured.

Angie asked Elliot, "What then?"

His gaze traced the nearby orchard fence and the barbed wire along the top of it. "Do we have any wire cutters in the back?"

21

E lliot lay in a hollow between two flowering wattle trees on the south side of the highway where it curved around the spur.

His elevated position up on the high shoulder provided a clear view along both sides of the spur. The taser burns on his gut prickled and stung. The wattle pollen was making his face itch and his head ache. He cursed and blew his nose into his hand, wiped it on his pants.

"What the hell is taking so long?" he muttered, though he didn't really want some of the potential answers to that. The chorus to his old regiment's unofficial theme song played on a loop in his mind— *The Waiting is the Hardest Part.*

The other three were in the positions he'd assigned them, though two of them didn't truly hold Elliot's confidence and trust.

Mafia, in particular: far too casual.

The former kneecapper leaned against a solitary eucalypt over on the grassy verge near the orchard fence. He flashed Elliot a thumbs-up. Then he checked the safety on the MCX that Elliot had loaned him. Elliot could only hope he would lie down as instructed when he heard motors. He'd given the man one of the spare mags, unwilling to give up more ammunition that he might want to use himself.

Once they got through this, if they prevailed here, short ammunition would continue to be a major issue. They could collect more weapons from whatever SERPs they took down, but the BearCat he'd taken had no extra rounds to reload the magazines they had. What if the one they attacked didn't either? That led to other questions. What did the SERPs have left after two or more years of fighting the undead? Was it only what they carried on them? Or was an entire underground floor of that facility chock full of bullets and flashbangs that the rest of them could use against Elliot and his small team?

A fresh thought hit him, so hard and so raw it caused him to flinch physically—he couldn't believe it had never crossed his mind to date. Did Tasmanian cops have an armory before the Collapse? If so, where?

Okay, put a pin in that one, team leader. That's a thought worth coming back to later.

Besides, the SERPs no doubt thought of that one, too ...

For now, they had to work with low ammunition. Once that was gone, it would be a return to the Middle Ages if they couldn't learn to manufacture gunpowder and cartridges fast enough. Mafia and Spider had left their bows and arrows in the Mazda, grinning like kids on Christmas as they'd taken hold of their loaned weapons. Mafia had the MCX and Spider the .22 along with a .40 cal handgun.

With the BearCat parked in bushland five hundred metres east toward The Downs, they'd tucked the hatchback into an old roadside fruit stall to the west. Angie and Spider were out of sight near the small car's hiding spot, a hundred and fifty metres to Elliot's left. Angie had placed herself up on the shoulder like Elliot; the raised position provided a better angle for firing down on the enemy—and a better chance that friendly crossfire wouldn't hit her. Her sling-satchel contained her sawn-off double-barrel. Favoring her Glock and its huge double-drum magazine, she had turned down the offer of an MCX. She would do fine; she would *be* fine.

She has to be fine.

None of mine are dying this time.

Spider mirrored Mafia's position, situated on the other side of the road from her, but at least he was lying down, doing the right thing. Elliot had put the skinny Vike in the grass behind the orchard's wire fence after thoroughly checking the surrounds for drybones. Of the two Vikes, Elliot trusted Spider more and had allowed Spider to have one of the Molotovs in case escaping SERPs tried to overrun his position or take shelter in the orchards. But he had strict instructions about its use. And Mafia had been unhappy about not getting one of his own, despite the power-discrepancy between his rifle and Spider's. A gap they'd cut in the wire allowed Spider a quick escape if he needed it. It also provided him fast access to the road when the trap sprung.

The trap.

There was no point second guessing it, but he hoped to Christ it would work. The three thick cords of

PETE ALDIN

barbed wire traversed the road five metres to Elliot's left where a driver wouldn't see them until they were on them. They were anchored either side of the blacktop by heavy planks of wood, so they didn't curl upon themselves until a set of wheels hit them. It was that simple. And it would work. It had to work.

"I hope," he muttered. He'd been doing a lot of hoping these last two days; so far luck had been a roller coaster.

Across the way, Mafia scratched his back against the tree, yawning. Elliot checked the sky—

Six hours of daylight left, plenty of time, no need to get antsy.

—thin cloud cover, little chance of rain. The trap was wide enough that even if the second vehicle swerved around the other, there'd be plenty of barbed wire left for it, too. He yawned, growled and shook off a sudden wave of wooziness. Time for sleep later. And what the hell was keeping Kyle? What was he doing?

Keep calm, soldier. Don't waste energy. Conserve your breath. Conserve your focus.

His regiment's favorite chorus reasserted itself in his mind, as if someone had turned up the volume.

Don't know how much more of this I can take, he thought. *Maybe Angie's right.*

He was running through options—find a fast-moving motorbike and head to the farm to entice Kyle back here; abandon the ambush site and take the fight to them after all—when he heard the rattle of gunfire in the distance. A burst of single rounds, fired by two or more weapons simultaneously. Over as quick as it started.

Before he could wonder about that, the buzz of engines came from the east.

The tension in his gut reached up to squeeze his heart, chasing away any tiredness. He shifted position. Mafia had caught the sound, too, crouching, weapon up. Elliot whistled and signaled him to drop onto his belly, to stay cool and not fire yet. Mafia nodded dismissively. The way he got prone seemed reluctant.

Elliot cursed as he took the safety off his SERP rifle. What if the Vikes screwed this up? Whether or not they thought they were helping here, if either one of them looked like harming Elliot's people, he'd put them down without a single qualm. They weren't his people. They weren't his …

Family?

That's what Claire had called The Settlers.

"Damn it, Claire. We should've found another way to fight that bug."

The engine noise grew louder. Two shapes appeared to the east, dark boxes moving fast. They were a kilometre away but at that speed, they'd be here in under a minute. Moments later, the blocky lead vehicle resolved clearly as another BearCat.

Perfect.

If the vehicles continued at this rate, they wouldn't have a prayer of avoiding that wire. The lead truck was almost at the place where the hill's crest and the road's curve combined. As the Vikes had indicated, a removals truck followed close to the BearCat … then began to drop back, the driver possibly lacking the confidence in his vehicle's ability to corner at speed.

The armored truck passed Elliot's position at thirty or forty miles an hour. A moment later, its driver locked up the brakes, seeing the wire-trap and unable to avoid it. The wire kicked up as the vehicle hit it, squealing like hell's minions, bunching beneath it and thrashing the sides.

Elliot smacked the earth beside him. "Yes!"

Sparks spattered from under the fuselage. The BearCat slewed to the right, away from Elliot's side of the road. Ten or fifteen metres further on, it hit the drainage ditch, bounced up and over, chewed up sods of earth across the verge, slammed into the farm fence. It came to an abrupt rest with cow catcher down in the dirt and thick grass and fence debris, motor revving, back wheels churning up more clouds of dirt.

A moment later, the slightly longer removals truck came around the curve. Seeing trouble, its driver also braked hard. Elliot tracked it along his rifle barrel and the rush of elation evaporated: the first truck had gathered and taken all the wire with it. The road was clear. The second driver—perhaps on instinct, perhaps following prearranged procedure—released his brake and gave his truck more gas. Elliot raised the MCX, tried a couple of rounds at rear tires and gave it up for fear of a ricochet into the fuel tank or a cargo bay no doubt filled with Settlers.

But although he'd stopped firing, someone else was at it, the sounds ringing out above the growl of truck gears. Mafia.

Elliot shouted "Cease firing!" He shouted it a second time and had his weapon turned toward Mafia before the Vike heard him and stopped—narrowly avoiding death.

Slinging the MCX, Elliot commenced a controlled slide on his heels down the embankment. Up the road, a handgun sputtered a few rounds then stopped. Angie trying for the driver. But the truck was past her position by the time Elliot had his feet on the tarmac.

Goddamnit!

Most of their people would be on that truck.

That's for later. Concentrate. BearCat.

Elliot's shoes pounded asphalt, following the black trail of tire rubber, the scrapes in the road. He had the MCX back in hand. Mafia picked his own way more carefully through the grass on the siding, though he kept up. No movement from the BearCat yet: wire had gathered around the front wheels and up along the sides to the cabin doors. They'd hit that ditch hard, stopped hard: what if everyone on board was dead? What if Lewis was badly injured in that cab or the rear compartment?

Along the road, the back end of the removals truck flashed him like a deer's ass before vanishing around the bend. Spider was on the outside of the fence down there, sprinting hard toward the BearCat. And Angie—

Angie was down from the embankment. But she was running in the other direction. Running after the vanished truck.

He sucked in breath, readying to shout her name. But it was pointless. She wouldn't heed him even if she heard it. And it would slow him down, eroding the advantage he still had. He knew her. She'd be going for the Vike car. She'd chase them. She might just make it.

Or she might get herself killed.

He was over the ditch and in the wet grass of the verge when one of the BearCat's rear compartment doors creaked open a few inches. Elliot caught a glimpse of red hair before the pitch of the vehicle's chassis caused the door to swing back again and slam. A rifle fired. A bullet pinged from that door.

Elliot did slow, turning his rifle Mafia's way. "Wait until you're sure!"

Elliot expected attitude back, but the Vike slowed to a stop, panting. He took one hand off his rifle to signal a curt acknowledgement.

Elliot pointed to a fence post to Mafia's right. "There. Cover the driver's door and don't fire. Unless they're firing at us."

The back door opened a little and a voice called Elliot's name.

"Who's that?" he called back.

"Me. Sturgis. Don't shoot."

Elliot picked his way through the broken fence where the truck had plowed on through. He called, "Hostiles in there with you?"

"No. But we've got injuries."

"Stay there till we come get you. Door shut."

Obediently the door clacked closed. Wondering desperately who else was in there, Elliot moved out wide, rifle trained along the vehicle's left side—the passenger side in Australia. He whistled to Mafia and pointed to the rear right-hand corner of the truck. Mafia nodded, moving forward.

Spider was getting closer, too, but he'd slowed with a hand to his belly as if he had a stitch. His bare feet seemed as tough as boots. The .22 was slung and his Glock bobbed by his thigh as he moved.

An engine revved as Angie speared the Mazda out onto the road, fish-tailing to get it pointed the right way. The small motor screamed as she started working through the gears. By the time Spider was off the asphalt again, across the ditch and onto the verge, the small car had vanished around the bend in the road. And with his own vehicle a half click away, and with the current situation occupying all of his attention, there wasn't one thing Elliot could do to support her.

Concentrate!

Spider had a good view across the waving heads of the grass toward the cabin's side window—a window that began winding down. A pistol muzzle appeared there, so Spider raised his and fired, one-handed. The four rounds sprayed uselessly, wastefully, only one of them even banging off the truck. The hand inside the window returned fire, more steadily. Spider went down into the long grass. Elliot sent a controlled burst along the chassis, scuffing the ballistic glass. The pistol vanished and the window went up fast.

Back of the truck, Mafia shouted something and fired twice. "Got him!" he called. The driver must have tried an escape. Mafia stayed where he was and added, "Shit, he's back inside. But I got the prick."

Which one was Kyle, Elliot wondered: driver or passenger? Or was he in the escaped truck?

He steadied a shoulder against the warm steel of the chassis and raised his voice. "Yo, the cab! Three choices. One: we get our people out and set a fire under you. Two: you try to fight your way out and die exactly one second later." He sucked air, and finished, "Three, you ease that door open, drop all your weapons out. Then we see your empty hands. Then you slowly follow those hands out of the vehicle, walk three paces away from your weapons and get on your knees with hands behind your heads."

There was silence. The engine had cut out, he realized now. It ticked. Someone moved within the cargo space. He thought he heard a groan in there. How bad were his people's injuries? And had it been the crash that caused them, or the SERPs?

Spider appeared above the grass, limped forward. In thirty seconds the young Vike could evacuate the cargo space while Elliot and Mafia kept the cab covered. Thirty seconds was too long. Elliot's patience was already at an end.

"Time's up! Decide! Fighting or surrendering, do it now."

He tightened his grip on the MCX and hoped Mafia was ready and competent on the other side.

The passenger door parted an inch. A strained male voice came out of it. "Driver's dead. I'm surrendering, mate. All right?"

Gotcha, you roach-hearted sumbitch.

Weapons followed: two .40 cals, two MCXs.

"Your side?" Elliot asked Mafia, but the stocky Vike shook his head no then started forward down his side of the truck.

A man's hands appeared out the passenger door. The SERP shoved the door open with his shoulder and slid out to collapse onto all fours, wheezing. He was blond and stocky and Elliot had never seen him before.

For a half-second as the man collapsed, Elliot nearly fired, thinking him going for one of the weapons. But the struggle for breath was genuine. Maybe the seatbelt had snapped some ribs in the crash, despite the vest he wore.

Well, good.

"Hands behind your head," Elliot barked.

Spider asked, "Can I shoot him?"

"No, you goddamned can't shoot him. We need intel. Are you all right?" Elliot added.

"Grazed my elbow, but I'm not hit." He came up alongside Elliot, still limping.

The passenger had straightened himself up on his knees, his breath coming hard. He avoided eye contact.

Elliot said, "Can I trust you to watch this asshole without shooting him while I check the back?"

Spider's face screwed up like he could smell dogshit on his shoe. "Yes. But you're no fun."

"We good over there?" Elliot called to Mafia as the driver's door was opened

"All good! Guy's dead all right."

Elliot relaxed half a notch and yanked at one of the truck's rear doors, throwing it all the way open so it banged against the side. Five of his people were inside. All had injuries.

None of them was Lewis.

Nobody's injuries were life-threatening.

Apart from a black eye at the hands of the SERPs, Sturgis had nasty lacerations on and above his left ear from the crash, and had some gauze pressed to them to staunch the bleeding. Di, who'd arrived in a millionaire's yacht with husband Raj at The Downs lighthouse, looked anything but rich. Her face was bloody from a laceration above her eyebrow, and she had a banged knee and bruised shoulder. Rit had bumps and scrapes. Chariya had landed on Claire and appeared uninjured. Claire seemed to have a fractured wrist and a mild concussion.

"That's what I get for being Chariya's airbag," she told Elliot when he'd returned from securing the prisoner to the fence. "Hurts like hell. Good they had supplies." She nodded to the large medkits Sturgis and Spider were using on the others. Claire's wrist was in a sling and she was sitting in the shade of an apple tree. "I'd really like today to start over again."

"The entire week," Elliot said. He lowered his voice and crouched beside her. "This is total FUBAR, a disaster."

"Yes," she said, her eyes shining with tears. "It is."

"You haven't asked me about Angie or Jimmy," Elliot murmured after a short silence. "Or Woodsy."

"Time for stories later," she said, her voice catching at a pain in her hand. Her next words came out strained. "Things to do, still."

He glanced toward the SERP handcuffed to the fence. His name plate read DRISCOLL. Driscoll's head was down and he was still avoiding eye contact with anyone. He looked scared as hell.

Falling into enemy hands without a prayer will do that to you, asswipe.

None of the Settlers were talking to each other, focused on removing useful items from the back of the stricken truck. Sturgis and Spider were assessing the weapons and the kit taken from passenger and driver. Spider had a vest on now, the blood-streaked one from Mafia's kill; Elliot the other.

Elliot patted Claire's foot. "Quite a few things to do," he agreed.

"The first thing's back at Settlers Downs," she said.

"Nope. First thing is Mafia hurrying the hell up with my ride so I can get after Angie and the second truck." Once things were under control, Mafia had set off in a jog to retrieve Elliot's BearCat.

She narrowed her eyes at him.

"Angie's okay," he said. "So far. She took off after the other truck. Alone."

Once more, she didn't ask about the other two members of their mission. But before her eyes squeezed shut, he was sure the flare of pain in them had more to do with Jimmy than with her head or wrist.

"Well," she murmured. "You can chase them if you want. But there's another problem. Kyle and one of his men stayed back home along with all our sick people."

"*What?*"

"The … what are they, *cops?*"

"They were. Apparently."

"Well, the two cops stayed back to pack stuff—our stuff—into all our vehicles so others can come back and get it all tomorrow. And to—" She paused to groan and grit her teeth for a few seconds. "And to treat our sick with their medicine. Kyle made it sound like a great big favor. Even while he was herding our people into trucks. God! The Druids. Now these people?" Echoing

Angie from earlier without knowing it, she said, "What the hell is wrong with our species?"

For a moment her glare burned towards the prisoner before she forced her gaze up at the spread of the tree above her. "Love and light to those who have trespassed against me," she whispered, voice breaking. "Love and light." Her eyelids closed. Tears leaked from between them.

Elliot touched her foot again. "You rest. I'll … I'll figure out what to do next."

He stood, his scalp brushing against apple tree twigs. He reached up and twisted one of them, broke it off, flung it aside and stomped over to Sturgis and Spider.

"Two of them stayed back there with our sick?"

The former Navy officer lifted his face to study him. "You about to lay blame for letting them all in? Coz if you are, you can't say anything to me that I haven't already said to myself."

"Made plenty of errors myself," Elliot said. "Problems. Solutions. Actions. Let's keep it to that. Two SERPs back home? Not three, not four?"

"Definitely two. They brought three in each truck. Two got in the removals truck and these two got in this one. Their boss Kyle stayed back with another bloke."

Kyle. That sonofabitch.

Elliot raised his eyes to the road at the sound of engines. Nothing was coming down the road from the west; it wasn't Angie. He turned his head the other direction: Mafia turning the other BearCat onto the highway.

"Are you good to fight?"

With his free hand, Sturgis patted one of the two new MCXs. "Bloody oath, I am."

"Spider here followed instructions just fine. You take him back home and deal with it. Rit stays with the ladies. Sorry it'll be two hour's hike for you to The Downs, but I'm taking Mafia and the BearCat to go after the other truck. If I can get back in time to help you, I will, but don't count on me. We'll leave our prisoner handcuffed here till we decide what to do with him."

That would not be a difficult choice.

Sturgis said, "I'd rather have Rit, too, or Chariya. Make it three."

"You decide. You'll have to go in the back way. Spider, this man was Navy. He knows his shit."

"Not today, apparently," Sturgis muttered.

"Hey!" Elliot snapped his fingers. "Concentrate."

"Right. Yes."

"You follow his lead," he told Spider.

The Vike gave a thumbs-up. "No probs."

The BearCat was nearing now, but slowly, as Mafia got used to driving it. *Hurry the hell up*, Elliot thought. To Sturgis, he added, "Whoever stays here keeps a handgun."

"Maybe they should head to a safehouse." He nodded out through the orchard. "Closest one's forty-five minutes' walk that way."

"Yeah, good idea. We can join them later. I don't think Settlers Downs is going to be secure for a while." They'd had such a good thing going, a tough life, but a good one. A working community. He shook it off. "Whoever goes with you, you're the boss. Make sure you locate both hostiles before committing to action. When you do, you put them down. No mercy."

"Don't have to convince me of that."

"Me either," Spider said.

He pointed to Claire and Chariya and Di. "Then you take whatever supplies you can to these guys and wait for me there. For *us* there."

"For how long?"

"Judgment call. All yours. If you're worried, there's always Barnabas island."

Sturgis looked unhappy about that.

"Here's my ride, finally," Elliot said and shouldered his rifle. Mafia had just pulled up along the centerline. Elliot passed through the fence and across the verge toward the waiting truck, patting the spare mags in his vest's pockets. He had an armored truck with more horsepower than that removals truck or Angie's hatchback. He had a rifle and a sidearm again. He would catch up, he would deal with it, he would—

"Oy!" Mafia shouted out the window. He'd wound it down about four inches, had his lips pressed to the gap. "You were gonna shoot me."

Elliot froze.

"Weren't ya?" Mafia insisted.

Elliot took another step. "You nearly shot one of my people. It was a reflex."

"I was helping you."

Another step. Elliot steadied the swinging rifle against his side, and raised his other hand placatingly. But his danger sense was alive and alert; he dearly wanted both hands filled reassuringly with a weapon.

"C'mon, man. We're on the same side. Let's talk it over on the w—"

"You have no honor!" Mafia snarled. With that, he dropped the clutch and took off, tires squealing. He hooted a laugh out the window.

Elliot swung the rifle from his shoulder, aimed, fired at the departing vehicle. It was useless against the protected tires. It had wasted ammunition. His people by the crashed vehicle instinctively ducked for cover, even though he wasn't shooting near them. He roared at the sky in frustration, stormed back to the others, locking eyes with Spider.

The skinny Vike was also crouched, his eyes wide. He put down his .40 cal and raised his hands. "Not on me, man. Not on me." He looked from Elliot to Sturgis and back.

"What the hell was that?" Elliot shouted. "What the *hell* was *that?*"

"Please, man." Spider was genuinely scared now. He shuffled awkwardly back on his haunches to keep his distance as Elliot came to a stop at the fence. "It's on him, not me."

"Get him back!" Elliot snarled.

"What? How?"

Now that was a damn good question. Off to the side, the prisoner snickered at it. Elliot turned the rifle his way—the man bit off his laughter.

Elliot relaxed the rifle and told Spider, "That shit-stained prick took my truck."

"I—I'm sorry, man. But it was him, not me."

"You're the same people."

"We're not. I told you we're not." Spider swallowed. "We're just a bunch of losers who tried to come up with some kinda society that would work for us, you know? Vikings had rules and they had honor. He, Mafia, he feels like … well, whatever. Honor, yeah. But we're all messed-up individuals really, and he makes his own choices. And you know about my girlfriend—"

Elliot took two steps closer and Spider quit babbling. Sturgis was standing now, his weapon pointed at the ground near Spider's feet. Elliot said, "If Mafia meets up with Angie out there? Tell me he's gonna be polite. Convince me."

"He won't hurt her, promise. Look, Mafia was a founder. He and I always disagree on shit—like that guy Bourbon does—and I got voted into a decision-making position which pissed Mafia off. That's why he left me here. He's got a beef with me and with you. But he's got no beef with Angie. He didn't shoot *you,* after all. Just nicked your truck."

That much was true.

Elliot took some deep breaths to calm himself, but it didn't help much. The only working vehicles he knew of were back at The Downs. "I'm coming with you," he told Sturgis.

Sturgis said, "That's what I thought. How much time do we have? If, you know, that truck gets back to *their* home without Angie catching it."

"Six hours, maybe. Ten. Damn, we have to move."

"Another question: is he still coming?"

Spider started to rise, but Sturgis warned him off it by pointing the MCX at his leg.

"Fellas," Spider said, settling. "Let's think this through. I saw a truck taking your people away to be slaves. Three years ago, the Death Druids took my brother and his wife. I don't want that happening to my girlfriend. My baby. I have a baby," he told the others. "Plus, one of my so-called friends just took off and left me here. That means, I got two things to live for. Helping you kill some of these slaver-pigs, and getting back to *my* home so I can punch Mafia in the face. Let me help you and we all get what we want."

"His buddy did just dump him here," Sturgis said.

"Which means he's part of a lawless group of screw-ups and ex-criminals with swiss cheese for brains."

Elliot stooped and picked up the .40 cal that Spider had dropped.

"Deal's off," he told him. "Leave the .22 and the vest. Start walking home. And when you see Mafia, you give him a second punch in the face from me."

PART FIVE

I'VE NEVER BEEN A
FAN OF LONG HIKES

22

I t was a long walk through bushland before the three men made it to the back of the farm. Rit and Sturgis entered first, pushing their ballistic vests ahead of them through the "back door", a disguised tunnel beneath the wire. On the way through the tight space, Elliot scraped his taser wounds hard on the packed earth, hissing in pain. Two dogs—Fido and Wilma—met them with hackles up until they heard Elliot's voice.

"No talking," he reminded the men as he gave each dog a cursory once over. They seemed uninjured.

"Got nothing to say," Rit murmured and got his vest back on. Then he refitted his black baseball cap, turning it sideways against the sun.

It was indeed the first time Rit had spoken since his rescue from the BearCat; Sturgis had told Elliot quietly that two of the Settlers had resisted the SERPs and paid the ultimate price. One of those had been Kim, Rit's brother-in-law. Kim had been a good man— a damn good man.

And they could remember him later. Along with the other dead. When this was done.

Elliot made the dogs stay; Fido took more convincing, being younger. He had checked Sturgis's watch the other side of the fence: a little before 14:30. It had threatened rain during the hike, but the clouds had blown over, leaving the sky a vivid spring blue. The air smelled of wet grass, fertilizer and faintly, the ocean. The clean air, the spring colors and scents, they made it feel like a good day; it should have been a good day. And it wasn't. He was aware of the whisper of wind on grass, the tread of his colleague's shoes as they started after him, bleated inquiries from the sheep paddock two hundred metres right, some noise from the twenty-odd cattle venturing closer in hopes of food. Elliot hoped the stupid creatures would keep out of their way for the final fifty metres to the next fence and gate. More concerning was the *lack* of noise coming from north of their position, the area where he kept his camp and the dog pens. He didn't want to think about what that silence might mean, what the SERPs might have done to his animals.

Sturgis and Rit, stacked behind Elliot as instructed, followed his hand signals and quiet commands, sweeping their piece of the pie as they followed him along fence lines and buildings, helped him clear the Community Centre in middle of the property. The men proved efficient and steady. Sturgis spoke only once, as they moved past the infirmary, asking should they check it? Elliot shook his head no. They would come back there.

Disciplined, focused, the men moved on with him until eventually they reached the back of the giant open-aired tin-roofed sheep shed that stared out into the Yard where the first Battle for The Downs had taken place.

And here comes another battle, he thought sourly.

Using hand signals, he directed Rit to head along the back of the building. He murmured one word: "Garage." Rit moved off without comment. From the garage, Rit would have better cover than he and Sturgis, along with a wider angle on the Yard; with zero combat training, Rit would need it.

Very slowly Elliot opened the door to the back of the sheep shed, wincing as it creaked a little. Crouch-walking, he followed a service sidewalk around the inner left-hand wall with Sturgis at his back, their rifles trained on the Yard beyond. The cement floor reeked of decades of urine. They stopped at the front corner of the building, crouching low at the steel railings.

Some of the community's vehicles—a tractor, Ford pickup, two quad-bikes and a diesel-minibus—were still parked over by the homestead. The SERPs had parked four other cars side by side, twenty metres out from Elliot's position, and at a right angle to the holding pens: two Land Rovers, the Ute with the plow-catcher, the Audi SUV. The vehicles' tailgates lay open and facing into the barn entryway.

"Bastards," Sturgis murmured, leaning around Elliot. "*Bastards.*"

The two cops stood in the midst of the cars at the barn, sharing a smoke and a bottle, chatting relaxedly. One voice definitely belonged to Kyle. An inch or so of each man's hair was visible above the large vehicles' roofs; if they had brought along helmets and MOPP masks, the pair had taken them off while working.

One of their rifles was visible lying across the Ute's hood, further testament to their confidence. The cars appeared near-to-full with resources. Downs' resources. Elliot wondered if even their cigarette was one of those he'd given to Shaz the other day.

He'd told the others that he'd prefer to take Kyle alive, for various reasons. But unless Kyle or his buddy were lying prone, unarmed and begging loudly for mercy, the instruction was to shoot them dead and be done with it. No more chances.

With Sturgis covering him, Elliot slid beneath the railing and onto the dirt and gravel of the Yard, keeping his taser wounds from scraping on the ground. From there, he crawled on knees and elbows left toward the corner where barn met sheep sheds, rifle across the crooks of his elbows. Sure as shit, it was a risk being out in the open—and felt like it. But the sheep run rails offered almost zero cover, whereas stacks of tires lined much of the barn, covered with tarps that rippled and snapped in the light breeze. From that position of relative cover, he would have a clean line of sight between cars and barn door when the men returned to work. There would be a two- or three-second window. Plenty of time. As long as they both stepped into the open together. If they didn't—or if one of them made it inside the barn—there was always the smaller doorway at this end of the structure Elliot could use to follow him.

Snatches of conversation drifted his way, as carefree as his movements were careful. The subject matter was mundane, the pair trading sports anecdotes the way the two Daves might have. Shooting the breeze after shooting Kim and Dylan.

They were still at it when he reached his new position and got his left shoulder and body in cover of the tires. Rifle pointed securely down the fire lane past the door, he selected full-auto, and glanced right. He could see Sturgis' weapon poking from under the rails; the man was prone, too. Rit was not visible but should have been in position now.

"Should be easy," he whispered to himself, mindful of many things that could go wrong. "Please be easy."

He thought about flushing them out by firing on the vehicles, but that would likely drive them to ground. Occasionally he'd catch sight of a boot or two beneath the cars, never long enough to safely take down both men. He might have used Rit's or Sturgis's flashbangs, except he'd have to get in much closer to toss them: the damn things only had three-second fuses. He considered himself a proficient shooter, but not enough to have tried headshots through the windows of packed vehicles.

Patience. You've come this far. Do it careful and do it right.

The enemy were out in the open. His team were relatively sheltered with overlapping fields of fire. They had this.

Footsteps!

He braced. One of the men was headed for the barn—he could see the boots moving.

But the other man wasn't.

Not easy, then.

The first SERP—not Kyle!—stepped out of cover, wisecracking over his shoulder. Elliot had no choice but to fire on him before losing him inside the barn. Mindful of the enemy's ballistic vest, he fired at knee level. The contact's legs buckled under him. Elliot added a few more rounds as the man hit the ground. Blood spattered up into the air along with chunks of dirt and what Elliot hoped was brain and skull.

And then another plan went to hell.

Gruff cursing came from behind the cars. Feet moved, but quickly disappeared behind wheels. He kept the rifle trained that way, half his attention on the downed man. If Kyle came back this way, Elliot might hit him, and if he ran for the homestead or gate, Sturgis and Rit were awaiting him.

Instead of either of those happening as he expected, a car door creaked open. The Audi.

"Great."

Movement right: Rit breaking cover, fast-walking across the Yard with his weapon up. He fired a three-round burst. Clumsy grip: the recoil pushed his muzzle up so the rounds missed the car and punched through the barn's tin siding. "Damn." He adjusted his hold, rifle stock firmly against his shoulder.

Elliot got up into a crouch.

The engine turned over, then started. Rit fired a second burst, then a third. The car revved, wheels crunching on gravel as it started off. Sturgis fired a single round from the sheep sheds. Rit fired a fourth burst, then lowered his weapon as the car fishtailed around in a long and shallow U, coming to rest with its driver's side toward the smokehouse near the gate.

Sturgis was sliding out from the sheep run. Rit kept on walking but his rifle drooped groundward.

Elliot shouted, "Weapon up!" and kept his own rifle trained on the man fallen by the barn, advancing on him and shifting his selector to single fire.

Shots came from the car by the smokehouse, a pistol. Rit and Sturgis hit the dirt, fast. *Wounded?* Elliot wondered. Rit got his weapon up and fired another burst, the weapon bobbing in his hands. He got it firmer against his shoulder and fired another. The rounds made tinking sounds as they punched through the smokehouse walls and kicked up debris from the production line set up outside it.

Sturgis was belly-crawling hurriedly into the cover of a Rover, rifle scraping along beside him.

A shadow bolted between stalled car and smoke-house door. Elliot squeezed off a round, missed. The smokehouse door slammed closed.

"Shit," he and Rit said in unison.

Sturgis peeked over the front of the Rover. "He got inside?"

Elliot reached the other end of the same Rover. The hostile he'd shot was one hundred percent dead. One down and one sheltering in a wooden building with one door and no windows. "Cover that door," he told them. He bent and slipped the flashbang off the dead man's vest, then checked inside the back of the Rover. Grunting in satisfaction at what he'd seen, he clipped the grenade to his belt and told Sturgis to toss him his flashbang, too. Once that was also on his belt, he swung the rifle to his back and reached into the

Rover's cargo area for two of the four-litre jugs of kerosene in there.

"Watch that door," he repeated and marched across the open Yard to Kyle's stalled car. He crouched and put the kerosene jugs beside him in the lee of a wheel.

There'd been no activity from the smokehouse: Kyle could be wounded, dead, radioing for help, thinking up options. Elliot had one of the SERP's knives from Jericho. He used it to punch a hole in the lid of each jug, then tossed one underhand to land at the end of the building furthest from the door. Clear fluid began to spill against the wooden wall and across the concrete foundation-slab beneath it.

"Come on out, Kyle," he called.

Silence.

Was the man dead? Looking for another way out?

Then Kyle called back. "You're a dogged sonofa-bitch, Elliot. I knew we had someone special with you. Sure you don't want to join us? " He was in the middle of the building, no doubt crouched like Elliot behind something to protect against gunfire.

"Join you? I'm not the one holed up in a wooden building with no way out." He took a flashbang from his belt.

"That's true. But you're the one without a prayer of getting his friends back unless he plays by our rules."

"Not so sure about that," Elliot said and pulled the pin on the grenade.

Where it landed, he didn't see. He was hunkered down with his fingers in his ears, his eyes closed and his mouth open to protect against the pressure wave as the grenade detonated. He peeked over to see flames spreading through spilled kerosene before the bottle itself exploded against the wall.

"All *right*," Sturgis exclaimed. He hadn't changed position. Rit had shifted across the Yard toward the homestead, perhaps for a different angle.

Within the smokehouse, something metallic banged—Kyle wrestling with a fire extinguisher. There'd be no flames inside yet, but the smoke must have been showing.

"You can do that," Elliot called. "But there's only two extinguishers in there. And your MOPP hood's out here. We'll keep adding more fuel until you're overcome."

"If it's the waiting game you want to play, Elliot, you do that." Kyle had changed position inside, but Elliot wasn't sure enough of it to waste bullets. Besides, he didn't need to.

"Waiting game, huh?" he called.

"Let's see what happens first. You smoking me out. Or my guys coming back here."

"If you had guys coming back here, you wouldn't tell me."

Another series of heavy clunks from within. Kyle might have been trying to batter palings from the opposite wall; he'd find the building too sturdily built for that. And then two gunshots. Kyle still had his handgun. No fresh holes appeared Elliot's side of the building so no doubt the SERP was punching breathing holes elsewhere.

"How's the air in there?" he taunted.

The next two shots did come through his side, then. One was low, kicking up dirt to the side of the Audi. The other shattered one of its side windows.

Elliot pulled his head down, cursing quietly. He could spray bullets in return, but he wanted those rounds. He reached for the second kerosene jug, stuck a couple more holes in it and tossed it onto the roof, following it immediately with the second flashbang. Moments later, flames spread and crackled across the wooden slatted ceiling.

And finally Kyle had had enough. "Coming out! Coming out, Elliot! Chucking my weapon first."

The door opened. A handgun landed on the dirt beyond the fire. Kyle came out in a fast walk with hands raised. Elliot fully expected one of the others to fire on him. They didn't. He didn't.

First, he made Kyle kneel and put his hands behind his head.

And then he came forward with his own handgun holstered and his rifle slung.

And he used his fist to break Kyle's nose.

Two other bodies lay on the ground: Kim and Dylan had been shoved over by a rectangle of straight fence poles. It was an area of the Yard where farmers had once piled dead stock for later disposal. The dark irony didn't escape Elliot and he gave the handcuffed Kyle an extra kick in the back as he stowed him in the back of a Land Rover.

Sturgis had told him that when the SERPs gained access to the Yard claiming to represent the new government—after they'd gathered everyone into the turning circle on the pretense of inoculating them, and after they'd then revealed their true intent—Kim and Dylan had tried wrestling a rifle from one of them. The two men had paid the ultimate price for it.

Kim.

Dylan.

A brave father and a young man Elliot had never thought of as brave before today.

He felt someone at his shoulder as he slammed the door and avoided looking at the bleeding SERP inside in case he killed him.

"I can't go over there," Rit said. "I know I should. That's my brother-in-law lying where this bastard tossed him like … like a sack of garbage. But I can't go look."

Inside the cargo space of the Rover, Kyle shifted, trying to get comfortable. Elliot resisted the urge to put a round through his head. Not yet.

"You don't need to," Sturgis said from nearby. "If we had time, Elliot and I would bury them, properly. But we don't have time and they'd understand that."

"Yeah," Rit sighed. "They would."

Sturgis turned to Elliot. "I'll go check the sick."

"We both will." He turned to Rit first. "There's empty water bottles in the barn. Fill as many as you can and strap them on top." He patted the Land Rover that Kyle was bound and gagged inside.

To himself he said, *Get these guys moving, get the dogs, get them all to a safehouse, then get after Angie.* A hell of a lot of time had passed since she'd gone. A hell of a lot. But he had to try.

Rit adjusted his baseball cap. He hadn't moved an inch toward the barn. "Elliot, I told you before we came here. I got other things on my mind. My kids and Kim's kids are out there. I helped you. I have cars available. I want to go find them."

Rit and Sturgis had explained that the kids—being quarantined on the far northern boundary of the property—had escaped initial detection by the invaders. And by the time the SERPs had gone looking, Krystal had led them all out another bolt hole, heading for one of the other safe houses they'd established. Meanwhile, Lewis had stayed in their hut in case he was needed to stall and delay the SERPs. Which was exactly what he'd done. While the kids got away, Lewis was taken to the truck.

You heroic little bastard.

The SERPs had arrived a little after nine a.m., Krystal taking the kids soon after that. Elliot imagined a bunch of children traipsing over hills and through native forest between Settlers Downs and the closest safehouse that side of the property. They'd had enough time to make it there if they navigated correctly. Of course, there were other dangers out there besides SERPs.

"Elliot," Rit said, insistent.

Shit.

If Rit went, if Rit took off on his own, that only left Sturgis to manage one vehicle for the three women, plus watch those two prisoners. Sturgis would need Elliot's help. And Elliot wanted to chase after Angie. That was selfish. There were people *here* who needed resettling before he headed out on another wild goose chase. What was it Angie had said in the truck before they met the Vikes? *I can live with a lot of things on my conscience, Elliot, but not with knowing I got good people killed.*

"Wait a second," he said to Rit and bent to pick two walkies from the pile of equipment he'd stripped from both SERPs. He selected a frequency and passed one to Rit, pointed his one at the minibus across the Yard. "Take that. You find them, you don't find them, you buzz me. Don't mention specific locations, but use references I'd know. We'll find each other."

Rit nodded his thanks and started toward the garage. "Tell Chariya where I'm going."

He hooked the walkie onto his waistband. "Of course, pal. Godspeed."

With Kyle securely trussed up in back of the Rover, he handed Sturgis a MOPP hood and followed him back through the sheep shed toward the Infirmary. For protection against infection, they put on the hoods as they reached the three front steps.

The door was wide open; he hadn't noticed that when they'd first passed by.

It meant he saw what he saw before he reached the top step and moved inside.

And he'd half-expected it.

But it took his breath away, all the same.

Back in Al-Kasrah, when the relief had finally arrived, they'd brought medics. Too late for the boy who'd lost his arm; Elliot hadn't been able to keep him alive long enough. Doing penance, Elliot had helped bag pieces of his team before finally allowing the medics to take him away. As he'd left the town, the local survivors had been arranging their own bodies in lines. The boy's had been closest to the market entrance.

Rows of bodies.

The Settlers Downs Infirmary held twelve beds, six either side of a walkway down the middle.

Rows of bodies.

The closest bed to the door held a boy.

Elliot smelled copper and smoke. Smelled the phantom rot of deaders. Felt the heat coming off the bright lights above Jericho's Night Court. Watched dusty Syrian air creating a haze in the gloom of an Australian late-afternoon. Saw two boys in the bed near the door, one superimposed upon another, one with one arm, one with both.

He blinked it away, only to see a hospital tent, hastily erected in Libya this time, dead and living bodies of soldiers filling the cots. The ghosts of medics and nurses rushed between them. He stepped aside to let one leave as she raced out for a fresh IV, then realized that she wasn't there. Neither was he. He was here. He was now.

Sturgis was outside on the steps, puking beside his discarded MOPP hood.

Elliot's pulse raced. His ears rang with tinnitus. He tasted stomach acid, glad he hadn't eaten for a long time, nothing to puke. He was going to get through this. He made himself focus on each of the ten people in the Infirmary, murdered by gunfire. He said their names in his head, remembering them.

Macca. Farmer.

Piers. Gardener.

Raj. Di's husband.

Tony. Little Ben's father.

Garry. Tony's friend who'd saved father and son in the early days of the Collapse.

Ilse. Sturgis's sister-in-law.

Little—

He had to stop a moment. Had to swallow hard on the emotion rising like reflux and force himself to keep on.

Little Abby. Three years old. Sturgis's niece. Ilse's daughter.

Ben. A six-year-old boy. Tony's son. *Goddamnit.*

He hurried on, eyes ranging up the rows, feet anchored by the door.

Jen. Cook. Seamstress. She'd had a crush on Elliot. She'd made him a sweater. And Elliot had never given her so much as a smile.

Faye. Nurse. Claire's mentor and friend. Elliot's friend.

Elliot's *friends.*

Elliot's *family.*

He pulled the door closed, tossed the SERP MOPP hood into Sturgis's pile of puke. Sturgis was still bent double, ribs heaving. The vomit was all Elliot could smell now. The tinnitus was fading.

He put a hand to the back of Sturgis's neck and squeezed gently. "More to do, buddy."

Sturgis got out the word, "Yeah" before heaving again.

When he was done, Elliot said simply, "I'll meet you by the rain tanks. If we're gonna hide at a safehouse, we'll need water."

Sturgis straightened a little, wiping at his face. "Okay. Right. Okay." He didn't move any further, though, his breath coming hard.

Elliot said. "Just meet me there when you're ready."

"Okay."

"Okay," said Elliot with a last glance at the Infirmary door. Then he set off in a run. The water was important, but first he needed to go for his dogs.

Fido and Wilma followed him eagerly, healthy, alive, and anxious.

The dogs in the pens were all dead.

Sturgis was filling one of two ten-litre water bottles at the rainwater tanks when he got back. The navy man's face was pale, eyes red-rimmed and puffy. He maneuvered the second water bottle under another water tank spigot and said, "Holy shit, Elliot. They shot them all. Women, kids …"

Elliot signaled the dogs to sit and keep watch. He said nothing, wondering if Sturgis had been over to take it out on Kyle.

Well, if he had, if he'd killed Kyle early, then so be it.

Sturgis opened the spigot, locked it in place and straightened as the bottle started filling. Then he punched the plastic wall of the tank. "They *shot* them! Abby and Ben—they were just children. They shot *children*."

"I know, bud, I know." Children shot and blown apart and torn apart: of all the twisted shit he had seen in his life—and he'd seen plenty—they were always the worst. Always.

Sturgis ground the heel of a hand into one eye. "I started to ask myself, how can people do that? These people were cops. And then I remembered. I was just as bad."

"No, man. I've told you before—"

"I've tried to tell *you* before. This time you'll let me finish, damn it. I stood on that dock beside Meg when you came to us for help three years ago. You and a boy and an old man. And we turned you away. I know you've forgiven that—"

"You've made up for it, Sturgis."

"—but I'll never forgive myself. And I never ... I mean I've been scared. But I haven't felt like this, like you guys must've felt. My little son's out there in the bush with only a teenager looking after him. My wife's on that truck. And I can't..." He put both hands to his mouth as if he'd puke again.

Elliot flashed to a landing field in Turkey, Radler with hands cupped to *his* mouth, facing a nearby group of Marines and serenading them with his rendition of *Anything you can do* while Mac and Eames attempted the worst harmonies in history.

He said to Sturgis, "Whatever the rest of that sentence is, it's not true. You *can* do it. We can. We will get 'em back."

Hooah, said McGovern's ghost.

Elliot shut off the first spigot, screwed the cap back on the bottle. Sturgis could take care of the second when it was full; it would keep him busy. Elliot reached out and grabbed his wrist, tightening his grip until Sturgis gasped and pulled free. "Do not do this to yourself."

"You don't think I should feel like shit?" Sturgis demanded.

Elliot had beaten himself up a lot over the years. A lot. This week was teaching him that sometimes it didn't matter how well you trained or planned or armed yourself. It didn't matter whether your head was on a swivel or stuck in the sand. Didn't matter what decision you made. Didn't matter how much you concentrated. Shit was *going* to happen.

"Are any of the rest of you sick?" he asked. "The people in that removals truck? No? That figures. See, I could now say that everything we did was for nothing. No one else got sick and we put everybody in harm's way trying to get meds we didn't need."

"We do need—"

"Not my point. My point is the time for guilt is over. We did our best." He told this to Sturgis and he told it to himself. "Now keep on doing it, man."

"We *will* get 'em back," Sturgis said through gritted teeth.

And Elliot said, "Hooah."

He lifted the full bottle onto one shoulder, pushed himself upright, and headed for the car, wondering just how in hell they were going to do that.

They had been a community drawn together by fate and by the good in all of them, if one was to believe Claire's spiritualist horse twang. They had worked hard to forge a good thing here. And now they were dispersed to the winds, fragmented into small groups in varying degrees of danger. Krystal and the children in one direction. Rit out looking for them. Three women now heading to their own safehouse with a dangerous prisoner in tow. A dozen decent people murdered at Settlers Downs. Seventeen more crammed like cattle into a freight truck, including a young man who'd put his own life ahead of a group of children.

And a woman pursuing that truck in a clapped-out Mazda.

"Godspeed, all of you," he said. But the only face really in Elliot's mind was Angie's.

Elliot and Sturgis each drove a Land Rover back toward the ambush site. Near that site there lay a side road that would take them to Claire's safehouse.

Beside Elliot, Fido occasionally whined, reassured by a brief rub of his ears and neck. With little room in the back of the cars—and with Kyle stuffed in the back of Sturgis's, Elliot had split the two dogs between them.

They were two kilometres out when a dark shape appeared on the road ahead, slowly cresting a hill. Bourbon? Or Da Silva and Erikson?

Elliot jammed on the brakes, angling his nose toward the Centre line. Reading him well, Sturgis came around him and did the same, the two vehicles forming an arrowhead. Even a BearCat's driver would have to be deranged to ram through two 4WDs at high speed.

They got out and up the bank into safer firing positions before Elliot saw the vehicle was not a BearCat. He swore.

"Is that…?" Sturgis started.

The removals truck approached, grinding down through its gears to help it slow down. The dogs began barking from the Rovers. Elliot unsafetied the rifle.

His frown deepened. Bullet marks starred the truck's windshield; they hadn't been there earlier. It pulled up ten metres out from the Rovers, the driver door opened and a woman's voice called, "Hold your fire."

Oh, thank Christ.

His rifle drooped as a blond head appeared.

Angie.

As she climbed down, a second welcome surprise came when another face appeared in the doorway above her.

Lewis.

"Thank God," said Sturgis and slid down the short embankment. He sprinted toward the truck, obviously hopeful his wife was in the back.

Angie stayed at the nose of her vehicle with a wary expression, waiting while Elliot double-timed it toward her.

Without so much as glancing Elliot's way, Lewis joined Sturgis to help open the back of the truck.

Angie said, "Listen, I know I shouldn't have taken off like—"

Elliot reached her, pulled her tight against him and pressed his lips against hers. A second later, her hands clutched at his shirt. Her lips responded hungrily.

A swell of tired cheers came from the people pooling out back of the truck. "About bloody time," someone called.

Angie broke contact first, pulling away enough to smile tentatively at him and brush her hair back behind her ears.

"You got them back," he said.

"I did."

"You gonna tell me how?"

She glanced back at the truck, expression darkening again. "Maybe."

And then a further surprise for Elliot. The truck's passenger door opened and a third person dropped to the road. A skinny guy with a bad haircut appeared around the truck with a sheepish grin. "D'ja miss me?" Spider said.

Elliot drew breath to curse him out until Angie pushed all her fingers against his lips. "Not now," she said.

"I was hitchhiking," Spider called, "and she was kind enough to give me a lift."

Angie's fingers pressed harder. Murmuring so Spider wouldn't hear, she said, "Let's give him another chance."

Elliot grunted and rolled his eyes. Satisfied he wouldn't argue, Angie removed her hand and pecked him on the cheek. "Good boy."

Many of the released Settlers came nearer now, closing around him and Angie, squeezing their shoulders, kissing their cheeks. Instead of moving on, the Settlers stayed, the pack thickening. Farmer Nancy called out, "Group hug!"

Elliot and Angie found themselves pressed in the middle of a scrum of laughing, crying people. The melee tightened to the point that Angie gasped up at him and he had to fight for his next breath.

Then one of the Daves said, "Geez, we all need to get a room."

The scrum broke up with more laughs, forming into smaller groups, embracing, comforting, reassuring.

Elliot leaned into Angie once more.

With her warm and soft against him, with the smell of her hair, the taste of her lips, and the clamor of celebrating friends around them, Elliot saw a Hollywood happy ending that could never happen in this world.

He separated from her and saw in her eyes that she knew it, too.

He pointed to the cab of the truck. "It'd be so good to carry you in there right now and—"

"I know, but—"

"We better—"

"Yeah."

They turned to stand side by side.

"People!" Angie called and Elliot added, "We got things to do!"

23

The majority of the surviving Downs' residents gathered into a rough circle in the middle of the highway. Many stood. Some—like Claire, brought back from the safehouse minutes earlier—sat on the cold asphalt. Side conversations were few and they were muted. A few had Downs weapons that the SERPs had piled into one of the Rovers; Sturgis had distributed those earlier. The two dogs moved from person to person, soliciting belly rubs and back scratches.

The sun nuzzled the trees; despite a clear sky, night would fall quickly.

And still so much to do, Elliot thought.

Some were already working. West along the highway in a new blind spot, Spider, Lewis and the Daves were making another barbed-wire trap in case Da Silva sent another truck.

He scanned the circle: young people, old people, those in between. Many men and women had tears on their cheeks, but all seemed steady. They were tough, these people. Tougher than he'd thought.

Her hands locked with those of her bereaved sister, Chariya nodded readiness to him. Her husband Rit had radioed Elliot that he'd found the eight kids alive and well, though distraught. Elliot had told him to sit tight at the second safehouse until he called them in.

Di had just found out her sick husband had been murdered. But she was functioning; Elliot could hear her murmured conversation with Nance about making soup to feed the troops.

Heng shuffled on the spot, hands in pockets, eyes on the ground. He had a black eye, but seemed otherwise unharmed. At least, physically.

Claire slumped on the tarmac, sleepy from the painkillers they'd given her.

Sturgis stood stiff and angry to Elliot's left; Tina's arm was wound tight around her husband's. Their boy would be returned to them soon.

Angie sat cross-legged to Elliot's right; Alyssa sat next person over with her head on Angie's shoulder.

The two captured SERPs stood fifty metres down the road, cuffed to the roof rack of one of the Land Rovers. Neither looked too cocky now.

"With permission, Claire?" Elliot said.

She gave him a sad smile and gestured for him to take the floor.

"You all know what the bastards did to our sick people? To little kids."

Nods from the crowd. Grunts. Some people's expressions softened, others hardened. A few of them sniffed and wiped at eyes. There were no sobs. No comments.

"So, we all know what we're dealing with. First question I have for you all is: where do you want to go? Not many choices. There's home, of course, Settlers

Downs. There's our safehouses. We can try finding somewhere new up in the hills around St Mary's. Or we can ask for help from Nine Mile River or from Barnabas Island."

"They won't help," said Shaz. Abducted by bikers three years ago and now by cops, she looked less traumatized than murderous. Something fierce glowed in her eyes.

"Damn straight," Heng mumbled, still staring at the road. "No friend there."

Beside him, Sturgis cursed quietly under his breath.

"St. Mary's?" Elliot continued. "Plenty of mountain hideouts around there. Tough terrain for us to enter, but tougher for anyone trying to sneak up on us once we've dug in."

No one spoke for a moment, then Angie cleared her throat. "Which means that anyone who already went up there three years ago has had three years to dig in and ambush *us*."

Elliot nodded approvingly. Exactly what he'd been thinking. It was good to know that Angie at least was on the same page. "So anywhere we go, we risk people thinking we're coming for them and blowing our heads off."

"What do *you* want to do, Elliot?" asked Neil, the former accountant.

"Yeah," Shaz agreed. "Your call."

Elliot exchanged a glance with Angie. Why would they look to him? He'd left with three people, come back with one. Why would they trust him? Angie's stare was unrelenting, reminding him of their talk on the drive back. *Your role is to lead*, she'd said. *Your role is to get the rest of us to help you fix this.*

"All right then. A few of you will be joining the children at their safehouse. The rest of us ... the rest of us will be defending our home."

A murmur of approval passed quickly around the circle. There was no dissent.

"Whatever you need us to do, mate." This was from Mike the Builder, a guy Elliot couldn't remember ever actually speaking to before.

"You say that, you better mean it," Elliot told him.

"I mean it."

"Me, too," said a few others simultaneously.

Over Mike's shoulder, Elliot could see the booby trap builders jogging back. Lewis was a little ahead of the others. The young guy had gotten fitter over the last few years. He'd also not had to harm anyone; Elliot wondered if he could work it so things could stay that way.

Probably not, he told himself. *Innocence is a luxury. And this is not an age for luxuries.*

"Twelve dead," said Di. It sounded more incredulous than aggrieved. "My poor Raj."

"But twenty-five adults and eight kids alive and well," Elliot said as gently as he could.

Di nodded.

"Twelve dead," Sturgis whispered.

"Sturgis." Elliot's tone turned stern. Besides Angie, Sturgis was the best asset Elliot had. He needed this man and he needed him to channel his anxiety and anger in a productive way.

"Will they come back?" Neil asked. "Those bad cops. How many more of them are there?"

"That, I don't know exactly. There's at least ten of them left. They also have … I guess you'd call them collaborators. People on their side." Like the aging farmers who'd once tried to hand Elliot, Angie, Heng and Lewis to the Druids. There was always someone willing to sell their soul for their relative safety.

Elliot pointed to the setting sun. "Time to move. For tonight at least, Chariya, Huy, Shaz, Tania and Claire: you're going to relieve Rit and look after the kids. The rest of you, if we're defending our home, we have things to do."

"We need a ceremony for the dead," Claire murmured suddenly, rubbing at sleepy eyes with her good hand. "We need to name them."

"We will," said Di and reached down to touch her hair gently.

"We definitely will," Angie added.

Elliot said, "But later. For now, we're heading home to fortify it. Hate to say it, folks, but I need most of you back in that truck."

The group broke up. Angie stood and pecked him on the cheek.

"What's that for?" he asked.

She smiled tiredly. "Good luck." She headed for the truck, intending to drive it. He watched her jeans move and thought how undeservedly lucky he already was.

Walking beside Angie, Alyssa glanced over her shoulder and gave Elliot a thumbs-up. Elliot returned it with a wink.

"Are you okay in that truck, honey?" Sturgis told his wife. "I could move crap out of the Rover for you."

"I'm fine." She hugged him briefly, kissed him and followed the crowd.

When she was out of earshot, Sturgis looked back toward the two captive SERPs. He asked, "Did you mean what you told me?"

"About the Jericho slaves?"

"Yes."

"Yes. Once our people are secure."

"We'll need help."

"Who's gonna help us?"

"Spider's guys, maybe. Barnabas. Nine Mile. They all have reason to."

"They might not see it that way."

"We have to ask. None of us can let the SERPs get any stronger. You said you saw 'collaborators'? That means Kyle's crew are recruiting and not just enslaving. That goes on too long, they'll grow too big for us to take down. They're probably already too big. For just the few of us."

"Maybe yes, maybe no." Elliot found himself yawning. "Let's talk about it tomorrow."

"All right," Sturgis said. "And our friends there?"

Elliot followed his gaze back to the captives. Driscoll had both arms on the car, leaning his head against them. Kyle was standing straight, his face swollen around the broken nose. He returned Elliot's stare without expression. "Our friend Driscoll will answer some questions tonight."

"Not Kyle?"

"Kyle won't talk. He'll pride himself on it."

"So …"

"I'll take care of it. Tomorrow."

Sturgis spat to the side. "Tomorrow then. And I get to be there."

"Fine." He scratched his chin a moment, then said. "I got another reason we should pay the Vikes a visit when we get the chance."

"What's that?"

"I want my fucking BearCat back."

They could get it, he thought, while they were there picking up Spider's family.

Elliot turned back to watch his people climbing aboard the removals truck. Lewis was there, waiting patiently at the back. After a moment, he noticed Elliot's scrutiny. Like Kyle, he regarded Elliot without expression. And then, just before he climbed into the back of the truck, he gave Elliot a nod.

It wasn't much.

And it was everything.

24

The Ute's dash clock read 09:16 as Elliot parked along the country road's centerline. He cranked on the handbrake and put his head against the rest for a moment. He'd caught two long naps overnight, taking turns with Angie, while the other directed sentry arrangements and the finetuning of spike traps along the property's boundary. Settlers Downs's defenses had been developed when there was a threat of biker attack. They'd become a little neglected over the years since that threat faded away. Out in the cold night air, his people had made amends for that lapse in caution and care, laboring to repair old traps and create new ones. Bundled up in layers of sweaters, people had taken turns watching the coastal road. None complained. They were hardening up. Again. And this was very good.

He reached for his MCX. Angie's eyes were on him. "What is it?" he asked.

"Just thinking."

"About what I'm about to do?"

"About how stupid human beings are. All of us."

"That's been a given for a while now."

"Look at us. The Settlers, the Nine Mile River group, the Barnabas Islanders, the scav-rats, the Vikes." She hooked a thumb at the cargo pod on the back of the Ute. "The SERPs. We all survived the end. I mean the *end*. Civilization got trampled underfoot by the undead. Power grids broke down. Water stopped pumping. The outlaw gangs who were ready to take over everything, they eventually disappeared, too. And there's us left. Normal people." She checked the side mirror outside her window, maybe looking at Spider climbing out of Rit's Rover behind them. "Mostly normal. We made it. But we're fighting. Instead of helping each other, we're screwing each other over. I mean, literally fighting for *no reason*. The only things left in this world are actually an abundance, more than enough to sustain us all, but we're fighting as if … I don't know. These dirtbags want slaves, but if we worked together we'd get it all done anyway. Probably better. Maybe it's humans who are the monsters."

She blew hot breath on the glass, drew a face in the condensation with angry eyes and a wide O for a mouth.

"I don't understand, Elliot. I don't understand why … the day we met … those old people, those farmers were selling us out and we had to kill them."

She fell silent, leaving Elliot to pick up the thread of her thoughts. "And now it's ex-cops who are no better than the Druids. Yeah. It messes with your head. So, take my advice and don't think about it."

"How do you do that? Not think about it? Coz I know you *do*. I know that's got something to do with when you blank out."

"But I don't blank out twenty-four-seven. I get breaks from it. I make myself busy. I think about what there is to do."

"Yeah, you're not real good at chilling, are you?" She smiled tiredly. "I try that busyness thing too. Maybe I'm just really tired, but the last two days, I can't keep the thoughts out. Especially ..." She shrugged then punched her own thigh.

Elliot usually had to squeeze his will around the panic that always burned at his core, the tempest that raged alongside and above the still, deep well of his anger. But today, he felt the opposite of what Angie had just said. He didn't have to squeeze at anything. The memories were there. And they were dangerous. But the sudden flare of cordite smoke in his nostrils and the feeling of a hot Syrian wind against his skin seemed not so threatening. And the sight of Radler's remains and Eames's and McGovern's and the death of Birdy and the ghosts of Tommy Harrison and Uncle John—it was there and it was bad and the next day it might swallow him whole, but now, right now, it was just there, an unwanted companion, but for the moment a tame one.

He didn't know how to tell her all of that, but one day soon he would try. The face she had turned toward him was more vulnerable than he had ever seen it before.

He said, "There's life the way it should be. There's life the way it is. The best we can hope for is to move it closer to what it should be. And for that, we have to fight."

She reached out and none-too-gently patted his cheek. "Good pep talk, Sarge. Write me some poetry some time?"

He jerked a thumb at the back of the Ute the way she had. "Sure, like that's gonna happen. Right now, I have to do this thing."

"I'll help."

They climbed out and went around back.

Spider waited, his gaze raking the countryside around them, holding a SERP .40 cal. He now wore a duffel coat and sneakers, symbols perhaps of distancing himself from his former "tribe".

Rit gave Elliot a nod from behind the Land Rover's windscreen, focused and calm now his kids were safely under their mother's care.

Sturgis leaned against the outside of Rit's door, his face hard.

Elliot readied his own .40 cal while Angie opened the Ute's cargo pod.

Both captives were in there. Kyle blinked out at them, apparently emotionless, resigned. Driscoll by comparison shivered enough to make his handcuffs rattle; one side of his face was swollen, purple and red from contusions and abrasions. He hadn't held out nearly as long as Woodsy had.

Angie moved inside and jerked Kyle from his seat by the elbow. Elliot blinked in surprise at her strength; Kyle was not a lightweight; perhaps her sudden strength was born of rage.

"You, we'll keep a little longer," Elliot told Driscoll and closed the pod.

"I wouldn't trust anything he told you," Kyle said. His voice sounded off, warped by a broken nose full of dried blood. "He'll say anything to stay alive."

"Shut up," Elliot said and helped Angie march Kyle to the side of the road where the grassy verge dipped toward the fence. "I'll take it from here," he told her.

"But—"

"My job."

She bit the inside of her cheek, wrestling against her objection, then snorted and raised her hands in a *whatever* gesture.

"You morons can't save everyone," Kyle said. "There'll always be—"

Elliot shoved him down the small slope. Soundlessly, the SERP boss rolled to the bottom then got himself upright immediately, his cuffed hands out before him for balance. He hadn't sworn, hadn't so much as gasped in pain. In another man, Elliot might have respected that inner grit. In Kyle, it made him even less human.

Elliot had parked the Ute near a gate he hadn't noticed last time he was here. He opened it, shoved Kyle through, and followed him into the field.

As they trudged, Kyle spoke, affecting a whiny voice. "Where are you taking me; you don't have to do this; we can work this out; let's be friends." He laughed and resumed his normal haughty tone. "Guess that's the kind of bullshit you expect me to try on? Most people whine and plead when facing sentence. Like Woodsy, eh? Like Driscoll up there, the soft little turd. Not you and me, Elliot. We accept what is. No point fighting it. I've lived a few years longer than I expected to, that's for sure." He laughed again. "The only thing I *would* like to ask is: can we please stop walking and get it over with? I've never been a fan of long hikes."

Not so many days ago, Elliot had been thinking that some deaths were meant to happen, that some kills were good kills. He'd been correct. And he'd been wrong at the same time. This *had* to happen, it was the right thing to do. But there was nothing good and nothing satisfying about it.

"You listening to me, Elliot? I said, just shoot me and be done with it."

Elliot didn't reply, pushing his prisoner deeper into the field of high, dry grass. Following. And when he'd gone as far as he dared, he closed the distance between them, kicked Kyle's knee from under him. With a surprised grunt, Kyle toppled onto one side, fought for purchase with elbows and knees. Elliot pointed the .40 cal out into the field and fired a single round.

"What in …?" Kyle started asking. Then he caught the sound the same time Elliot did. The rasp of clothing against dry grass. Someone was coming. Some*thing* was coming.

"Oh, shit," Kyle said.

A growl then. From Elliot's two o'clock. A mewl from his ten. He drew his knife and tapped it hard against the pistol, like a man calling his dogs in for dinner. He took a couple steps back as the grassland came to life. If he could call it life.

Kyle was up on his knees and for the first time, there was panic in his eyes. There was real fear. He put his cuffed hands out in front of him, a grim and desperate supplicant.

"Elliot, please."

Finally, Kyle was afraid. He was feeling exactly what he'd made others fear. He gasped and shuffled a few inches forward as the first two deaders stumbled from of the screen of vegetation, falling over each other to land out of reach of him.

"Your wish is my command," Elliot said and put a bullet through Kyle's head.

Kyle pitched backward to land between the two deaders. They rose and pounced upon this boon.

Elliot turned and strode away as more bodies crashed through the grass behind him, as the flesh tore wetly from Kyle's bones, as the undead began to remove all trace that Kyle had ever darkened the earth with his presence.

Four people met Elliot back on the road, standing between the two cars. They had weapons in hand, black ballistic vests or coats, hardy boots. Sturgis, Spider, Rit, Angie.

There'd been other vehicles on other roadsides, other warriors waiting for him by them.

There'd been a team in Syria waiting as he walked between the Major's tent and the Humvee, ready to drive to Al-Kasrah. Though he would never have admitted it to them, they were men he liked. Friends. His *last* friends.

There'd been another fireteam for a time after that, though he hadn't led it. There'd been increasingly risky and covert missions placing Elliot in situations where an enemy's bullet might save him the trouble of doing it himself. After a year of those, when the nightmares didn't ease and the flashbacks got worse, there'd been transfers to less-demanding jobs. And then finally the day that Elliot had decided he wanted a different life. A quieter life.

For a time, he'd had that quieter life, too.

But he'd had no more friends.

Until now. Until The Downs. Claire and Heng and Alyssa and Lewis...

And these four fellow soldiers waiting on a Tasmanian roadway, watching him climb the fence and walk back up to the cars.

Sturgis.

Spider.

Rit.

Angie.

A new fire team.

His new fire team.

"You shot him first?" Sturgis asked as he reached the asphalt. "Before *they* got there?"

"I did."

Sturgis sniffed. "I'd have hobbled him. Left him alive while they did ..." He gestured to the tall grass thrashing behind Elliot. "... that."

"Ditto," said Rit.

Both men's faces twisted with hate.

Elliot—who had once shot a pedophile child-killer in the throat and stared into his eyes as he'd died—shook his head. "There'll be plenty of chances to kill SERPs soon if you want. Trust me."

"Yeah, well, you didn't watch them kill my brother-in-law," said Rit.

313

"Or throw my wife in a truck."

Elliot opened his mouth to reply but Angie beat him to it.

"No, he didn't. But we didn't see what happened to Jimmy. Or what Kyle did to Woodsy. Elliot did."

Rit and Sturgis dropped their gazes a moment before returning them to the field past Elliot.

Spider cleared his throat. "Bad joke, but … speaking of lunch …"

No one laughed. People back home were cooking hard and packaging much of it in case of evacuation. Or siege. Elliot had to admit that, despite what he'd just seen in the field, the machine that was his body needed fuel. It was hungry.

"Home then," he said.

"I'm driving," Angie said and Elliot followed her as the other men climbed into their Rover.

Behind the wheel, she eased a crick from her neck, waiting while he got his seatbelt on. "I know you're thinking of going back to Jericho," she said.

He winced. "Sturgis told you."

"Sturgis? He didn't need to. I know you. And before you think I'm going to argue, I won't. People need help there, right? And we still need the meds that started this whole shit storm."

"Yeah. We need to finish what Woodsy started."

"You're blaming him?"

"Not as much as I was."

She started the engine. "Never thought I'd hear love for Woodsy from you."

"Pity, Angie. That's all. He didn't make it to Settlers Downs with this asshole." He gestured to the remaining SERP in the cargo pod. "Not nice to think what might have happened to him."

Driscoll hadn't known the answer to that question. And Kyle hadn't been telling.

She commenced a three-point turn, a tough ask on the tight rural roadway. Back a ways, the Rover started the same thing.

Angie asked, "And Nine Mile River?"

He nodded. "A checklist of crap back home to finish. But, yeah, maybe tomorrow: Nine Mile. Barnabas, too."

She completed her turn and waited for Rit to complete his. "You sure?"

"They at least deserve to know about the bad guys. And who else besides Spider's moron buddies can we ask for help?"

"They won't give it."

"Probably not. But we gotta try. I hope to Christ this is a short war, but any war needs soldiers. More we have, the better."

"War," she sighed. "I guess it is."

"Well, we got one advantage." He offered her a grim smile and tapped his chest. "Those SERP assholes haven't had a decent opposing force to deal with so far. But now? Now they're messing with a truly devious sonofabitch."

"Wow," she said, looking anything but impressed. "You want that on your tombstone?"

"Sure. In about fifty years."

Angie hit the gas, expression softening. "Attempting contact with Nine Mile again gives me one of those bad feelings that movies used to talk about."

McGovern had said something similar on the day he died. Elliot hoped it wasn't a portent.

He replied, "Everything gives me a bad feeling these days." She shot him a warning glance, so he reached over to play with a loose strand of her hair and corrected himself. "Almost everything."

ACKNOWLEDGEMENTS & COMMENTS

My thanks follow at the end of this section. Before that, I make comments on three things …

Firstly, I apologise to members of the police force in Tasmania and elsewhere. My police here are not intended to represent any real law enforcement or emergency services personnel. They are a fictional device; their original genesis was the questions "Who in gun-wary Tasmania would have hardcore weaponry apart from outlaw bikers?" and "Who might have reason and opportunity to lord it over other people?"

Secondly, the place where Elliot stands between two ecosystems (pine forest one side of the road, rain forest the other) was an actual place I visited in Tasmania. It awed me and freaked me out. It was self-indulgent of me to include it in *Came Monsters*, but it accurately captures the constant mini-ecosystems crammed up against each other in Eastern Tassie.

Thirdly, the way Elliot kills the guard by using the man's rifle: I anticipate objections to this. However, this method is an unusual but very *real* special forces technique. It was described for me by James Jackson of The Ward Room (wdrmmta.wordpress.com). Elliot's action with the strap-and-rifle would exert pressure against the victim's trachea and the C section of his spinal column. Eventually the man's trachea would collapse and/or his neck break. Usually, I'm told, this is all over within 6-8 seconds. I took the liberty of making it a little quicker in this case, to keep the story moving. And before you say, "But the strap would break", JR told me (and I quote):

> *Funny thing is, the companies that make those slings market the product with claims that you could rappel or abseil (using the sling) and that it can hold up to 300lbs before failure. Neck failure results long before the sling would ever break.*

So there.
Do not try this at home.

As I've said elsewhere, you can't write anything half-decent without the generous support and advice of others. As I continue working on this series, I offer heartfelt thanks to …

Janine. For everything. Absolutely everything.

Zompoc author and military advisor to writers, JR Jackson. Amazing insight and corrections, as always. This series would be a joke without him.

Tamra Crow for some awesome proofreading and funny Messenger conversations.

Authors D Robert Digman, Krawleigh Adams, Shannon Lawrence, Noel Osualdini, Tim Annable. For reads and re-reads.

Mark Stallings. For helping me correct that prologue.

The Feendz. You know who you are and you share my love for things that happen beyond The End.

God. Yes, seriously. God. One of my sons almost died during the period I wrote this project. Miraculously (and it's a long and personal story), he did not. I am eternally grateful. A major theme in *Came Monsters* is family: perhaps you, dear reader, can understand why this theme is so important to me.

Some errors and untruths in this novel represent an author taking liberties, bending Truth to serve Story. Others, I'm sure, are simply errors.

CONNECT WITH THE AUTHOR

Connect with Pete at www.facebook.com/PeteAldinAuthor and www.petealdin.com.

If you'd like occasional bonus content and news about the series, please sign up for the newsletter at http://www.subscribepage.com/Doomsday'sChildNews . Your email address will only ever be used by me to send newsletters out to you. I hate spam, and I hate companies on-selling our data to others. I'd never do that.

FIRST BONUS: Newsletter subscribers receive the eBook prequel novelette "Half Past Doomsday" upon sign-up. This story is **free and exclusive to subscribers**, and not available for sale.

HALF PAST DOOMSDAY

PETE ALDIN

Before Elliot met Lewis …

PAPA ED

Bonus short story

The End came years ago when we was all children. A buncha kids from eight to eleven left to face a new world. All just kids, cept for Papa Ed.

It was him what found us in that school. Him what got us to his bus. Him what got us forty-nine screaming young uns outta danger.

That trip was bad, real bad. The bouncing and skidding. Them bastard Kooks beating on the windows and sides like a thunderstorm. Them bastard Kooks wanting to eat us. Us wondering where our parents was. Kids pissing their pants. The older ones swearing and Ed yelling at em to shut the hell up so's he could concentrate.

It was Ed what got us here to this chunka land just off the mainland. Petal Island, like a flower, but there weren't a flower in sight, least not when we came. He set fire to the land end 'a the causeway just after we'd crossed, then made us stay in the bus for hours while he killed every single Kook on Petal. He used bombs to blow up more 'a the bridge the next day. We dunno where he got them bombs. He never answered

323

questions like that, questions like, "Where'd ya get all the guns, Ed?" and "Where'd the Kooks come from?" and "Where's our parents?"

And, "When can we go home?"

When ya little and there's only one giant left in ya world, and he's a guy who can do anything—find food, build shelter, grow crops, and besta all protect ya from the Kooks—then 'a course ya trust him. After a while, ya kinda forget ya own parents, ya own family. Ya forget what they look like. Ya forget to remember them.

And ya new protector, he becomes Papa.

Dunno who first called him that. Don't care. It fit. He was a good Papa. He made rules and explained the why of em so we understood. He taught us to do stuff like growing food, keeping chickens. With forty-nine 'a us, he still had time to talk to ya everyday—though he'd usually make ya help with something while ya talked.

And we loved him. He was grey bristles, thick arms, a booming voice telling stories at sunset before bedtime. He was eyes the colour 'a sunwashed ashphalt, the color 'a cigarette ash gone cold—eyes that didn't miss a thing.

Course, it didn't last, the good times, the safe times. Same as our life before the Kooks, it had to end. There was something in us, something stupid I guess, maybe the same nuttiness what caused the End over there across the waters. Six of my birthdays passed, I reckon, before we grew outa childhood into something else.

As we started doing dumb things, upsetting our Papa, I'd wonder if we was infected too, if we'd turn into Kooks. Scared the shit outa me, that idea did. But it didn't stop me. Or the others. Everyone—cept for the six nerds who stood by Ed, who stayed in his school—we started telling him to get stuffed, telling him we hated maths and science and history and writing.

Secretly I missed it.

Jacko was the first to find a container 'a smokes. We made ourselves sick, then got up and did it again the next day. A few days later, he broke into a house that Ed had double locked and we discovered alcohol. When Ed found us smashed off our faces, he hit the roof. Best I don't talk about that, because it hurts to remember him so mad and so unable to stop us, to really stop us. If we'd listened to him then …

Papa Ed locked the booze up good and tight then destroyed all the smokes he could find. Jacko and his mates weren't gonna take that. They was bored. Us girls was happy just to chill, to talk, but the boys wanted to *do stuff.* They remembered there's a whole world back across the thin strip 'a grey-brown channel, a worlda smokes and beer.

"Kooks don't smoke or have piss-ups," Jacko said. "Plenty waiting for us over there. Sides, s'no Kooks over there nomore anyhow. Been years. They's all dead'."

"Idiot," I said. "'A course they're dead. That's the point."

"I mean *dead* dead." He was angry with me. Didn't like a girl challenging him. I put my hands on my hips and dared him to hit me. He'd hit boys before, but if he

PETE ALDIN

tried it with me, I'd 'a kicked him so hard he'd never get on with a girl ever again.

"How ya gettin over there?" Gail asked and the moment passed.

Oh, Jacko had it all figured out. Had a boat. He and Micky had been practicing with it. And they'd nicked one 'a Ed's guns.

The word *persistent* is a good word, a book word, and I often think 'a it when I thinka Ed. On the evening Jacko and Mickey slipped the boat outa the moorings, Ed came looking for us with a storybook under his arm. The row boat and boys was a blob halfway across to the mainland. Gail and Jane and I was climbing the hill from the shore to find shelter from the wind.

"Hi, girls," said Ed. "Story time in half an hour, up at the Big House."

"Too big for that now," Gail said with a sneer.

"Too *old*," I corrected her and caught Ed's gaze.

Gail and Jane stepped round him, but I was pinned there.

The helpless look in Ed's eyes stung, like someone ripped a band aid off my heart. He'd lost me, said his look. I wasn't his no more. Which meant, he wasn't mine neither.

And then his eyes turned hard as they found the stupid boys out in the channel.

"Oh my God," he whispered. His face filled with colour. His chest inflated with anger. He tossed the book in the grass and ran like I've never seen him run, down along the coast and out of sight.

326

I didn't know if I should follow. So I didn't. I sat back down and soon Gail came back and we discussed how dumb the boys were and what Ed could be doing now and how we was all gonna get it for this. It was dark cept for the moon by the time we heard the motor. And there, coming round the point of the island, was a light moving fast across the field of black.

Ed going after Jacko and Mickey.

"Holy shit," Gail breathed.

I said it too.

We watched and we waited. A couple more people joined us, Jane and Troy, wondering where we was. A bit laters, three more came. Our eyes strained in the dark but there was nothing to see after Ed's light had went out. Maybe an hour later we heard the gunshots. Nothing else, just gunshots. Three of them fast. Another three. A different gun firing once. Then lotsa nothing for a long while. Just the shoosh 'a the water on shale and the wind on grass. We asked each other stupid questions about what was happening over there and made up stupid answers. What the hell did we know?

I musta slept coz next thing the sky was pink and grey and I was dribbling on Gail's shoulder. I sat up straight and shook her awake.

We heard the motor before we saw the white speck on the water. The boat returning. The boat getting bigger and bigger, bouncing over the waves. The boat coming straight at us. The boat smashing hard into the shale right below where we stood.

Two people got out, a man and a boy, Ed and Jacko. They stumbled across the shale and fell against the grass slope near us. We ran to em but Ed yelled at us to stay away. He rolled onto his back and the blood on his shirt made me gasp.

Jacko stayed on hands and knees like a dog, looking like he'd puke. "Where's Mickey?" Gail asked him, but the answer was obvious and Jacko didn't bother answering.

I crept closer to Ed and gave a little cry. The blood was his, his shirt was torn up, and the blood was still coming out.

I found his eyes as they found mine. "Bit, sweetheart," he nodded with a sad smile. "I'm bit."

Jacko took his pistol and put it by Ed's head. He yelled at the rest 'a us to get the *bad word* away from there. They all left, running. All but Gail and Troy and me. We had to see. We had to be there as our world turned inside out for the second time in our short short lives.

Jacko turned Ed's head face up. He pressed the gun into his forehead which was a mercy, coz we didn't see the back 'a his head come off when the gun barked. We just saw Ed jerk and lie still with a small red hole above his eyebrows.

Just like that, our Papa was gone.

Gail and I had to grab each other to stay standing.

Jacko sighed—an outa place sound, like he'd just woken up and was doing a morning bed-stretch—and he stood and he went to the water and he waded out until it reached his hips and he put the gun against his heart and it barked again and Jacko slid into the water then bobbed sideways along the shoreline until he vanished around the curve 'a the beach.

And then we called some others back to help us bury Papa Ed on the hill overlooking the causeway. A long time ago, he'd destroyed that causeway. To keep the Kooks away.

Most 'a what we know bout Ed, we know from what we found in his room, a place none 'a us had ever been before. Beside his bed was a box 'a journals, a photo album bout a woman and three small kids, and three bottles of port wine. In the week after we buried him, while everyone else cried and argued and smoked and drank and picked fights, Gail and I hid in Ed's room reading his journals and sipping his port. It was hard to imagine the old man drinking—Drinking with a capital D. He'd never touched a drop in our sight and we hadn't known about the port wine. I started reading the oldest ones first while Gail started at the other end and read back towards me.

When she picked up a notebook marked *Jun 2022-Apr 2023*—those years he had little to say, though what he did say was fulla anger and doubting himself and fear—a yellowed piece 'a paper slid free from the book and glided to the floor. I slipped off the bed to grab it. It was a printed "email", a kinda message people used to send each other, although this one was written more like something from a book. It said children was like puppies and teenagers like cats—I think it was meant to be funny but it wasn't. It was actually kinda rude to us teenagers. Until I got to the last line—the one that said that eventually ya cats will become puppies again and they will come back to ya. Ed had underlined it in three different coloured inks and underneath he scrawled the words, *Please God let them come back.*

And we did. We all came back to him. We gathered at his grave, we made a huge cross and wrote on it. Those who couldn't write properly told the nerds what to write and they did it for em. *We* did it for em.

Every night since, we gather there at sunset and take turns reading stories or bits 'a his journals. We're real careful about the mainland now and only go back in big groups for things that we need bad, things we can't find on Petal.

And as us girls've started getting preggers—babies having babies really—we've learned how to make a new world on Petal Island and how to be parents ourselves. Learned from the things that Papa Ed taught us.